A MATTER OF BLOOD

Tom Walsingham Mysteries
Book Six

C. P. Giuliani

SAPERE
BOOKS

A MATTER OF
BLOOD

Published by Sapere Books.

24 Trafalgar Road, Ilkley, LS29 8HH,
United Kingdom

saperebooks.com

ISBN: 978-0-85495-599-2

To my dear friend Milla, who always listens, and laughs, and bounces ideas, and talks reason and wisdom — about Tom, and everything else.

ACKNOWLEDGEMENTS

Fates be thanked — as Tom is fond of saying — for librarians and archivists! First of all, the wonderful people at the inter-library loans desk at Biblioteca Baratta, Elena Montanari in particular: they never tire of seeking out bizarre titles for me all across Italy and Europe... And this time we even crossed the Atlantic! Thanks go to Alex Webb and Valerie Mendoza of the Harold B. Lee Library, at Brigham Young University, all the way in Utah. I also wish to thank Vincent Thauziès, librarian at the *Archives Historiques du Diocèse de Paris*, who pointed out to me something that, in time, will likely become another story.

Once a murder is conceived, it's still quite hard to execute it in a way that is both plausible and effective, even only on paper. Thank you, Adolfo Vaini and Francesco Cantarelli, for sharing the medical knowledge needed to stab and poison several people; and thank you, Fausto Lusetti, for the invaluable help and endless patience in staging the ambush and consequent swordplay. Any remaining mistake and implausibility is mine — but I hope that, with rapier, dagger, and poison, I've done justice to the skill and knowledge of you all.

And then there was The Great Computer Disaster. I'll never be thankful enough to Guido Scaravelli — together with Angela, Enrico and Silvia — for resuscitating my poor hard disk, and to Almo and Michela Dalzoppo for the technical (and emotional!) support. You all really saved the day — and the book.

Last but not least, thank you, Rosie, my unwaveringly patient and cheerful pillar.

PROLOGUE

Tom Walsingham stood straight, his eyes fixed on the flames of the twin candles on Sir Francis's writing table, and wished himself elsewhere. The winter evening was windy enough to make the flames dance, and to shake the window's shutters on their hinges — a fitful rattling that sat well with Mr. Secretary's mounting rage. Tom tried not to wince as the storm gathered in his kinsman and mentor's voice — and silently thanked the Fates that it wasn't directed at himself. Frozen before Mr. Secretary's writing table, the victim, head-cypherer Phelippes, stared at the floor.

Sir Francis read aloud from the letter he had received from Sir Edward Stafford, the Queen's ambassador in Paris. *"We have letters and a notable cypher that Phelippes sent to Gilbert Gifford."* For one possessed of a temper that was the matter of legends, Sir Francis Walsingham, Secretary of State to Queen Elizabeth, showed it seldom enough. Right then the legendary wrath was swelling as Sir Francis read aloud the news from Paris. *"And certain letters Gifford wrote to Phelippes have been intercepted and decyphered."*

The guilty Phelippes said nothing.

"And worse —" the paper rustled as Sir Francis shook it at his errant head-cypherer — "Sir Edward says: *It is told to me that things are discovered of the death of the Queen of Scots and the apprehension of the gentlemen that were executed.*"

The wind in the chimney made the flames hiss in the fireplace, and Phelippes's pockmarks turned purple on his pale face — always a sign of great distress with him. The cypherer gaped.

Keep quiet! Tom frowned in warning at his friend. *Hold your foolish tongue.*

But no — the half-wit must go and blurt out: "Gifford was never supposed to keep the letters."

"Nor be arrested, I'm sure!" Sir Francis thundered, the storm breaking at last. "What is it you wrote to that scoundrel? What is it the French have?"

Phelippes shifted his weight. "Old letters, for the most part..." he began — and had the belated sense to fall silent under Sir Francis's sharpening glare.

"Not that old, if they discuss Mary Stuart's death."

For Mary Stuart — the deposed Queen of Scots, polestar of all Catholic intriguers, and a lifelong danger to England — had met the executioner's axe some ten months earlier, to much outcry in France.

"I..." Phelippes blinked against the candlelight, likely trying to recall what he had written.

Sir Francis hit a palm on the tapestry-covered table. "You had to discuss it in writing — and Babington's fate too! Is there a lack of ill-will against England, in Paris?"

It was hard work, Tom found, not to cringe. The death of the Queen of Scots and that of the traitors who had plotted to free and enthrone her — Anthony Babington at their head — had not endeared England to the French — and to have Mr. Secretary's hand in it all revealed like this...

"Please, Your Honour," Phelippes tried again. "It seemed necessary that Gifford should know."

Oh Lord! Was the fool trying to rile Sir Francis on purpose?

"Gifford," said Sir Francis, leaning across the table, "is the unchanciest man who ever took Her Highness's coin — and mine. A seminary priest who doesn't know where his own loyalties lie, unless you count loyalty to himself. Easy to fright and touchy as a rabid squirrel — and you write of secret things to him, and set him to spy on Ambassador Stafford *without my knowledge!*"

These last three words were roared so furiously, they made Tom wince — and *he* was innocent. He spared a glance for the stiff-shouldered Phelippes, as his cousin sat back, gathering his composure about him. Few ever saw Mr. Secretary like this, forcing breath after breath through flaring nostrils, red rage staining his cheeks — but then, they'd come to the crux of it, hadn't they? For Sir Edward Stafford was no friend to Sir Francis, and sure to pounce on any weakness he saw — eager to make trouble for others if he couldn't lessen his own, no matter the damage to England. And now Phelippes, for all his skill and keenness, had offered Stafford just such an opening by exposing Sir Francis's secret part in the execution of the Scots Queen.

For a mercy the cypherer had enough wit, or enough fear, to keep quiet at last, and wait until Sir Francis spoke again, very bitterly.

"Sir Edward writes —" he tapped a forefinger on the Ambassador's letter — "how Gilbert Gifford brags that he kept intelligence with Her Grace herself — through you! What must I worry about — that you went behind my back, or that you are a fool?"

A question with no good answer, if ever there was one.

"He made that up!" poor Phelippes stammered, knotting his fingers together at his stomach. "It's true that I set him to spy on Sir Edward of my own counsel — but that was all." He stopped and swallowed hard, just as Sir Francis tilted his head, one eyebrow raised.

"Unless you had him report to you alone — so that you could pass on his reports as though they were Gifford's own notion," Mr. Secretary said — and it was no question at all. "Our Deacon Gifford lacks many things, but not some wit."

Under the cutting evenness, poor Phelippes wilted so that Tom couldn't help himself.

"Still," he ventured, "not even the French would swallow the notion of Gifford keeping intelligence with the Queen herself, Sir — no matter what tale Sir Edward will tell."

Great as Sir Francis's irritation towards his head-cypherer was, he still had some left for his cousin. "Wouldn't they?" he snapped. "Why, does it matter if they do, when the gist of that intelligence is true?"

"Your Honour, please!" Phelippes took the smallest step forward. "Let me travel to Paris. I'll repair the harm I've done. I'll —"

And the rest was lost as Sir Francis exploded: "To Paris, you blundering idiot? Back to your work — that's where you'll go. And if you value your position, you'll do naught of your own counsel."

Under such a slap of a dismissal, the cypherer blanched. *Oh Lord, Philippus! So sharp-minded, so cold, so calculating — and now this...* The scurrying retreat was painful to watch.

Sir Francis slumped in his high-backed chair with the smallest grunt of pain, the moment the door clicked shut. "What possessed him, I would like to know!" he groused, and shook his head. "Would you have thought it of him, Thomas?"

Would he? A nagging memory stirred in Tom's mind — one that perhaps should have pricked him sooner. "He did name Sir Edward once or twice last year, Sir — when we were dealing with the plot of the ambassador's brother, so maybe that should have been a sign." *And I wondered for a moment whether I could trust Phelippes.* But never in his life would Tom have questioned the man's loyalty to Sir Francis. "I'm sorry, Sir."

Sir Francis gave an impatient wave of his hand. "Phelippes must be sorry, not you — and I, for giving him too much his head. He's clever, he's ruthless — but none of this is antidote to the megrims of overreaching."

"In fair truth, Sir, it's not Phelippes's fault that Gifford was arrested. And cyphers there had to be, if the man was to be any use."

"But trusting Gifford in the first place — and to spy on Stafford! And now this matter of Charles Arundel's death..." Sir Francis winced, half turning to Tom who hovered at his elbow. "Oh, do sit, Thomas!" he ordered, irritation flaring again. "It's you I want in Paris."

As Tom bowed and went to sit, Sir Francis drew the candlestick closer to read aloud from the letter again. *"My cousin Arundel fell suddenly sick with such extremity that I never saw; so that I think Paget and his companions have poisoned him..."* Sir Francis paused. "Arundel fell ill just after Gifford's arrest, just after promising to recover the man's letters for Stafford — and not a week later he was dead. There's food for thought, in that."

Tom very much agreed, for, kinsman to Stafford or not, Charles Arundel had been a Catholic, an intriguer and a traitor, and a leader among the English exiles in Paris, just like Lord

Paget and his brother Charles, two schemers with a hand in every Catholic plot.

"It's true they never saw eye to eye, Arundel and the Pagets," Tom ventured. "On Mary Stuart, on Cardinal Allen, on the Jesuits… But was it enough to do murder? And why now?"

"Indeed." Sir Francis nodded over his steepled fingers. "You'll have to look into this, Thomas. And needless to say, you can expect little help from Edward Stafford, and solicit less — because the worst of it all…"

The worst of it all was that Phelippes hadn't been wrong to have the Ambassador spied upon — untrustworthy, contriving Stafford, who wanted to be devious, and lacked the wits to be. What sort of game had he been playing with a Papist like Arundel? Or was there worse still? Tom waited as Sir Francis folded the letter, smoothing each crease with utmost care.

"I should have told you this before, perhaps," he sighed at length. "When did you first hear of Edward Stafford's gambling debts?"

"When Rogers came back from Paris last summer." A returned spy, grimly reporting after many months of posing as a discontented Catholic exile. "He called it a pit deep enough to swallow a man's loyalty." Blood rushed to Tom's cheeks; his own debts were a prickly matter — although his loyalty had never been under suspicion.

"Yes," Sir Francis said. "But the rumours had been around earlier than that — or they would have been, if my Lord Burleigh hadn't had Rogers' letters diverted, and the tidings withheld."

Lord Burleigh, the Queen's Lord Treasurer, had once been Sir Francis's mentor, and was now his rival in the Privy Council, and Stafford's patron. There little Tom put beyond Burleigh — or Burleigh's unpleasant son, Sir Robert

Cecil — but this… "This is unconscionable!" he blurted out, earning a twitch of the lips from his cousin. "Beg pardon, Sir."

"Oh, it *was* unconscionable — although I'm sure His Lordship would disagree — and of little use, for in time Rogers travelled home, and told his tale anyway. You must have wondered why I didn't act on what the man said? Why I didn't have Stafford removed from Paris at last?"

"I was sure you had good reason, Sir."

"In trying to shield his man Stafford, you see, Lord Burleigh had furnished me with the means of greatly embarrassing him with Her Highness — and that, in time, I traded for His Lordship's acquiescence, if not his help, in the matter of beheading Mary Stuart."

It was childish, surely, but Tom couldn't help the laugh of triumph at his cousin's cunning. "I never trusted His Lordship's shows of friendship last year."

But there was no triumph, not even satisfaction in Sir Francis's manner, as he frowned at Sir Edward's letter. "One should never trust a Cecil too far." The onyx ring caught the firelight as Sir Francis tapped his forefinger on the folded paper. "Much less now that the tables may be turning."

"Turning?"

"Don't you think that Lord Burleigh will make use of this disaster of Gifford's? Now the question is, what he does or doesn't know about the younger Stafford."

Tom's heart sank. Learning of young Will Stafford's regicide plot had convinced the Queen to send Mary Stuart to the scaffold — but there had been no such plot, beside what Sir Francis himself had woven to force his sovereign's hand. Were she to learn this, through Stafford and Burleigh, there was no telling what the consequences could be to Sir Francis.

"But would William Stafford risk his neck by talking?"

"I misdoubt it, or that the Stafford brothers confide much in each other, even if communication could be held. And yet…" Sir Francis looked up. "Are you sure Robert Cecil still believes you, Thomas?"

Was he? Tom pictured the lamprey of a fellow — the smile that never reached the cold black eyes, the hunched shoulder, disguised well in stillness, but showing in the walk, the threat couched under colour of friendship. "I've always thought I'd know, Sir — the day I found myself in debtors' prison." And as evenly as he tried to say it, and as foolish as it was to resent it, it rankled with Tom that Cecil should think to own him, through the moneylender he couldn't repay.

Fool that he was, he hadn't even kept his bitterness to himself, and there was a sharper edge to Sir Francis's instructions. "Before you leave for Paris, you'll tell Sir Robert how furious I am with Phelippes — who overreached himself and lost my trust by it — with Gifford, who can rot in a French prison for all I care, and with Stafford, who will now have to be rescued. Don't mention Arundel unless Sir Robert does. As for what you'll do when you arrive in France…"

It had been one of Sir Francis's teaching devices, to let a much younger Tom deduce his instructions. Feeling seventeen again, he tried not to wince. "I'll assure Sir Edward of your continued trust, Sir," he said. "I'll convince him it's in his best interest that I talk to Gifford and look into Arundel's death. And I'll find out, very quietly, just what sort of games he's playing."

It was a great relief to see Sir Francis nod, and sit back in more comfort. "A tightly knotted tangle, yes. Accomplish what you can, and it will all go towards paring down Lord Burleigh's claws — at least for now. But, Thomas…" He leant forward again, a dark-veined hand flat across the papers. "Be very careful. The Lords of Guise are far too powerful in Paris, and fanning the people's anger against England. We beheaded Mary Stuart, we paid mercenary troops for the Protestants... I wouldn't put it beyond the good Parisians to harm an Englishman in revenge."

CHAPTER 1

3rd of January 1588, Paris

"*Be glad it's Sunday,* 'e says," groused Nick Skeres, hunching lower in the saddle as he scowled at the thronged street, the cheerless grey piles of the Hôtel-Dieu, the spire of Notre-Dame beyond them, piercing the heavy sky, and the whole choking, muddy, restless Île de la Cité. "*Be glad there'll be less of a crowd...*"

And because he was drenched to the marrow and cold in the freezing drizzle, in spite of his new fine grey Dutch cloak, Tom glared at his servant. "I said so back at the Porte Saint-Denis, and it was true enough. Now..."

Now Tom frowned at the sodden crowd that clogged their access to the Petit Pont and the Left Bank of the Seine, a roiling of men and women in their Sunday best, and black-garbed students, and friars of all hues, and shrilling children. He'd lived in Paris long enough, years ago, to know Parisian crowds as constantly dense, noisy, and inclined to mischief — and yet this one, this day, had something about it as it boiled around them, something that kept Tom's horse twitchy and flat-eared under him, and the traffic to the bridge impossibly slow.

A sullen irritation thrummed in the winter air — but then what would one expect, with war coursing through the kingdom like a fever, and the Guise Lords and their Catholic League fanning the flames?

When Notre-Dame began to boom three o'clock, it had been the better part of an hour they'd spent traversing half the city, and the forbidding fortress of the Petit Châtelet, looming at the bridge's other end, still seemed as far away. The great cathedral was followed at once by church after church, until the wet sky rang with chimes, drowning for a while the din of the crowd. Before it was done, the slow traffic towards the bridge came to a halt yet again, and at once those waiting began to trade insults and shoves.

Tom's mount fidgeted in the press, and grew more nervous still when Tom tightened the reins. "One can tell you're a French horse," he muttered, and, after nodding in apology to an old man who thought himself incommoded by the brute's distress, turned in the saddle to see how his servant was faring. Skeres had fallen back, staring with his nose in the air at the sky that quivered with the last of the chimes. On hearing himself called, he nudged his horse forward — and never mind the grey-robed friar who was pushed into a pile of ordure — and still he squinted up at the stern-faced statues of the Hôtel-Dieu that loomed overhead.

"Are you sure it ain't Christmas Eve 'ere after all?" the lad asked hopefully.

Ah, but it was hard to put a notion into that thick head, at times — for all that it had been five years since Pope Gregorius had bethought himself to change the calendar this side of the Channel.

"How many times have I told you, Dolius? They're ten days in advance of us, here. Christmas is well gone."

This darkened Skeres's mood into grumbling again. "What I say is, just because the Pope says so…"

Ah, well — at least the lad had the sense to keep it to a mumble.

"Well," Tom said. "They *are* Papists here. Now hold your tongue and be of good cheer: with any luck, tomorrow the Ambassador will —" and he went no further, because at that moment a commotion erupted a short distance ahead, and the crowd pressed on in an unruly wave.

Reining his mount hard, Tom half-stood in his stirrups. Were those English words he could hear in the clamour? There it was, past the wall of heads and bodies: a bearing chair leant against a wall at the bridge's head like a washed-up boat, and by it a horseman in a dark green cape, leaning from the saddle to shout at a pair of figures in coats of dull red. Didn't the man see the long verges they carried? Even not knowing them for sergeants out of the Petit Châtelet, he should have known better than to bellow at them half in bad French and half in English.

"Lack-wit wants a beating," Skeres muttered.

"Come, Skeres!" Tom nudged his horse ahead, forging through the press. Fates be thanked, it was a short distance. Busy jeering impartially at the sergeants and at the foreigner, the bystanders parted in no worse than protesting annoyance, letting Tom reach the Englishman just in time to stop him from drawing his sword.

And see if the fool — a very young fellow, too young for a beard — didn't turn on Tom, eyes wide with rage and fear.

"Are you mad?" Tom hissed. "Drawing on the King's men!" And, moving his horse to stand in front of the hothead's sorrel and the chair, he dismounted to face the sergeants.

"*Mes maîtres!*" Tom said in his fine French and his most commanding manner. "Have forbearance with a foreigner newly come to Paris — and only a boy at that, with little or no

French." Now let the young fool's command of the tongue be truly poor, for he didn't seem the sort who'd take kindly to being called an ignorant boy. "I'm sure no harm was meant — on either part."

A bold show of authority, Thomas, may well do instead of authority itself, Sir Francis was fond of saying — and the maxim held true in France as in England.

Finding himself addressed in French by a well-armed and well-spoken gentleman, the junior sergeant blinked in half-relieved uncertainty, while his more seasoned colleague bunched his pockmarked face in consideration. He observed Tom, and then the seething young man on horseback, and then Skeres, who had pushed his way to his master's side, burly and businesslike.

And before the sergeant could consider too much, Tom asked, all brisk reason, "What is the matter now? Nothing that can't be solved with some goodwill and charity, I'm sure?"

Did he sound dreadfully like a Huguenot, in this city of rabid Papists? Not too much for the grizzled sergeant, who nodded and instructed his underling to send everyone on their way (and how the poor man was to do it alone, Tom didn't know), and then gestured for one of the bystanders to step forward. This was a stocky fellow of five or six-and-thirty, wearing the woollen russet and fleshy jowls of a prosperous butcher.

"That chair," he said, pointing at the offending vehicle, to much encouragement from the bystanders. "They near ran down my niece. And when I —"

"What's the scoundrel saying?" came a voice from behind Tom's back, and he quietly hissed for peace over his shoulder.

"Was your niece much injured?" he asked the offended uncle.

The man raised his shoulder, and it was plain in his face the reckoning of how thick he could lay it — a reckoning brought short when the sergeant, with a great snort, gestured again, and from a gaggle of clucking women a girl of about thirteen emerged.

"We did nothing to her!" the Englishman cried — and Tom quite believed it, for the girl's cheeks reddened more in excitement than fear, and she showed no worse marks than a stain of mud on her blue skirt. Still, the crowd didn't like the outburst, and eddied closer, with a few cries of "damn the murdering English", enough to make the younger sergeant ready his verge, the youth dismount in readiness to join the fray, and Skeres tense.

"Lack-wit's going to 'ave *us* beaten too, Master," the Minotaur growled, earning an outraged gasp from the lack-wit himself. He then glowered at the bristling press. "Do I trounce 'em?"

Trounce a whole mob — oh Lord!

"Peace — both of you!" Tom ordered. "And blades in your scabbards!" And then he applied himself again to smoothing the trouble. "The young lady looks well enough to me, and thank Heaven for that," he said, giving the girl a nod that made her blush crimson amid the women's giggling.

Of course, the uncle wasn't so easily placated.

"But she was much frightened, *Monsieur!*" he cried, pointing again. "Almost to her death, she was — and this man —"

"*Allons, allons!*" the sergeant broke in, shouldering the fellow aside with the calm of long practice. "The *demoiselle* is unharmed, yes. But your friend, he wanted to hit her uncle, and us, when we arrived. He as good as…" He gestured to his own hilt.

Which Tom had seen happen — and averted — but still…
"But, *mon Maître*, consider. He has no French. He found himself surrounded by a shouting mob, the chair…" For the first time he observed that one of the chair's carrying poles was broken, and no porter was in sight. "The chair was damaged, and all these people shouted and threatened. What would you have done, *mon Maître*?" And, as he spoke, he discreetly slipped his purse out of a sleeve, and fingered it.

Whatever else he might be, the sergeant wasn't slow. He rubbed at his short beard. "I see," he hummed. "I see…"

And the butcher, or whatever he was, saw too, and pushed forward again. "But *Monsieur* — my poor niece!"

"Of course." Tom took two quarter-francs from the purse, and handed them to the sergeant. "Would you see to it, *mon Maître*? I'm sure something can be done for those ruined skirts."

The sergeant looked pleased, and the butcher appeased, if nothing else.

Being neither, the Englishman grabbed Tom's arm. "What do you think you're —" he began, and stopped, blushing under Tom's glare — and Skeres's.

Oh, but this young fool was a penance! "You can repay me when we're out of this scrape," Tom said through gritted teeth, and then suggested to the sergeant that, if all was sorted out, they might be on their way?

The fellow was obliging enough to say that, the porters having fled, he would see to the wrecked litter, which Tom translated for the young man.

"Unless you know how to recover your porters?"

The matter of the bribe had deflated the fellow's arrogance.

"They ran at once…" He gestured helplessly around. "I wish I hadn't hired this contraption now, but my sister is unwell, and there are no coaches to be had in this infernal place." He had grown louder, and when Tom shushed him, he wrenched his narrow-brimmed hat from his very fair head, and then crammed it on again. Very young indeed he looked in his distress — no more than eighteen, if that.

And Tom, who at that age had been galloping on the roads of France and England, carrying secret dispatches sewn into his clothes, felt a twitch of impatience for this coltish boy.

"The streets of Paris are no place for coaches," he said briskly. "Do you think your sister can ride with you?"

At this the youth straightened, and set his jaw. "She'll have to," he said, and went to knock on the litter's door. "Anne?" he called. "You can come out now."

A gloved hand appeared, and then a small, triangular face framed by a dark hood.

The youth opened the door and, leaning on his arm, a young woman clad in the severest grey stepped out of the chair a little unsteadily.

"I was so afraid, Clement!" she said, shivering in the drizzle, and then turned on Tom a pair of impossibly huge eyes, of a clear, golden hazel. "It's you that we must thank, Master…?" She hesitated, the strange eyes darting over Tom's face and person, gauging him — for what, there was no saying.

Well, whatever it was, there was no time for it, for the crowd still pressed around, watching the English with the unamiable curiosity of crows.

"Thomas Abbot at your service." Tom supplied the smallest bow. "But, Mistress, we'd better go. Can you ride?"

Much as her brother had done, she straightened, pinching her small mouth to answer, in a voice that would have been pleasant, but for a hint of shrillness, "I am Lady Anne Gawdy, Mr. Abbot — and yes, I can ride with my brother."

She ruined it all by stumbling as she moved towards the sorrel horse — and the hand she put out to catch herself on the bridle trembled a little. Cold, perhaps, or the remnant of fear... Still, when her brother lifted her up, Lady Gawdy slipped into the saddle with the ease of one well used to the exercise, unimpeded by her voluminous grey cloak — and her sideways seat was effortless while the youth mounted before her.

Countryside gentry, Tom decided, remembering himself and his sister Mary doing the same countless times, whenever Mary didn't get her way to ride on her own. Meanwhile, Skeres had recovered their horses, and stood ready — good Minotaur. Tom had his foot in the stirrup when the older sergeant came to stand at his elbow, a hand on the horse's neck.

"I'll see your papers, eh, *Monsieur*?" he said.

If there was any surprise in this, it was that it hadn't occurred earlier — for there was nothing French officials of all ranks liked better than to wield this particular power over foreigners and travellers.

"And those of your friends," the sergeant continued — only to stop as he took in Tom's courier's passport. "*Diantre!*" he softly exclaimed, and raised a brow at Tom. "And you all...?" The man described a small circle with his forefinger, encompassing the whole group.

Tom tilted his head. Let this fellow think what he chose — most likely that he'd better have these people belonging to the English Embassy off the streets.

With a snort, the sergeant refolded the pass and gave it back. "I think, *Monsieur*, that I'll see you to the other bank."

They crossed the Petit Pont in some magnificence, escorted by the sergeants with their verges, ogled and pointed at by two wings of good Parisians who, squeezing against the apothecaries' shops that lined the bridge, made gleefully free with the opinion that the English were being arrested, until they were swallowed by the cold gloom of the Petit Châtelet.

Petit they might call it, but there was nothing small to this squat, severe fortress, through which one passed to the Left Bank — and even less that was pleasant. The clattering of the horses' hooves echoed under the vaulted passage that smelt of wet stone, while an icy drizzle rained down from the square of open sky over the bleak courtyard. In that grey light, Tom caught sight of Anne Gawdy trembling, and clinging to her brother — and small blame to her.

The sergeants abandoned them at this point — and what they thought they'd helped with their brief escort, Tom didn't know — and let them pass on, out onto the Left Bank.

"At last!" young Clement exclaimed. "These meddling dunces — worse than the constables at home! If it hadn't been for them, we'd have had no trouble at all."

Of this Tom had his doubts, nor was he so relieved at the lack of safeguard — for the streets on this side of the Seine were no less crowded, and their reputation for mischief much worse. "Where are you headed?" he asked.

"Our cousin lives near the Porte Saint-Germain," Clement replied, pronouncing the name English-wise. "If you only point to us towards where that lies, we'll thank you and be on our way."

"Good riddance," muttered Skeres under his breath, but truly, conscience forbade Tom from abandoning these two children among the press that milled restlessly about.

"I'm not sure it would be prudent," he said, as softly as he could — but not so low that Lady Gawdy didn't hear it, and her pale eyes flashed from the depths of her hood.

Her brother was less anxious. "But it's full daylight," he protested. "The streets are full of people, and I'm well armed."

Skeres snorted. "Much they care for daylight, these French ruffians! Look at 'em, all spoiling for a fight, and you so ready with your —"

"Peace, Skeres!" Tom snapped — but he wasn't sorry to see some alarm dawn on young Clement's face. "This is a very big city, and very unquiet these days, for France is at war with itself, and the Lords of Guise are forever stirring discontent, and calling the English enemies."

"We're not at war with them, though, surely?" Lady Gawdy said, a little tremulously, over her brother's shoulder.

Jove, did these two know nothing? Who had thought to send them to France all on their own? "We may not be, but the Protestants have been paying their mercenaries with English gold. For all that the mercenaries were routed at Auneau back in November, I much doubt we're forgiven yet."

"But," Clement began, but whatever he'd been about to say, he thought better of it. There was something in the glance he exchanged with his sister, though, that made Tom wonder: had he stumbled upon two of those Catholic exiles who had fled England? Well, if they thought themselves safe from danger on account of their faith, they were bound to wake up roughly, and soon.

Skeres must have been thinking the same thoughts — though not to the same conclusion. "Send 'em their way, Master," he grumbled, in that tight-lipped manner he always seemed to think Tom alone would understand. "Do we lack trouble, that you must borrow more?"

Which was, it must be said, only good sense — and yet there they clung to each other on horseback, this unwary, arrogant stripling and his fearful sister, and all around them roiled the Left Bank, ready to swallow them whole... Ah, well.

"Let me see you safe to your cousin's door," Tom said, ignoring the Minotaur's groan at his back. "The Porte Saint-Germain, is it?"

"You are very kind, Mr. Abbot," said Lady Gawdy, her voice soft and just a little shrill from inside her hood — and the decision was made.

Once, Tom would have turned right into the Rue de la Huchette as the shortest way — but now, mindful of his own words, he led his little party along the Rue Saint-Jacques, which was large and well-peopled, if nothing else. Also, once, he would have regarded the Sunday crowds at this hour of the day as slightly more respectable. Instead, elbowing their way among the churchgoers and the idle, many black-garbed young men marched in clutches in the ankle-high mud, loud and brash.

"Who are these people?" Lady Gawdy asked, as the press pushed Tom's horse close to her.

"Students of the Université," he explained. "As bad as the apprentices in London — only better read."

Anne Gawdy gaped a little as she caught a strain of doggerel a dozen miscreants shouted. "Why, 'tis Latin!" she cried — a well-educated creature, but a tad too loud.

One of the students heard her, a Frenchman well in his cups, judging by his rosy cheeks and nose, and the unsteady forefinger he wagged at the horsewoman. "*Latin, ma belle. La-tin*," he corrected her in the French way, and reached for a fold of her dark cloak. And here was young Clement again, reaching for his hilt...

"You fool!" Tom snatched at the sorrel's bridle. "Come away."

But fear heeds no sense, of course — and Lady Gawdy, finding herself clutched harder, gave a sharp little cry and kicked at the student, who stumbled back into the arms of his companions — some laughing, some not at all.

"Come away," Tom repeated, and tugged at the bridle, while Skeres, who had been keeping to the rear, pushed his mount between Lady Gawdy and the miscreants.

And then there was a surge in the crowd, like the tide swelling, and the shouts around were not of laughter — but must Clement wrench free of Tom, and make his horse swerve, displacing Skeres?

"Away, you rogues!" he shouted, as English as you please, and elbowed aside the folds of his cape from his half-drawn rapier.

The closest students shied away, only to be shoved back against the horses, as the rabble yelled against the murderous English — and Lady Gawdy shrieked again.

Oh, devil take it! Where were the sergeants when one wanted them?

"Skeres!" Tom called — needlessly, since the lad was already pushing his big bay against the students. On the other side, Tom grabbed Clement's bridle again, and this time the youth let him, gawping around half in rage, half in fear, and reaching back to hold his sister tight.

War horses are trained to fight their way through a skirmish, a soft voice echoed in Tom's mind — his beloved cousin Frances, recounting some feat of her now-dead soldier husband.

"Well, love — post horses are not!" Tom ground out, as he spurred his nervous mount, and tried to drag Clement's behind him. Then, in the unreasoning way of crowds, the wall of bodies gave of a sudden, just enough that Tom broke through with his charges and plunged into the nearest alley.

"Skeres!" he again called over his shoulder, and again it was needless, as the lad, crimson-faced and panting, rode just behind them, leaning from the saddle to slap at pursuing, shouting heads.

Now where? The unpaved street curved a little ahead, made narrower still by the awnings and the jetties of the tall houses on either side where shutters were slamming open, and heads sticking out, but Tom knew where it led: the Place Maubert — and, not much past that...

"The Embassy!" Tom shouted to Skeres — and ignored young Clement, who twisted in the saddle and gaped.

For the students hadn't tired of the game — why, they ran after the trotting horses, their black gowns fluttering wing-like, as they jeered, and snatched at stirrups and cloaks, and called to the people that leant out of the windows above: "*Anglais! Anglais!*"

A cry of "*Gare-à-l'eau!*" and a sudden explosion of French curses made Tom glance back to catch Skeres laughing, and past him a sodden student shaking himself. Someone had emptied a chamber-pot from above and, whoever the intended target, the pursuers had been doused, much to the Minotaur's joy. They may not be so lucky the next time, though, and Tom was glad to see the alley's end ahead.

"Stay close!" he shouted to Clement. "We'll soon be safe."

And then the horse's hooves struck cobblestones under the mud — and the blessed width of the Place Maubert opened before them, where the Parisians walked in clutches in the sideways rain. Feeling Clement stiffen at his side, and gather the reins, Tom tightened his hold on the sorrel's bridle. "Trot," he ordered. "Nothing more than that."

A backward glance showed a dozen students still in pursuit — devil pinch them! — and by now the street urchins were picking up the shouts of "*Anglais*! *Anglais*!" The whole rabble followed across the place, and down and up a small curving rue, and it was not long before the first missiles sailed after the fugitives. Something squelched against Tom's back — let it be no worse than mud! — and Lady Gawdy, hood knocked askew and face buried in her brother's shoulder, was sobbing hard. Bringing up the rear, Skeres turned his horse around to roar at the pursuers — who only grew louder, and drew closer, until at last the Embassy's ochre-coloured wall was in sight.

"Ahead, Skeres!"

At Tom's order the lad spurred his horse into a bounding canter, reached the carriage gate, and began to pound on it.

Under the pelting rain, Tom pushed his horse between his charges and the stubborn pursuers — no more than a dozen now, students and urchins, and keeping all the way across the street, but rabid enough that they had begun to hurl stones and shout, "Away with the English!"

Skeres went to join his master. "Cuds-me, Mr. Tom — but you are one to find trouble!" he groused, and he began to hurl insults of his own at the assailants. "Do I trounce 'em?"

"Mind that they don't trounce you," Tom called, just as the gate's peephole opened and a man peered out.

"Let us in!" Tom ordered — and, as the man hesitated, "I'm from London — for the Ambassador!"

The face disappeared, and in the din Tom wasn't sure it was a drawing of bolts that he heard, but the postern opened a sliver.

"The gate, fellow!" Tom roared, just as a stone caught him in the shoulder, and a string of curses from Skeres denounced another hit.

Still the servant dithered — bless him with hot water! — and young Clement dismounted, half dragging his sister off the saddle with him, and bustling her none too gently towards the postern.

Perhaps the sight of a woman in distress had decided the man inside: this time, there was no mistaking the rasp of bolts, and the gate began to swing open — not a moment too soon, for the ruffians were closing in, one student brandishing a piece of wood.

And then, through the cries and jeers, pierced a woman's shriek of "Clement!"

The youth was clinging to Tom's stirrup, hatless, and holding his hand to his bloodied temple — hit by a stone.

Leaping out of the saddle, Tom flung an arm around the boy and dragged him through the opening. Two men stood there, and a third came running from the house. Pausing only to push Clement into the nearest man's arms, Tom rushed outside again, calling for Skeres and snatching at his horse's trailing reins.

Skeres spurred his own mount through the half-opened gate, leading the Gawdys' beast behind him — and in doing so nearly flattened the Embassy servant who stepped outside, brandishing some sort of ancient pike.

A thick-shouldered giant, this man stood wide-legged and hard-faced, shaking his weapon at the mob and roaring, as Tom recovered his skittish horse. Why, he even took a couple of running steps, shifting his hold on the shaft as if to charge — which sent the students a-scatter.

He waited until Tom reached the gate, picking up young Clement's hat as he ran, and then retreated steadily towards it, all the time holding the pike like one who knew how to do it.

Another moment and they were inside the Embassy, the gate slamming shut. In the street the cheering swelled, and some more stones thumped against the wood — but they were safe inside a walled garden with a silent fountain, and an open gallery on one side.

"Mr. Tom, what were you thinking?" Skeres cried, shouldering away the huge fellow with the pike.

"Hardly a pitched battle, was it?" Tom said, annoyed at himself, for he was short-winded, and his hands shook a little as he took out his courier's passport.

He looked around, seeking someone to receive his credentials. The huge pike-man was obviously a servant, and so was the old fellow helping Lady Gawdy to support her brother, but the gentleman in clerical black and falling band had to be the chaplain, Tom decided. And the chaplain was nervous either of the affray or the newcomers — or perhaps both, for he stood shifting his weight from foot to foot, and fingering his little yellow beard. "Mr. Ambassador's secretary is coming," he murmured, peering across the frost-coated stretch of knot-beds and winding gravel paths, towards the many-windowed, steep-roofed house, with the bare branches of some climbing plant marking the front like lines in an old face. He looked greatly relieved when a tall man appeared from a door under the gallery: a man about Tom's age, with a fair complexion and a bearing of stiff importance that Tom knew from London — where he'd seen it crumble under no great pressure. It was a heartbeat before recognition flared in the hooded eyes, and the man made to speak.

"My name is Thomas Abbot," Tom hastened to say, holding out his papers. "From London."

And see how William Lyly blinked and faltered in the motion of taking the passport — this who was supposed to be Sir Francis's man! He frowned at the Gawdys and back at Tom — and Lord knew what he would have said, hadn't a lady sailed, all unattended, out of the house, a green cloak billowing around her as she hastened through the garden.

"Mr. Lyly!" she called as she drew close. "Who are these people?"

"A Thomas Abbot, Madam," the secretary answered with a bow. "From London — for Sir Edward…"

"Sir Edward is at the Louvre for the day." The lady studied Tom. "You're new," she said. "I don't think I have seen you before."

She had seen him, in fact, as a drab boy of sixteen in Sir Francis's wake — not one she would remember. Tom, though, remembered Lady Douglas Stafford very well. The deep voice like a viol, the proud head on a swan-like neck, the fine, imperious features… She'd been the dowager Baroness Sheffield, back then, and Lord Leicester's rumoured mistress. Ten years later, at five-and-forty, she hadn't lost a whit of handsomeness, nor of disdain in her manner.

Tom bowed. "I'm new, Madam. Thomas Abbot. My letters will —"

He got no further, for at that moment Lady Stafford observed Anne Gawdy, huddling with her brother on a marble bench by the wall, where the chaplain had led them, and her sternness remade itself at once. It was a different woman who clicked her tongue, and hastened to Anne's side.

"Poor child!" she cried, seizing the gloved hands in her own. "Were you chased in the streets? How horrible! And this poor boy...!"

"My brother is hurt, Madam." Anne sought Tom around Lady Stafford's shoulder. "Had it not been for Mr. Abbot..."

Lady Stafford stroked Anne's pale cheek. "Thank the good Lord he was there. But come, my dear — you need a fire and a posset!" She raised the young woman and led her towards the house, only pausing to call to Lyly over her shoulder. "Have Maître Hennert called, Mr. Lyly. And, Mr. Abbot, if you'd continue your good work..." And, seeing that Tom was going to help Clement already, she strode ahead, sweeping Anne with her.

The youth stumbled a little between Tom and the chaplain, but the gash on his temple had stopped bleeding.

"How are you faring, Gawdy?" Tom asked.

"Framlingham."

It was said so weakly, Tom had to bend closer to hear.

"Gawdy is my sister's husband. I'm Clement Framlingham, and in your debt." The youth's voice had grown a little stronger by the time they entered a dim, flag-stoned hall, with a spiral staircase of white marble at its end, down which a maidservant was hastening with a branch of candles. There were several richly carved settles as well, and on one of those Tom sat young Clement, who tried hard not to slump.

"I'm sure that Mr. Abbot has no thought of any debts," the chaplain said, patting the youth's arm. He had the sort of noble brow and chiselled features that seemed made for benign concern. "How pale you are! But Her Ladyship's sent for the physician..."

At this young Framlingham sat up straighter. He swallowed and rubbed at his forehead, which must have been hurting. "I'm very thankful, Sir, but we should be on our way. Don't you think, Anne?" He looked up at his sister, who was clinging to Lady Stafford's arm, bone-white, with her hair a-tumble and shadows under her eyes.

My sister is unwell, he'd said to explain the litter…

"I don't think it's wise," Tom tried, and Lady Stafford, bless her, came to his aid.

"Not at all!" A tinge of bitterness crept into her voice. "The good people of Paris have yet to forgive us all for the Queen of Scots' death. Besides, today is Sainte Geneviève's feast, and they've been deprived of their procession. As though they were to be less dangerous, crowding the streets without their relics!"

Sainte Geneviève — of all days! Tom remembered the flocks of mad-eyed faithful in rags or silks, who clogged this half of the city for a whole day, praying and singing, and reaching for the gleaming casket of bones… "I can't believe they'd be happy," he said.

The toss of Lady Stafford's head encompassed the foolishness of crowds and kings alike. "And it's growing dark. No, dear Lady Gawdy, there's no thinking of it: you and your brother will bide here tonight — and, come day, my servants will escort you."

Clement would have protested, perhaps, but Anne nodded gratefully, and the decision was made. Not that there had been much doubt: half an hour in her presence, and Tom was ready to swear nobody crossed the Baroness Sheffield.

The ladies disappeared up the staircase with their candles and Tom, young Clement, and the chaplain were left in the grey gloom. The chaplain — who had introduced himself as the

Reverend Mr. Richard Hakluyt — was murmuring to a blank-faced Clement. Before Tom could grasp the subject of the conversation, the elderly servant appeared from a side door, bringing two candlesticks.

"Why, Mr. Hakluyt, all in the cold and dark!" the man exclaimed, loud in the way of those hard of hearing — and put one of the candlesticks down on a side table. "I've had a bed put up in one of the small rooms, so Master Hennert can see this poor gentleman... Up-a-day, young Master!" He hoisted a wincing Framlingham to his feet, and smiled to Tom. "And please you, Master, wait here. Your man's in the kitchen, and Mr. Lyly will be here in a moment; he'll see to you."

It was no empty assurance: the old man and the chaplain had just led away the injured youth, when William Lyly arrived, a little breathless — a lean fellow, with hooded eyes in a long face, better dressed than he'd been in London, in clothes of dark blue mockado and a fine lace collar.

He tried for haughty composure at first. "You caught us at a bad time, Mr...?"

"Abbot," Tom repeated. "My name is Abbot — and it is a bad time, I'm sure."

Lyly shifted his weight from foot to foot, the candlelight glinting off a silver aiglet at his shoulder. "What I mean is that Sir Edward's at the Louvre."

"Yes, so I hear. When will he be back?"

"He meant to come home late tonight, but..." He frowned at the door, as though he could scent the unrest past it. "I'll give him your packet in the morning." He held out a hand, stiffening when Tom shook his head.

"What you'll do is tell your master that the new courier begs the favour of a word with him." Tom lowered his voice to a whisper. "And mind: to you I'm none but Abbot, unless Sir Edward tells you otherwise."

Here was another thing about William Lyly: it took little to discompose him.

"But…" he began, in a fluster. Was it the fluster of one who'd spoken of what he should not?

"Come, now! I'm sure you'd rather keep from Sir Edward our acquaintance in London." Tom stepped close to whisper: "Unless, of course, you've already betrayed Mr. Secretary's confidence…"

"On my word…" And at that Lyly faltered. Oh, yes — the word of one who, for not betraying one master's confidence, must have betrayed the other's trust.

In his younger, more innocent years, the fellow's predicament would have made Tom uneasy. In his younger years, he wouldn't have kept silent, staring hard while Lyly looked away.

And then a brisk little man walked in, clean-shaven and wearing the knee-length black coat, yellow gloves, and ermine collar of a Paris physician.

"*Monsieur* Lyly, I've —" he began brightly, and stopped at the sight of a stranger. "Beg pardon. I was told…"

Oh, the relief with which Lyly welcomed the interruption! "Do come on in, Maître Hennert. This is Mr. Abbot, who rescued your patient from the mobs."

A grander description than the facts deserved, perhaps, but it lit a benign smile on the physician's round face.

"And a good work of it you did, *Monsieur!*" Maître Hennert said, with a Flemish colour grating in his French. "The young gentleman is shaken, and a little scratched, but nothing worse than that. I've bled him just a little, to purge the humours — and now I'd advise warm wine and a good night's sleep. He worries much about his sister, though, and won't rest until he is reassured of her wellbeing."

This last was directed to Lyly, who took it with the eagerness of one seeing his escape.

"Of course. She was most upset. Her Ladyship brought her upstairs, and I'm sure she'll want you to see her."

He started towards the stairs and stopped when Maître Hennert patted his arm, as if he were another patient.

"Don't worry, *Monsieur.* I can find my way. You see to your guest, eh?" And with a little bow at Tom, and a murmur that these were trying times for a foreigner in Paris, he climbed up the stairs with unhurried purpose. Would he bleed poor distraught Anne, too?

So they were left alone again, Tom and the secretary, studying each other in the uncertain light. Was it worth questioning the man before he could consult with Stafford? Then again, if Lyly was of a mind to consult with the Ambassador, was it wise to have him uncover in advance Mr. Secretary's intentions?

"I've had a long day, Mr. Lyly," was what Tom said in the end. "Can I prevail on you for some supper and a bed? Oh — and my man's whereabouts?"

And why Lyly should flinch, the good Lord only knew. Had he truly thought to throw out into the street a courier — and this courier among all?

But perhaps he had, for it was with the greatest and grimmest resignation that, after some apology, he said he'd see Tom settled for the night.

CHAPTER 2

Tom awoke to frost-flowers on the small windowpanes, to a concert of bells, and to Skeres's grumbling that, back at home, it would be Christmas Day.

Sometimes it was like having a small boy in tow, instead of a manservant. "Won't they bake ginger cakes, your friends in the kitchen? Go and find out," Tom ordered a little briskly — and, having so disposed of the distempered Minotaur, he dressed, took the packet from London and went in search of the Ambassador.

Instead he found Lyly, shepherding Clement and Anne across the hall, though it was hardly light yet. And, it had to be admitted, Skeres hadn't been wrong: when she was not bedraggled and distraught, Anne Gawdy had a sort of wan prettiness, with her luminous eyes, and her hair gleaming honey-coloured in the candlelight.

Bowing to her and nodding to her brother, Tom offered a hope that both had recovered from their ordeal, and perhaps Skeres was right again, and Anne Gawdy's wits leant askew — for what had Tom said that she should stiffen so, and press her lips into a thin line?

Taken aback, he floundered a little, and looked to Lyly for enlightenment: had something else occurred?

Whether the secretary would answer, Tom never knew, for young Clement stepped forward, with half his face bruised black.

"Yes, thank you, Mr. Abbot," he said — and darted a glance at his sister. "It's been a day of trials. I've left with Mr. Lyly what I owe." Another glance. "Your money... Yesterday, at the bridge, you'll remember."

You can repay me when we're out of this scrape, Tom had snapped — and now it sounded petty and ungracious enough to raise a blush. "But there's no need for that!" he exclaimed. "I never meant —"

"There *is* need, Mr. Abbot. This is one debt we can repay to you." In losing some of its shrillness, Anne's voice had gained a steady coldness that ill-suited what should have been words of thanks.

What had he done now? Tom exchanged bows again with these baffling young persons and watched them walk stiffly through the door the huge servant had opened for them. Lyly seemed bent on seeing them away — so Tom stayed him to ask about the Ambassador.

Lyly hesitated between the departing guests, and the troublesome one who was remaining.

"Have the goodness to wait," he said, and then turned to yesterday's pikeman. "Hobelot, show the gentleman to the little parlour."

He hurried out after the Framlinghams, and Tom was left with the giant Hobelot, who closed the door with quiet care.

He had the biggest smile, this former soldier, who had walked against an angry mob armed with nothing but an ancient pike. "This way, please you, Master," he said — slow but perfectly intelligible — and, still beaming, he showed Tom into a parlour that wasn't especially little, finely panelled, and well-lit by two large windows. It had a number of chairs, a faded tapestry hung between the windows, plenty of sideboards carved in the flowery French manner, and a fireplace that was, alas, dark and empty of all but cobwebs in the corners. Whether the fine furniture belonged to the

Staffords or the house, it was becoming clear that little money was spent on firewood at the Embassy. But surely it was to be a short wait, not worth asking the servant for a fire — or a bit of breakfast? The man stood by the door, like a big pillar in dun-coloured livery, frowning as though uncertain of what he should do next. He lit up again when Tom addressed him.

"Hobelot, is it?" he asked. "Has your master returned? Is he at home?"

Hobelot grew solemn at once. "Ay, Master," he said. "My brother Adkin drove him home last night — him and Mr. Grimeston, as is the secretary. Very, very late, it was."

"And is Sir Edward up, do you know?" he asked.

Before Hobelot could answer, the door opened to admit Lyly.

The secretary looked displeased — but when had Tom ever seen him, here or back in London, looking otherwise?

"Sir Edward will see you, Abbot," he said — the Mr. dropped, as would be natural between a secretary and a courier.

"There, Master, see? His Honour's up!" Hobelot observed, and beamed happily as Tom followed Lyly upstairs.

The fireplace was roaring in the study upstairs, and by it stood Sir Edward Stafford, Her Highness Queen Elizabeth's ambassador to the French King Henri, the third of his name. He stood with his back to the door, looming large in a much-padded and much-embroidered doublet of fine damask, the colour of pale oranges. When Lyly announced the courier Abbot, he whirled on his heel in a display of the stiffest displeasure. The haughty scrutiny he must have meant for the courier went awry, though, as his brown eyes widened in recognition. Well, Lyly had held his tongue then — and Lord be witness that Her Grace's ambassadors were not beyond pouting! Or at least, this one was not.

"Ha!" Stafford exclaimed, striding to meet Tom. "And I wondered that your uncle should send a new man, now of all times!"

"Cousin." Tom had mostly given up correcting the general assumption that Sir Francis was his uncle — not that it mattered much, after all — but Stafford rubbed him the wrong way. "My father was Mr. Secretary's cousin."

And then he wished he hadn't, for the Ambassador's pout turned into a no less petulant sneer. "This then, William," he said, not quite for Lyly's benefit, "is the son of Mr. Secretary Walsingham's cousin — sent, I imagine, to undo some of the ills that Mr. Secretary's people wrought from London."

Unus ... duo ... tres... This Tom had learnt from a childhood tutor: counting in Latin before he spoke in anger. *Quattuor ... quinquies...* There was a heavily worked writing desk at the room's centre, encumbered with ornaments. With the most precise care, he laid the packet on it, beside an ornate hourglass of gilt bronze, filled with pale red sand. "I'm under Mr. Secretary's orders, Sir," he said, "to keep the name of Abbot while I'm here."

It was no great surprise when Stafford's brow darkened further. "While you're here!" he repeated. "Which means you're not riding back, I take it." He snatched up the packet and handed it to Lyly. "But no — if Mr. Secretary wanted just a courier, he'd have sent a courier, wouldn't he?"

Having known the younger Stafford, and suffered through the chore of governing the man's skittish humours, Tom saw the same manner in the elder brother — unstaid and touchy. If this was Lord Burleigh's notion of a good ambassador, Lord help England!

"I'm sure he would have, Sir — but Mr. Secretary is most worried and displeased over this matter of Gifford."

"Displeased!" Stafford flung himself into his chair, cheeks flushing against the yellow-starched ruff. "Over Gifford's arrest — as though it were my fault?"

"Mr. Secretary would never think of blaming you for the arrest, Sir." *Though he'd dearly like to know who informed the French on Gifford.* "And, I assure you, it's Phelippes who is the object of his displeasure."

"Oh yes, Phelippes!" Stafford sat up straighter, seizing on indignation with both hands. "Tell me of Phelippes, Mr. *Abbot*. My predecessor told me precious little of the state of things when he left — but one thing I remember: that you and this cypherer were the best of friends, back in your Paris days. Perhaps you can explain the man to me. I never saw him. I had a letter from him once, I think, but never did him good or harm — and yet see what he did to me!"

Well, this had been bound to come up, Tom supposed. "Phelippes is a good man who overreached himself most grievously. Mr. Secretary didn't know he had set Gifford to report particularly on you."

If he noticed the careful turn, Stafford didn't remark on it — though perhaps he was too incensed to notice. "How I wish it were only that!" he exclaimed, and gestured to Lyly. "William, if you please."

Over a chest beside the fireplace sat a cabinet, so intricately inlaid that it stood out even among the Ambassador's abundance of over-carved furniture. With the stride of one ordered into battle, Lyly went to it, his back to Tom as he unlocked the finely worked front flap, to reveal several rows of small drawers. Turning again to better conceal what he did — as though Tom were some foreign spy! — he extracted a small sheaf of letters and, after closing everything again with the utmost care, brought them to Stafford. And see how soldierly he stood at his master's elbow, stare fixed ahead, while Stafford sifted through the papers, and held one up for Tom to see.

"They took his papers, on arresting him."

But surely these couldn't be…? Tom stepped forward and reached out to take the letter. "I thought Mr. Arundel died before he could procure them for you?"

"And so he did." Stafford didn't quite snatch the letter away, but put it back on the table, tapping it with a testy forefinger. "These are just notes of things that Gifford wrote in them, and of things he tells the French. Such as, it was on Mr. Secretary's orders that Phelippes set him to inquire of me and my actions."

"Which, as I said, is not true," Tom tried — and it wasn't, not that it mattered, for Stafford ignored the interruption.

"That he found me a sly child — his own words: a *sly child*! — and that I courted the exiles' friendship, and set Lyly to pose as one of them, all to betray them to London —" He stopped short, as though he'd heard the sudden rising of his voice.

In the silence that followed, Tom asked, "And did you?"

"No, by God, I did not, as you and your father's cousin should well know!" Stafford brandished what Tom recognised as Sir Francis's still sealed letter. "I did propose to play such ruses, and was refused! Refused like the greenest —" Cutting himself short again, he flung down the letter, scattering the small pile of papers across the table.

Peevish, grudging coxcomb! If he knew how Sir Francis had predicted his passion of protest, and forearmed Tom with answers…

"Her Grace and the Council feared that such a bold game could be overturned too easily, Sir — just by some mishap, like this of Gifford."

"You hear, William?" Stafford gave a bitter laugh. "It was for my protection that they let Gifford discredit me and mine, to paint us all as the worst traitors on this side of the sea!"

Gifford and several others, if only the man knew — though, for a mercy, these others' dispatches hadn't been seized by the French. "Do you have this in writing?"

"I have not." Stafford's lips twisted around the sour admission. "But I know that he's talking to the French, hoping to gain favour. Telling them that, if he wrote to England, it was to discredit me as a fool beset by traitors: Lyly — my own right hand!" He reached to grab the man's elbow. "Lyly a secret Catholic, Grimeston a man of evil life, even my coachman a spy!"

And trust Deacon Gifford to play half a dozen games at once!

"Well, Sir, he's lying: he never wrote to London of Mr. Grimeston or your coachman."

Had Lyly noticed the omission? Had Stafford? But then, was he listening at all?

"And Arundel!" he cried — and one would be tempted to believe the anguish in the brown eyes. "He reported poor Charles Arundel as the rankest traitor, sent to haunt me by the Spanish Ambassador!"

"Another lie." At least the Spanish part — for Gifford had denounced Arundel as a man of the Duke of Guise, never of Don Bernardino Mendoza.

"What does it matter?" Shoving back his chair with a screech of wood, the Ambassador sprang to his feet, slamming both palms down on the table, hard enough to make the hourglass totter. "The French want to believe him! The King, the Queen Mother, the whole house of Guise … there's not one of them who won't rejoice to have me so discredited — and, through me, Her Majesty, and England! Don't you see the harm of it, young fool?"

Once more it struck Tom how much Edward Stafford resembled his brother in his fear. For it was fear reddening his face, loosening his pout into a shapeless grimace. Even Lyly, in his sentry's place, appeared ill at ease with the outburst.

Tom held the wild glare in what he hoped was a good likeness of Sir Francis's disapproval.

"What I don't see, Sir," he said, slow and cold, "is how you can be so certain of these reports of yours. Notes of letters — not even copies — and hearsay… How did you come by all this?"

And perhaps the likeness was there, enough of it that Sir Edward Stafford, who could claim distant kinship to the Queen, averted his gaze. He collected himself and sat back — Lyly pushing the chair for him — and drew a hand across his face. When he spoke, it was with the slightest tremor.

"Mr. Walsingham, you must pardon my distemper. This *is* an ill wind, blowing nobody good…"

Nobody but the enemies of England, of course.

"Truly, nobody regrets it more than Mr. Secretary. He deplores this breach of trust, and sends me to mend what can be mended. So, Sir —" *if you want back the trust* — "these notes…"

Whatever had made Stafford check himself, it didn't last long, for he flared at the unasked question.

"In the midst of all this," he hissed, "there are still some who love me, and have found means to come by Gifford's letters. They promise copies — but it's no easy thing. And there's one letter from your Phelippes..." He leant forward, palms flat on the table. "It says that Gifford ensnared Babington and his friends into a plot against the Queen, so they could discover and compromise the Queen of Scots!"

Oh Lord! "But this cannot be true!" It *wasn't* true — for Babington's plot had been genuine, as Tom should know, having played a part in defeating it — and, true or not, surely Phelippes would never...

"It proves that Gifford did so at Mr. Secretary's behest, and with Her Majesty's knowledge!"

The downright absurdness! It was all Tom could do to swallow a laugh. "What it proves, Sir, is that someone is lying to you. An overreaching fool Phelippes may be, but it would take a traitor to make up such scandals."

Stafford caught his breath and blinked — an appropriate reaction for one who had just suggested treason within Mr. Secretary's household. "Perhaps..." He shuffled the papers aimlessly. "Perhaps this is what they would make known here, twisting the meaning of the letters to create these scandals of yours."

Scandals of his! Truly, the man's gall... But then, it mattered little whose scandal it was, and what truth there was to it, if it was used to whip up more hostility against the Queen and her ministers. And if Stafford could boast access to the letters — or their content — why not Lord Paget and his brother, leaders to many English Catholics in Paris?

"Who are *they*, Sir?" Tom asked. "The exiles or the French?"

A mirthless chuckle. "The exiles, the Queen Mother, and that she-devil, the Guise's sister — *Madame* de Montpensier, and God knows who else. There's no lack of rogues eager to make mischief for Her Majesty, and for me as her minister!"

And trust the man to have himself in mind! Tom swallowed his impatience. "Yes, it is a chancy tangle. And if it brought about the death of Mr. Arundel…"

Stafford had been nodding, accepting the recognition of his troubles, but at this he sat up straight like one stung — sudden enough that, at his shoulder, Lyly flinched.

"Brought about…!" the Ambassador breathed.

"Didn't he fall ill just as he was helping you with Gifford's correspondence? You even wrote it must be Paget's doing."

It was plain that Edward Stafford now very much wished he'd written nothing of the sort. See how his mouth twisted and worked, how he sought Lyly's eye.

"I only wrote that in the first burst of grief and anger," he protested. "Poor Arundel was a kinsman, and a friend, for all of his misguided notions — and well on his way to rejoin Her Majesty's cause, for he was helping me greatly."

And perhaps then he wished he hadn't said that, either, when Tom said, "Which makes his death all the more dubious. Have you had means of confirming your suspicions?"

"How would I do that?" Stafford scoffed.

"You wrote that several physicians attended Mr. Arundel — including your own."

"And they all spoke of purple sickness."

"Did you mention your suspicions to them?"

"Good Lord, no!" Stafford all but jumped to his feet, and went to one of the intricately barred back windows. "It's an unchancy word, poison. Especially…"

Especially in the Paris of Catherine de Medici? Especially amidst all the mistrust?

"Nevertheless, Sir, I'm sure you see that I'd better speak to these physicians. You say that Mr. Arundel was helping you: if he was poisoned, then we must consider just how far the Queen's enemies had penetrated his schemes."

"What you call his…" Stafford stopped — a dozen answers playing across his face. *There are no schemes. There are schemes and you'll wreck them. There are schemes and still I'm not trusted with them.* After a moment, he came to lean with both elbows on the back of his chair, eyes narrowed at Tom.

"Walsingham's wolfhound," he murmured. "I've heard it said of you: hounding murderers for Mr. Secretary. Is this what you were sent to do?"

Walsingham's wolfhound! Who called him that? The Cecils, likely. Should Tom take offence? He tilted his head in neither assent nor denial. "I was sent to speak to you, Sir, and to look into things. The matter of Gifford — whom I will have to see — and that of Mr. Arundel too, for it seems to me that they may be tied."

Something shifted in Stafford's countenance, a moment's thought passing like a cloud on a windy day, as swift as it was opaque. At his elbow Lyly shuffled his feet, and was ignored.

"And it seems to me, young Abbot," the Ambassador said, "that asking questions may well make matters worse. I must think more on it. As for seeing Gifford, absolutely not. They're all watching to see what I shall do, what truck I have with Gifford… Well, I'll have none — nor anyone from under my roof."

"But surely, a way can be found. You have —"

"I said no," Stafford interrupted. "And now we'll have no more of this." He stood tall — the Ambassador dismissing an underling. "We keep Christmas, today, so we'll have a service — which you're welcome to attend — and a few guests for dinner." He held up a hand before Tom could ask who. "No one you need to worry about."

Of this, considering Stafford's choice of secretaries, Tom took private leave to doubt — but there was nothing for it, for one thing was clear: dinner with the guests he was *not* welcome to attend. Still…

"It's not Christmas to the French, Sir. The physicians —"

The raised hand again. "We must consider well, before you meet them. Still, if you want to hear of poor Arundel's death, William was with him at the end. I'm sure he can answer your questions, and we won't have to worry about raising the suspicions of strangers." He motioned to his secretary. "If you'd be so good, William?"

It was curious how he asked — as though for a favour — although it was clear from Lyly's stiff little bow that it was an order, and not a very welcome one.

Just how unwelcome the order was, and just what had so suddenly raised Stafford's spirits, Tom was still musing as he waited for Lyly to order his thoughts, or whatever it was that occupied his mind while he pretended to write urgently in the secretaries' room.

This, adjoining Stafford's study and serving as its antechamber, was a smaller room, far less richly appointed, but still very French, with its flowery cupboards and chests, and the two writing tables disposed so to profit from the two windows' light. Tom stood at one of these windows, looking down at the garden, where Hobelot was manning the gate, ready to admit the arriving guests.

And as he waited, he blew on his hands, so hard that Tom could see the clouds of his breath, and squinted at the bare shrubs, and at the silent fountain with such childish absorption… What would it be like to lose one's wits, and spend one's days slowly learning the world anew?

Shaking himself out of these bleak imaginings, Tom turned away from the window to see Lyly still pretending to work.

"Come now, Lyly," he said. "The sooner you tell me what there is to tell, the sooner we can join your master for the service."

This earned a quick resentful glance, and Lyly dropped the pen, together with the pretence of any importance in whatever he was scribbling. "And what is there to tell?" he asked. "Did I see anyone poison Mr. Arundel? I did not."

Tom went to perch on the corner of the unoccupied table, crossed his arms and waited. It didn't take long for Lyly to capitulate.

"I'm not sure what it is that you ask," he grumbled. "You'll know all sorts of things about how men die — but I…"

Walsingham's wolfhound hung unsaid — and if the fool hoped to vex Tom…

"What ailed Mr. Arundel?"

"Didn't Sir Edward write…?" And then, as his master had done, Lyly checked himself — remembering perhaps his last stay in England, and Mr. Secretary's long shadow — and shook his head. Taking a long breath, he began again. "He had a great fever that held him to the last, and those dreadful spots…" He touched his forearm.

"According to what Sir Edward wrote, he raved a good deal."

"That the Queen should know him for an honest man, again and again…"

Just as the letter said — but then, he'd likely written it under Stafford's dictation. Whether they'd made it up together, though…

"Always that?"

"I was sent there twice, to accompany Maître Hennert. The second time we found him raving. That was the day he died."

"Did you speak to the physicians?"

"Hennert, of course, and another, a Frenchman — whose name I don't know."

This last was added in a rush, lest Tom should go combing Paris for the fellow.

"And what did they say?"

They'd played the same game in London — question after sharp question. That they were now under the roof of Lyly's master changed little. Lyly kept his head down, fingering the pen and inkpot.

"They said that it was the purple ague," he said.

Again, straight from the letter — though not all of it. *The purple ague or worse...* "Is that all they said? With certainty?"

"I don't know of the Frenchman. And Hennert spoke to Sir Edward, not to me."

"And Sir Edward ordered you to tell me. To tell me as little as could be, I reckon."

This made the secretary stiffen. "You make very free with your opinion of Sir Edward," he said.

It was the same manner Lyly had had in the study, standing guard at his master's shoulder. Tom had himself stood like that by Sir Francis, and coldly glared at Mr. Secretary's foes — his kinsman's loyal man through and through. But what business had William Lyly doing the same for Stafford? It might have been fine play-acting in the Ambassador's presence, but now...

"Yes," Tom said slowly. "And I should not." *At least not before you.* "Tell me who else was there. Arundel's servants?"

But Lyly was on his guard now, stung into a tongue-tied wariness. "Yes — yes, there was a fellow, but truly, I was only sent twice."

Sent twice — and told to keep quiet.

"I think I've learnt what there is to learn," Tom said — and let Lyly make of it what he would.

Nothing very good, judging by his deepening frown — which didn't clear a whit when the door opened, and the Reverend Hakluyt appeared on the threshold, wide forehead creasing.

"Oh!" he exclaimed, peering inside and eyeing Tom. "I'd hoped to find you, Mr. Lyly, because Her Ladyship asks for you — but…"

Oh, how Lyly sprang to his feet, and welcomed the chaplain, and proclaimed himself at Her Ladyship's disposal. He would have run like a hare, had Hakluyt not stepped inside to let in another man who stood behind him in the door.

"But I keep Mr. Grimeston waiting…"

In waddled a stocky fellow, with cheeks the colour of raw meat, and thinning black curls. This one, too, Tom knew from London: another secretary of Stafford's, half-threatened and half-bribed into Sir Francis's service. And he knew Tom, but, unlike Lyly, made no sign of recognition.

"This is Abbot, from London," Lyly hastened to explain. "Mr. Secretary's new man, come in last night with the packet."

Grimeston nodded at Tom with little more interest than he'd afford a new chair, before he held up a small sheaf of papers. "He'll have to wait at least until tomorrow before he rides back. Sir Edward wants to go through these again, before he sends them. Meanwhile, if you'd be so good…"

Instead of producing whatever was expected — a key, most likely — Lyly drew tall, and reached for the papers. "Thank you, I'll put them away, Mr. Grimeston."

"Don't keep Her Ladyship waiting, Mr. Lyly. I'm sure I can be trusted with such a small task?"

There was a tinge of bristling to Grimeston's bearing, but quiet enough to make Lyly's sudden offence childish by contrast, as he called it an unseemly discussion, and led the way to the Ambassador's study.

"Dear me," murmured Hakluyt, once the door had closed behind the two secretaries. "I'd hoped... But I fear that this sad confusion has distempered us all."

A strange comment to offer to a mere courier! Hakluyt was a learned man, a writer of voyages, whose treatise had been read by the Queen herself. Surely he could never be this artless?

He blinked when Tom made a bland comment on the havoc that held Paris. "Havoc, Mr. Walsingham? Oh, there's plenty of that, for sure — but you must be aware..."

Mr. Walsingham! Tom raked his brain: had he met Hakluyt before — that the man should remember, and not he? "Aren't you mistaken, Sir?" he asked.

The chaplain had one of those fair complexions that coloured very pink. "Oh — but I assure you: were anyone present to hear, I'd address you as nothing else but Abbot. Sir Edward was most insistent on it."

Most insistent, was he? Jove rain on Sir Edward — and so much for discretion! "I'm sure he was," Tom ground out. "As I'm sure you'll be most discreet." And, after all, there being questions Tom Walsingham could ask that Abbot could not... "And yes, there's more than the Parisians' ill humour."

Three measured nods. "Poor Mr. Arundel, dead an exile and a heretic, and now Sir Edward's troubles..." He looked up and quietly clapped his hands once. "But it grows late. The Christmas service, you understand..."

And if he'd hoped with this to cut the conversation short, he was disappointed when Tom declared his complete understanding and followed along, asking about Arundel as they walked.

Hakluyt talked of the dead man in whispers as they descended the stairs, as softly as though they were standing at the graveside — or as though he feared an eavesdropper in every corner.

"My Lady Stafford's distant cousin, and Sir Edward's as well — but, of course, there couldn't be much in the way of intercourse, considering. A very sad thing, that families should be so sundered apart."

Foolish as it was, Tom found himself speaking softly in turn. "Still, Sir Edward sent him his physician, and Mr. Lyly was there at his death."

"That was mere Christian charity. Sir Edward would have sent me, if poor Mr. Arundel had wished for it, and I would have gone — but of course…"

"Of course. Mr. Lyly is rumoured to be a Catholic, so perhaps he made for more congenial company?"

The chaplain stopped short on the last step, his back stiffening. "Well now, Mr. Lyly…"

"There were rumours — even before what you call this 'sad confusion'."

The hall had two barred windows that looked out onto the street, and between them stood a sideboard. That was where the chaplain walked, slow of pace and grave-faced. Tom followed. There was an enamel candlestick on the board, and Lady Stafford's servants must have been lazy, for it was coated with dust, and a string of congealed wax clung to it. Richard Hakluyt ran an ink-stained fingernail along the dried drops.

"Your master, Mr. *Abbot*," he began slowly, "was good enough to give me instructions when I travelled here. Instructions to inquire for him into the voyages and discoveries of the French — not into the souls of those with whom I am living under the same roof." He fixed a pair of earnest grey eyes on Tom. "I am their chaplain. You surely don't expect that I should spy on them?"

Tom bit down a retort. What he expected was help in ascertaining the truth of a murder, but nothing the chaplain had said showed he was aware of Stafford's suspicions. Which begged the question of how the Ambassador chose his indiscretions — unless, of course, Hakluyt knew very well and was lying. Either way, better to fall back on a safer course, and on a manner of mild reason. "What I hope, more than I expect, is to clear Mr. Lyly of suspicion — if I can. Something must have caused the rumours — but the cause may well have been innocent."

And after all, perhaps, the man did have a trusting mind: see with what relief he grasped at this notion, nodding in sad sympathy. "You must forgive me, I feared... You are right. I wouldn't call young Lyly the most zealous lamb in my little flock, nor the most free-spoken — but I can see that he's much troubled by these rumours you mention."

"By the rumours, or by what he did to bring them about?" Tom asked, and earned a look of such dismay, that he hastened to add, "I don't ask that you should betray his trust — but reticence won't help him."

Hand to his chin, forefinger tapping his lip, Hakluyt considered. Did he wonder whose reticence was in question? Or why Tom didn't ask Sir Edward? Or did he weigh the dangers of displeasing Mr. Secretary's man?

In the end, he said, "I'd think he doesn't feel at liberty to tell ... and neither do I — not that I'd have much to tell if I did. But this I'll say: Mr. Lyly is loyal to Sir Edward, who trusts him deeply."

And kept trusting him while the man took Mary Stuart's coin, not to mention that of Sir Francis.

"Sir Edward trusts him with such tasks as visiting Arundel in his illness?"

The chaplain nodded once, slow and purse-lipped. "We all serve Her Majesty, don't we? You by winnowing truth from falsehood, myself by inquiring God's vast world, and Mr. Lyly by doing his master's bidding. If he puts himself in danger for this, must he be blamed? Or because he sometimes runs his master's errands of mercy?" All of this was said so nobly, Tom wouldn't have noticed the relief, if he hadn't known to look for it.

And then, pleading lateness, Hakluyt hastened away to his Christmas service, leaving Tom uncertain about the shape of a strict conscience and the loopholes men allowed themselves.

If Tom had hoped to observe the household during the service, he was disappointed.

He should have expected it, truly: no matter what Stafford had told the chaplain about Tom, Abbot was still nothing but a courier to most of those present, and therefore stood with the servants and the secretaries, near the back of the room that made do for a chapel. Cleared of all furniture and decoration, but for the ornate communion table, and two rows of chairs for the Staffords and their guests, the place had an air that was more austere than solemn. Even the abundance of candles in silver sticks and sconces did little against the greyness of the day, and the flames flickered in the chill draughts from the ill-fitting casements.

Tom shivered and fumed to himself in what must surely be a most unchristian manner. Of Stafford, his lady, and their guests, he saw no more than their well-dressed backs, while

Grimeston, Lyly and the servants he couldn't observe without turning around. All he could do was watch the mould that mottled the walls at the corners, and listen to the Reverend Mr. Hakluyt expounding — at uncomfortable and cheerless length — on the joy of the Saviour's birth. But then it had been a long time since Tom had kept Christmas with proper reverence. As for cheer... A sudden thought of Frances made his breath hitch. Frances, who'd never smile at Christmastide again, ever remembering the losses of her husband and her stillborn daughter. And here he was, bemoaning his own woes — heartless fool that he was! The rest of the service he barely heard, answering and singing by rote — instead praying in his heart that Frances's grief could be soothed.

After the last hymn, as he followed the minor folks out of the makeshift chapel, Tom found Skeres at his elbow.

"All the time I've tried to catch your eye," grumbled the lad, "but did you see? No — all glum and bedevilled!" *He* wasn't glum; in fact, Skeres sported such ruddy cheeks that Tom suspected he'd found some cheer already, in the shape of mulled ale. Still he had an air of purpose that made Tom stop them both in a corner out of hearing.

"And what did you want my eye for?" he asked.

Anyone watching them would think Skeres a villain plotting murder, as he peered over one hunched shoulder and then the other before leaning in close to whisper in Tom's ear.

"There's two secretaries, not one..."

Brows rising, Tom leant away from the festive breath. "Yes, Dolius — that we knew before leaving London: Lyly and Grimeston."

"Ha!" A portentous nod, a pointing finger. "Grimeston — that's the fat one with the red face! 'E says you'll find 'im at a place called the Plot a-Ten, behind the church of Saint Severin. For Christmas dinner, 'e says."

"The *Plat d'Étain*, perhaps?" Remembering Grimeston's uneasy London days, Tom hadn't thought him one for hugger-mugger. But then, what of the outburst in the secretaries' room? Unusual, judging by Hakluyt's reaction: had it been a play put on for the man from London? *See who is Stafford's man and who isn't...* "And when did he say so?"

"Sought me out in the kitchen before the service. Asked was I with the gentleman from London." A lopsided shrug. "So, 'ats and coats and all."

Thoughts of the Minotaur bellowing for good English ale in the middle of a *taverne* crossed Tom's mind.

"Mine, not yours," he said, and forged ahead before the lad could protest. "You stay here, and keep your ears open. And Skeres: you've wassailed enough."

Oh, the indignation! Skeres's flushed cheeks darkened in blotches. "When d'you ever see me sack-sopped?"

Seldom enough, in truth. But this morning Tom had only to raise a brow at his servant, who, when an attempt at offended virtue was cut short by a belch, could only look away — the Minotaur abashed.

"You stay, Skeres, and if you're sober enough, find out who it is that Stafford invites to his Christmas table."

And, having issued his orders, Tom hastened away.

CHAPTER 3

The *Plat d'Étain* — the Tin Platter they'd called it, with the Thomases — had been a pleasant place, once, with a brisk business and a cheerful air. Now the copper on the walls gleamed dully, and there were no fresh-cheeked lasses to offer welcome. Instead a gaunt fellow with a long face like a bad-tempered spaniel met Tom on the kitchen's threshold, eyes going cold on hearing even a shade of English accent, and colder still when the Englishman insisted on seeking an acquaintance among the customers — and failed to find him.

But there were all sorts of reasons why the secretary might be late — so Tom sat at a table in a quiet corner of the *grande salle*, ordered a jug of wine, and waited. The wine, it turned out, was thinned-out local fare, and the odour of tallow (it had been beeswax, once) hung in the air, so strong it drowned out the scent of cooking, and with every minute that passed, Tom's questions took a darker turn. Was this Grimeston more loyal to Stafford than he made out? Was this all a ruse to trick Mr. Secretary's man out of the way? And for what reason? Who were the guests Tom needn't worry about? Wouldn't it be better to hasten back to the Embassy, and surprise them all?

Even as Tom was beckoning the taverner to pay for his wine and leave, there he appeared: Grimeston, large and flustered, filling the doorway. He squinted through the candlelit gloom, lighting up in relief when he caught sight of Tom.

"Mr. Abbot!" he breathed, sinking onto a stool and wiping a kerchief across his sweaty brow. "I feared you'd gone."

"I was about to," Tom said, "for it crossed my mind that you'd been luring me away from the house." Although, if he had, then Grimeston would have been at the *Plat d'Étain* from the beginning, wouldn't he?

Unruly black brows, hands and voice shot up. "No, no! Why would...?" The secretary checked himself. "But you jest. I couldn't slip away before — and it was a good thing, in the end, because..." Stealing a glance over his shoulder, he hitched his stool closer, and then, not finding it sufficient, he rose to drop onto the bench at Tom's side. "You'll like to hear this, Mr. Abbot..."

He stopped when the spaniel-like server arrived to ask, "Would *Messieurs* eat?" Grimeston ordered Anjou wine and *pâté lorrain*, this French cousin of a pie — the Christmas dinner Tom reckoned he'd have to pay for.

"It's not worth drinking wine made in the *Pays de France*," the secretary said, gesturing at Tom's jug with a gap-toothed smile that made him appear younger.

The wine of the *Pays de France*, yes — it had been a joke among the couriers. "I'd forgotten that," Tom said. "Now, what is it that I'll like to hear?"

"Oh." Preoccupation aged Grimeston's face again. How old was the man? Not much more than five-and-thirty, surely? "There was a visitor for Sir Edward."

"I saw rather more than one."

Grimeston shook his head. "None of the English you saw at the service. This one was French, I think..." He leant a little closer. "He arrived just as the service ended, and brought some papers of Gifford's."

The secretary had been right: Tom liked to hear this very much. "The ones from Phelippes?" he asked, and was disappointed when Grimeston shook his head again.

"Or at least... I only know of two: the one I saw was a letter Gifford wrote to a cousin of his, a man in the Pagets' circle —

and to him he swears he played your master double; the other is a note from Sir Edward himself."

"A note!" Tom sat up straighter. There had been in Stafford's letter something about trying to warn Gifford in prison — but surely... "Surely it was never left with Gifford?"

Grimeston grimaced. "Sir Edward never told me to bring it back —"

"*You* went there?"

"Lord forfend Sir Edward should risk young Lyly going into the lion's den — but myself?" A bitter snort. "So I go to the Bishop's prison under the guise of an English merchant trying to arrange for young Gilbert's sureties at his father's behest, and bring letters back and forth."

So much for having no truck with the man! But the unspeakable stupidity... "And those from Sir Edward you left there."

"Only the first one. When Sir Edward thought to ask for it back — always through me — Gifford said he'd had it hidden where nobody would find it."

"Nobody except the French!" Tom sat back with a huff, watching the dark ceiling above, where ropes of greasy smoke floated up to coil between the beams. "What was in it?"

And Grimeston had thought to please Mr. Secretary's man with his tidings! "Sir Edward had me writing it in a counterfeited hand," he hastened to explain. "There were no names named. They've no way to know..."

Ay — and, as Skeres was fond of saying, pigs fly with their tails forward! Tom bent to catch the lowered eyes. "What was in it?" he insisted, and then was silenced by the arrival of their dinner.

As the maid fussed with trenchers and flagons, the secretary exchanged a few shy words with her. Once she was gone, he poured wine for himself and for Tom, and sat back with another sigh.

"Warnings to keep his counsel," he said. "An offer to get him out of prison — this was in the letter."

Oh, better and better! Tom unclasped his eating knife to cut himself a slice of pie, savaging the crust in his vexation, and finding it limp and soggy. "An offer the Deacon refused, I take it? Or one Sir Edward couldn't make good?"

And see how Grimeston squirmed, with sweat glistening on his brow and among his thin black ringlets. What else was there?

"I think…" He cleared his throat. "I think that those Gifford fears are outside the Bishop's prison. He says he knows who revealed him to the French, but won't tell."

The Deacon's malicious face painted itself in Tom's mind. How easy it was to imagine him, half-boasting and half-fearful!

"Gilbert Gifford believes that all are out to do him harm, but certainly he made plenty of enemies in France and in England." *You and Lyly, among others…*

"Not that he was slow in taking Sir Edward's money — but I—"

Wine will go down the wrong way when one catches one's breath while drinking. The secretary slapped Tom's back as he coughed and spluttered, while curious eyes turned their way all around the gloomy *grande salle*. Tom waved Grimeston back, and hissed, "What money?"

The man opened his mouth once, twice, and then: "I brought ten crowns myself this morning," he confessed in a rush. "Gifford says that money is all he needs to be freed, for they've nothing against him, nothing of true import."

"Nothing of true import!" But surely, they must all be dreaming? Gifford asked — and, knowing what he knew,

Stafford obliged! To think he was so scathing of them in London for trusting the man. "How you or Sir Edward can believe that, only the devil knows! But even if they had nothing against him, now you've given them written proof of intrigue with the Ambassador, and then a purse of money to cinch it."

And could it truly be that none of this had occurred to Grimeston? See how he blinked!

"But they don't know it's from Sir Edward," he protested. "I go under colour of finding him a French promotor, and never speak or write of Sir Edward other than as *the gentleman...*"

"And who else would do it all in secret, filching papers away under the Bishop's nose? What do you think they'll suspect, the moment they find your counterfeited letter gone?"

For a long moment Grimeston stared at the pâté, biting his thumb, and then he slowly looked up. "I don't know that they will, though. Sir Edward had me copy the other letter so it could be returned. Surely his was returned too?"

Why, yes — there was some reprieve in that, as long as nobody knew someone was at work to inform the English... Tom sat up of a sudden. Someone *was* at work! "You never told me: who brought these papers?"

Another shake of the head. "Sir Edward had me called to the writing-room, and bade me copy Gifford's letter in all haste, then went away. When he came back, he said my letter had been found. Mine — as though I were to blame!"

Which he was, for leaving behind the cursed thing in the first place, whether he'd been told to take it back or not. A piece of foolishness bad enough to have any Service man kicked out. But then, there was the crux of it. Tom contemplated his table-mate, who sat hunched, drawing lines with his knife in the soggy crust. Grimeston was no Service man. A scholar, and no fool by any means, but let him stumble out of the confines of long-sighted erudition, and he floundered. Would he prove more danger than help — to Sir Francis and to himself? If Arundel, fox that he was, had met such a fate... *If* he had met it at all.

But then, what would this fellow know? Ah, well... "Tell me of Maître Hennert," Tom said. "Will he answer truthfully if I question him?"

Whatever Grimeston had expected, it wasn't this change of tack. "Hennert?" he repeated, gawping.

"I assume Sir Edward trusts him, or he wouldn't have him at the Embassy." And much less at the bedside of a man who could betray them all when delirious.

The same thoughts must have been running through the secretary's mind, as he pursed his lips this way and that. At length he tilted his head. "If Hennert is in Sir Edward's confidence, why always have Lyly accompany him to see Mr. Arundel?"

But Lyly had told a different story, hadn't he? "Always?" Tom asked — and Grimeston mistook his meaning.

"Sir Edward himself, once — but otherwise..." He snorted. "Arundel's was a safe den for the boy to enter."

So many in the Service thought that Sir Francis shielded Tom like this — and they were wrong. But... "Lyly says he only visited twice."

"Then Lyly gives the truth a good shaving." Bracing both palms on the table, Grimeston pushed upright. "My appetite's gone — and I'll be missed if I don't go back. Perhaps you will be, too."

Would he be? Well, Stafford could hardly expect him to sit and mope in his room while the Christmas guests were entertained. Oh yes — the guests.

"Wait, Grimeston: Sir Edward's guests. He said I needn't worry about them."

"And you need not," the secretary said, as he donned his still-damp cape. "A couple of English merchants with their wives, and a kinsman of Lord Hunsdon's, passing through on his travels. But, Mr. Abbot..." He bowed to Tom as though in greeting, and whispered, "For one thing, Sir Edward told me who you are. And for another, beware: nothing you send to London and nothing you receive will go unread. Good day, Sir."

And, likely thinking he had acted with great secrecy and discretion, the secretary went on his way, leaving Tom to a cold pâté, and a host of unpleasant contemplations.

Pull the bell when you come back, Master, and I'll run and let you in, Hobelot had said on letting Tom out. The bell's last echo hadn't died down when the door of the right-side lodge swung open, and the giant stood there, with such a large, guileless grin that Tom just had to smile back. What sort of soldier had this one made? Or had what ferocity he'd once possessed been wiped away together with his wits? But no — for he'd had some left for the roisterers in the street.

Tom thanked the porter as he was let inside the lukewarm little vestibule, still pondering the matter of Stafford's letter-carrying friend. *Some who love me*, the Ambassador had said. Someone who had access to the Bishop's judicial papers — or perhaps good ears at Court, if truly the letters had arrived there. Someone who was French, and had an interest in keeping Stafford where he was...

"Hobelot," Tom called, taken with a sudden thought. "Is your master still with his French guest?"

The porter stopped in the act of drawing the half dozen bolts. "Why, no, Master. He's been long gone."

He looked worried of a sudden and — oh Lord! — surely it was a sin to make use of such innocence? Tom bit down the qualm.

"*Monsieur's* secretary is an old friend — I would have liked to have seen him again. Was Leduc with *Monsieur?*"

"Why, no, Master. *Monsieur* Simier always comes alone — but I've in mind that he lives quite near. Perhaps you can visit your friend? You must ask Adkin, though, for it's him as His Honour sends to light the way for the guests at night, seeing as he's big and strong."

Bigger and stronger than Hobelot himself? Tom thanked the fellow, and assured him that he would certainly ask Adkin — and then he made his way to the hall, mind awhirl.

Simier, then! Perhaps not so great a surprise: Jean de Simier, courtier and diplomat, King Henri's man, the Duke of Anjou's envoy to Queen Elizabeth during that prickly royal courtship — and, according to the spy Rogers, holding Stafford in a stranglehold over his gambling debts. The man had been Lord Burleigh's friend, back in England. Was he now scheming on the Treasurer's behalf? Tom always pictured his thoughts as pieces of coloured glass, clicking and flickering as they shifted into a pattern: at this moment, they lay in a shapeless jumble.

He had hardly the time to cross the garden before he found himself summoned by Stafford again — not to the study, but to Her Ladyship's parlour upstairs, where he found both the Ambassador and his wife. It was a goodly room, glowing with amber-coloured silks and many beeswax candles, hung with tapestries, perfumed with civet, and heated well past comfort by a roaring fire. In this rich nest the Staffords sat side by side by the hearth, a king and queen watching a supplicant.

The Baroness's idea, most surely — ruined somewhat by the fact that Stafford, under his padded silks, fidgeted and perspired in the cloying heat.

The Ambassador rose, bowing to his unsmiling wife. "My lady will excuse us."

He cut a very different figure in his lady's presence, with all the morning's bluster gone. When they were seen together, their ten years' difference showed starkly — not in that it made the wife appear old, but that the husband seemed at once less mature and more staid. How did she like it that they were now to walk out of her presence? Not very much, if one had to reckon by the tilt of her head: composed and graceful — but not pleased.

Barely acknowledged, Tom made his best Court bow, and followed Sir Edward to the secretaries' room — and all the while he pictured in his mind the Baroness rehearsing her husband on whatever grave matter he was to impart to Mr. Secretary's man.

But perhaps it wasn't just the lady's influence subduing Stafford's humours. Once they'd crossed his study to a severe smaller cabinet, where the candles awaited already lit, the Ambassador sank into one high-backed chair, and motioned Tom to another. His tone was still unblustering as he spoke.

"Mr. Walsingham…" He glanced at Tom sharply, as if expecting a correction. When none came, he squared himself in the chair, and began again. "Mr. Walsingham, there's a matter I would submit to Mr. Secretary. I wouldn't discuss it before Mr. Lyly yet — and I only tell you thinking that you're not ignorant of how the proposition will be received." He looked down and then up again. "I wish to resign my position."

Oh, he did not. Or perhaps he did in this moment, and would regret it if he got his wish. But what truly mattered was that Sir Francis did not wish it at all. So Tom made a show of doubtful consideration.

"Do you think it would it be wise, Sir?"

"Wise!" Stafford huffed, palms spread wide. "You've heard my plight: what use is an ambassador who doesn't have the trust of those who sent him?"

You'll have to soothe the man, Thomas... "But you do have Mr. Secretary's trust, Sir. I'm here to assure you —"

"And you'll still assure me, knowing how I'm discredited, thanks to your Phelippes?" He turned away, raking a hand through his brown curls. "You still assure me when I don't know how to deal with the matter, and they lie in wait, watching what I do?"

Why Lady Stafford had allowed her husband to make this plea alone, Tom didn't know. Surely she couldn't have hoped that he'd feel sorry for the man? But no. A glass piece clicked into place: in fact, she knew he wouldn't. Whatever her husband's megrims, Douglas Sheffield meant to stay in Paris. Whether this coincidence of her wishes with those of Sir Francis was a good thing, Tom put aside to consider.

"And what will *they* say if you go home now, Sir?" he asked. "One of two things: either that you do lack that trust and Gifford's lies are true, or that you had it, and let Gifford's lies send you home in a fury. Either way..." He trailed off, not surprised in the least when Stafford twisted in the chair to scowl at him.

"Either way I'll have played the fool, won't I?"

Very, very much, Tom didn't say. "Either way, Sir, think how much better it will be if you stand firm. You'll show yourself unmoved, unshaken in your standing. I see no better way to give Gifford the lie."

Instead of answering, Stafford drew in a long breath, and then another, and all the while he frowned at Tom and tapped beringed fingers on his fashionably padded peascod. Tom waited, as blank-faced as he knew how.

"I'll have to think on it," the Ambassador said at length, passion quenched for the moment. "To consider."

Just as he must consider more on the matter of Gifford — but that had been in the morning, before Tom had heard the truth of it from Grimeston.

"And, Sir — I truly believe that I could better help your case if I were to speak to Gifford…"

And there Stafford went scowling again — although not half as much as he might have. "You think it an easy matter?" he said. "Didn't I write that the man claims to be a priest?"

"He was surely a deacon three years ago," Tom said. "And he may well have been ordained since coming back to France."

"Well, then the Bishop had the right of it when he snatched Gifford from the King's Lieutenant Criminal, and put him into his own prison. Have you ever been at the For-l'Évêque? They're most particular as to who enters their gates. What if you went there, and they in some way or other tied you to the Embassy? Why…" He sat forward as a sudden notion hit him. "Gifford knows you, doesn't he? What if he told them who you are?"

"And who am I, Sir Edward? Gifford knows well that, no matter my name, I'm just one of Mr. Secretary's servants — like him, like Phelippes." Tom shrugged. Not that it was quite true — the Deacon being of those who still mistook Tom's place in the Service — but still… "He'd have no more reason to uncover me than anyone you sent. And he hasn't yet, I take it?"

Had Stafford been a fox, his ears would have pricked up. "Anyone *I* sent?"

"Your letter, back in December, said you hoped to have someone speak with him on the morrow..."

Did Stafford also count in Latin? Not very often, most likely — and not for very long. It took him no more than a few heartbeats to exhale through his nose and admit that yes — yes, he had.

"I've had one of my men see Gifford under the pretext of finding him a procurer." And whatever he saw in Tom's face made him bristle. "He does not go as my man, of course! I told you: I want no ties to be observed between Gifford and myself."

With the exception of a sum of money, and a most damning little note... "Well then, Sir, if your man succeeded in acting so secretly, there's no reason why I should not. Why, I believe I've more experience than Mr. Lyly in this sort of matter."

You'll often learn more by pretending ignorance or error, Thomas, than by asking. And indeed...

"Why should you think...? It's Grimeston that I sent," Stafford corrected. "My other secretary — a learned, staid fellow. I'm sure, whatever you want to ask Gifford, that he could do it for you."

"For a courier? Or have you told Mr. Grimeston, too, that I'm no such thing?"

It was unchristian, surely, to find some satisfaction in the way the Ambassador stared, wrong-footed.

"You told Mr. Hakluyt, Sir — and he didn't think to keep it from me."

With a harrumph, Stafford sprang up to pace. "You never expected that I should keep it from my wife and my secretaries?"

"And your chaplain."

"And no one else — but you make a strange courier, with a servant in tow, and asking all sorts of questions. They were bound to doubt."

And to speak unguardedly, perhaps. "This I won't deny, Sir — as long as you see that I must ask."

"I don't know that you can, though — not without risking more suspicion. What could you learn from Gifford that Grimeston can't? And from poor Arundel's physicians? They're French, God knows in whose pay…"

"Even Maître Hennert?"

The Ambassador threw up a hand. "He's a good man, and discreet — but still a French subject. What can you learn from him that would be worth the risk?"

What it is that you want to keep from me, for one thing… "I'd think, Sir, that it makes a great deal of difference whether Mr. Arundel died of poison or the purple ague. If the Pagets had him killed, it means your schemes with him are known to the enemies of England."

Stafford's pacing quickened. "Good Lord, I don't know that it was the Pagets' doing! And even if it was, poor Arundel and young Paget were like cat and dog. Why, once they even came to blows!"

"As I heard it, it was Arundel who drew his sword on Paget. But no matter: they may not have seen eye to eye, but their cause was still one, and Arundel is dead. *If* it was the Pagets' doing, it's more likely to have been over treason than out of dislike."

There was little that the Ambassador could object to that.

"Oh, this is going to distress my wife greatly. To think her cousin was murdered, and all because of Gifford! Would that…" He stopped behind his vacated chair, gripping the back. "Would that your Phelippes never thought to trust that knave with a scrap of paper!"

This from the man who, knowing what he knew, had trusted the knave with a damning letter and ten crowns.

"I'm sure we all very much regret it, Sir, and Phelippes most of all."

And had Tom meant this as anything other than yet another stroke to Stafford's ruffled feathers, he would have been much disappointed. The Ambassador drew himself as tall as he could, and looked down his nose with the utmost severity.

"Mr. Walsingham, it's Christmas today," he announced in a ponderous rumble. "On this of all days, as I would be forgiven by God, so, with all my heart I forgive your Phelippes. But, for sure, I think the stones will cry to God for vengeance on him. Not for seeking to make his own credit to undo me — but for my poor men, whose reputation is their living, which he disgraced and undid upon such a varlet's report."

Lord, what a pompous fool! Swallowing an urge to salute this noble speech with an amen, Tom nodded gravely instead. "Sir, I'll do my best to undo the harm," he said. "If only you'll allow me."

This earned no better than a twisting of lips — and wasn't it an irony that there wasn't one among his *poor men* that Stafford should have trusted any better than he did Tom?

CHAPTER 4

"Master!" Hobelot came trotting from the little lodge in the grey dawn, with another large man at his shoulder — and between them they filled the passage. Skeres, Tom could tell, was gauging the pair in wary consideration.

"This here's Adkin, Master," the porter announced, beaming as one presenting the Lord Admiral — and Tom remembered.

Adkin, the brother — and there was no mistaking it, for Adkin was another smiling, ginger-haired giant, if a little younger, and with intelligence intact in his eye. The coachman who would know about Simier's dwelling place…

Not that Tom had ever truly meant to ask — much less if there was anything to Gifford's claims. *A spy for the Queen's enemies…* Here was punishment for making use of poor Hobelot's innocence!

"Tell Master Abbot, Adkin!" Hobelot nudged his brother with an elbow that would have knocked down a lesser man.

Adkin was unmoved. "Ay, well," he said. "'Tis about Mr. Simier you're wanting to know, Master? The Frenchman?"

As though there might be an English Simier too, or Simier were the only Frenchman around… It could be that, in losing his wits, Hobelot had fallen from no great heights.

"Ay, him — I told you!" Hobelot insisted. "Tell him, Adkin."

So pleadingly he insisted, that Tom reformed his first judgment: the coachman wasn't so much slow as a little uncertain of what his brother said, and seeking confirmation. See how he patted Hobelot's arm in reassurance.

"Ay, Hob — I'm telling." He gave Tom a rueful smile. "Mr. Simier, now — he lives a stone's throw away, Master, in the Rue de Bièvre, just round the corner."

"So you can see your friend now, eh, Master?"

Ignoring his beaming brother, Adkin glanced at the window. "I can show you the door, Master, if you like — and if you care to go before I'm needed."

Because out in the garden, a flare of bright green in the dreary light, Lady Stafford was walking in her emerald-coloured cloak, inspecting the intricate knots of beds and paths with an unseasonable keenness. It was as good an excuse as any to decline the coachman's offer, and Hobelot's disappointment vanished when Tom vailed both brothers.

"You've made a friend there," Skeres chuckled when the two had gone their way.

Tom was a good deal less pleased. "And perhaps awakened a foe to my doubts about Simier," he said. "Gifford calls our Adkin a spy."

Over his shoulder the lad glowered at the door through which the brothers had disappeared. "Whose spy?"

"Lord knows. Another thing to ask the Deacon, if I ever get to see him." Tom couldn't blame the Minotaur when he snorted. Outside, Lady Stafford still surveyed her garden with the air of a displeased general. Her Ladyship, now. And Arundel. And Simier… "Go haunt the kitchen, Dolius, and make eyes to your scullion. I want to know what the servants think of the coachman."

Skeres's face, having brightened with the notion of the warm kitchen and the girl, darkened again at once. "And you? You ain't going out again without me, are you? 'Obelot says the Papists are all spoiling for a fight."

And why his servant must think him so helpless, Tom neither knew nor wanted to discuss. "I'm going nowhere for now," he said a little brusquely. "I've a sudden itch to speak to Her Ladyship again."

Being admitted to Her Ladyship's presence, it turned out, meant going through Lyly — and Lyly, huddled in his chair in the secretaries' room and staring dully at the one lit candle, wasn't in a helpful mood.

"At this hour?" he groused. "You must be mad! She won't even be up yet."

"I saw her in the garden a while back."

"Then why don't you ask her yourself?"

Tom did not, he decided, like William Lyly in the least.

"I'm asking you," he said, and they both knew he was not asking.

For a little while Lyly sat there, blowing on his fingers — and little blame to him, for Stafford didn't share Sir Francis's maxim of always keeping his scriveners warm, and the room had no fireplace.

At length he stood. "She doesn't like to be disturbed before breaking her fast," he tried.

"Then you'll tell her woman that Abbot begs for a word, as soon as it's convenient to Her Ladyship. Surely Sir Edward will have told her why I'm here?" *And surely he'll have told you?*

No matter how he fiddled with the ink-pot on his table, each thought showed plain on Lyly's face: could he get away with a lie? Was he being put to the test?

"Yes," he ground out at length. "Yes, he'll have told her. He told me and Hakluyt — and Grimeston too, I'll wager — and there's little or naught he keeps from her."

Nonetheless, when they tracked Lady Stafford's woman hurrying upstairs with a tray, it was Mr. Abbot's message that Lyly gave.

"The servants are not to be told," he explained once out of the woman's hearing — leaving Tom to marvel at Stafford's notions of discretion.

He had to marvel at Lyly's reluctance, too — when, for all of his sullen predictions, Lady Stafford sent for Abbot at once, and received him in the same amber-hued parlour as last night.

Daylight made it shabbier: it dulled the sheen of the silks, and showed the fray at the tapestries' edges. Still, the parlour was the best appointed room Tom had yet seen in the Embassy, and made a fine frame for Lady Stafford as she stood by the fireplace, tall and magnificent in sage green.

Tom bowed low, and waited while he was appraised with frank curiosity, and he remembered what a striking figure the Baroness Sheffield had cut together with the Earl of Leicester. Well, she was certainly still as striking on her own.

"You look nothing like your kinsman," she said at last, in her beautiful viol's voice, and so disapprovingly that Tom almost felt at fault.

"I take after my mother's side, Madam," he said, half in apology, half in amusement — as he recognised the irrelevance for what it was: *I know who you are.*

And she must have seen the way of it, because the shadow of a smile twitched at the corner of her mouth. It was a heartbeat, and then she sobered again. "So Mr. Secretary thinks that Charles Arundel was murdered," she said.

Otherwise, why send his hound? "Mr. Secretary won't discount the chance — mostly because Sir Edward suggested it in his letter."

"Sir Edward didn't…" The Baroness's lips tightened. "Since that letter, my husband has come to think differently on the matter."

"So he's told me — but I still think his first suspicion is worth investigating," Tom said. "If there was a murder, the understanding he had with Mr. Arundel could make Mr. Ambassador's position here in Paris unsafe or awkward. Why, if the French were to object to his continued presence, the Council would be forced to recall him."

A solid argument, when it came to Stafford's wife, and one that she would surely keep to herself. She stood considering, half turned away, tapping on the hearth with the point of an embroidered slipper.

"And if you can't prove it one way or the other?"

By all accounts Douglas Stafford was a friend to the Queen Mother, Catherine de Medici — the ruthless Italian schooled in the works of Machiavelli and the use of poisons. Tom found that the lady's imperious stare made him rather more nervous than all her husband's posturing. Let her not laugh at him, as he tried for Sir Francis's most even manner.

"We must hope that I can, Madam — and soon, for an unconfirmed suspicion would leave Sir Edward exposed to whatever doubts the French may conceive."

She must have been thinking at least a little of the same. *And a great nuisance you are with it*, said the tightening of her lips, and the tilt of her head on her long neck — the same ill-tempered elegance of the Queen's swans — but still, a nuisance who wasn't wrong, for she asked, "And how do you propose to go about it?"

Well, at least she didn't seem bent on opposing him — not that Tom would confide in her for it. "There are several ways,

Madam. First, though, if I'm to confirm or exclude the chance of poison, I must speak to Mr. Arundel's physicians."

Why he didn't go to her husband with this, she didn't ask — but the embroidered slipper resumed its tapping, and there was more annoyance than anything else when she said, "Why you should think that I know them..."

"I know from Sir Edward's letters that Maître Hennert was one of them." *But, not knowing what's good for him, Sir Edward dithers and I waste time...*

It all hinged, Tom supposed, on how badly the Baroness wanted to stay in Paris.

Badly enough, it seemed. "Very well, Mr. Walsingham. Lyly will tell you where to find the man — but..." A considering frown. "These other physicians... You'll know that poor Charles was much in the confidence of the Duke of Guise. The Duke could well have sent them to tend to him in his illness." *Or to poison him, on finding him unfaithful.* She clicked her tongue. "Oh, one of your name will know to be wary."

How could one respond to this, but with a bow? "And, Madam, what of Mr. Arundel's servants? They might have seen something amiss." *Or done something amiss, if they came from the Duke of Guise too.*

Lady Stafford huffed — if such a ladylike sound could be called so. "You set such store by poor Arundel being my kinsman! I'm sure you understand, we weren't such close friends as we both could have wished. He was too fervent a Catholic for a kinswoman in my position. It doesn't mean, though, that I wouldn't learn the truth of his death. Now I wish I'd paid more attention to his domestic arrangements."

"Could the Duke of Guise have sent him servants, as well as physicians?"

Another shake of the dark head — this time one of slow consideration. "Who can tell that he didn't? You'll have to tread warily, Mr. Walsingham, even with Hennert, for all that he has my husband's trust. As I said, Lyly will know how to find him."

This last was said with enough firmness that Tom knew himself dismissed. There was little for it but to thank the Baroness, and bow, and be content that he had her blessing in the matter of Hennert, if nothing else.

Finding Maître Hennert's house in the Faubourg Saint-Victor was easy enough; finding the man himself was another matter. Out doing his visits, the dour housekeeper said, and not expected home until the dinner hour. Cursing himself for not having thought of this, Tom vailed out of the woman the names of a few streets inside the walls where her master had patients to see — and, perhaps more promisingly, that of an apothecary on the Petit Pont, where the physician had matters to discuss.

So out into the pouring rain he stepped, and slogged his way back through the gate and into the filthy streets, scanning the crowd for yellow-gloved medical gentlemen riding a mule. He saw none — not that he'd truly expected it — and he was soaked to the marrow by the time he entered the gloom of the Petit Châtelet. Lord, but he loathed the place! Even being out of the rain was no relief in that damp, echoing, ill-smelling chill that shook him in a shiver. How the sergeants stood it all day, loitering in the shadows in red-coated twos and threes, peeking out of a wardroom's door, deaf to the cries of the prisoners… Although perhaps they looked bleaker than Tom remembered, these days. But then, all Paris did.

It was not uncommon to be stopped while crossing the fortress, but nobody challenged Tom, and he was bracing himself for more pounding rain, when the clopping of hooves sounded on the uneven pavement behind him. Stepping out of the way, he squinted through the gloom at the mounted figure, near-black against the grey light from the courtyard, and was disappointed to make out a large horse, and a bedraggled plume hanging from a wide-brimmed hat — a soldier perhaps, grimly going his way. Meanwhile, though, another rider was coming from the bridge, sitting astride a mule, and was he wearing yellow gloves?

He was, and nearly ended in the mire when the soldier's big horse half-shouldered the mule into the wall. To the sergeants' utter unconcern, the mule danced and brayed in protest, and the man in the yellow gloves scampered off the saddle, made awkward by his long black coat — half-muttering at the soldier's disappearing back, half-soothing his mount.

And there was no mistaking the Flemish rasp to the man's speech, was there? Thanking the Fates, Tom stepped close, and made to grab for the bridle and steady the mule.

"Maître Hennert," he called, and had to jump back as the brute's yellow teeth snapped a breath away from his sleeve.

"Have a care!" cried the physician, swatting at his beast. "Are you bitten, *Monsieur*? She dislikes to be —" His brows rose. "Why, but you're…"

"Abbot," Tom finished for him — from a safe distance, and see whether the mule wasn't laughing at him! "We met at the English Embassy."

"But yes — yes!" The frown cleared, and then creased once again in worry. "Your young friends have not suffered a relapse?"

"My…? Oh." The Framlinghams, of course. "They were well enough yesterday morning, when they left Sir Edward's house. It's regarding another matter that I seek you."

"Seek me?" Oblivious to the mule's antics, Hennert ran a considering eye up and down Tom's length — like one considering leeches.

"Not a professional matter," Tom hastened to say. "Or at least not one that concerns my health. Lady Stafford told me where to find you." *And yet here I am, chasing you in the streets.* Now let the man not take alarm…

He did not, this most trusting of fellows. "*Madame* is very good," he said, beaming under the wide-brimmed hat. "But you say it's not for your own health, *Monsieur*?"

On the way from London, Tom had readied his tale — a bland, plausible one that would take time to disprove, if anyone cared to do it. Now to see whether it held water. "Mr. Charles Arundel had a sister, *mon Maître* — Lady Bevyle. I'm sure you'll understand that she would know how her brother died."

The smile fell, accompanied by a little grunt that might have been acknowledgement, as though Hennert had been expecting questions on the matter, and wondering when they'd come. Whether he swallowed the matter of the sister, though… Could it be that he wasn't quite so trusting?

"Yes," he said, and squinted around in the echoing gloom, at the milling sergeants in their faded red coats, and then at the thickening rain outside. "This is no good place. Follow me, *Monsieur*. I've just come from an apothecary nearby. He'll give us shelter while we speak."

They ventured out into the downpour — and very soon they were ensconced in the fragrant back room of an apothecary's shop, sipping warm wine among the shelves of blue, white and green jars.

Hennert had grown sober. "Poor *Monsieur* Arundel — a very sad end. It was not a long malady — hardly a week — but he suffered much."

"Uncommonly so?"

"Yes, I'd say. As virulent a purple ague as I ever saw." A shake of the head. "Such a raging fever, such a malignant exanthema…"

"You can be certain that's what it was — the purple ague?"

"Ah, *Monsieur* — certain?" The physician spread his hands. "When can we ever be?"

A more honest answer than most of his peers would give, Tom suspected.

"And your colleagues agreed with you on this? Sir Edward tells me you didn't tend to Mr. Arundel alone."

"No, indeed. There were two others…" A frown. "In truth, with one of them I spoke but once, and very little. But yes, we all agreed on the diagnosis."

Now how to ask this without offending the man? "Is there any way, *mon Maître*, that I could speak to these colleagues of yours?"

There was a workbench under the one window, and on it stood a small stone mortar. Discarding his wine, Hennert went to occupy himself with it, lifting the pestle, peering at whatever was inside, smelling it — and all the while his jaw worked. There went jealousy — or, worse, suspicion…?

But no: when the physician put down the pestle, his eyes were crinkled in honest worry. "You think of poison, *Monsieur*. Like Sir Edward."

If Hennert was in Sir Edward's confidence, why always have Lyly accompany him to see Mr. Arundel? Grimeston had asked.

"You know the English are not loved here, and poor Mr. Arundel had … enemies of his own." Tom watched unease and scruple play across the round face. "A nasty rumour reached my Lady Bevyle, and she won't rest until she knows: *could* it have been poison?"

Hennert went back to the pestle, moving it lightly this way and that as he thought.

Tom waited, listening to the rain outside and the sounds of the apothecary's custom in the front, smelling the scented air — mint and lavender and comfrey, much like his mother's still-room back at Scadbury, and something else, something pungent and sweeter — the ambergris he'd sometimes smelt at Court. The physician gave a great sigh.

"In truth…" He paused, fidgeting with the pestle. "Poison should have been quicker in killing, unless *Monsieur* Arundel was dosed with it more than once, in small quantities, over several days. And mind, I can't say that he wasn't… But perhaps you'd better ask my colleagues, for I believe they saw more of the patient than I did."

And were better placed to poison him? Having thought the man so transparent until then, Tom found him suddenly hard to read.

"And could you acquaint me with them?" he asked.

It was like seeing wax melt: at once the mask-like stiffness dissolved, leaving Maître Hennert all eagerness again. See how he dropped the pestle, how he tapped his chin.

"I don't know about the *Docteur* Duret, a very learned man, professor at the *Collège Royal*, close to Duke of Guise. I can't say that I *know* him — or rather, he won't know me, for I'm a very small personage, and a half-foreigner, and a heretic to boot. But perhaps young Jourdain will know how to approach him. Maître Jourdain, I should say: he was *Monsieur* Arundel's habitual physician, and *him* I know quite well, and can make you acquainted."

Promising enough — unless… "He doesn't move in the firmaments of dukes and princes, your Jourdain?"

In his relief at finding himself no object of suspicion, the Fleming chuckled as he waved the notion away. "But no, *Monsieur*. Too young, too unimportant, and not much given to politics. Poor *Monsieur* Arundel could never have afforded one such as Duret."

Which still wouldn't prevent young Jourdain from being — or from aspiring to be — a Guise man. Caution would have to be exercised. And, because it would pay to be forearmed as well as cautious… "He never spoke of poison?" Tom asked.

Again that small grunt. "Well, not to me — nor to Sir Edward, not in my hearing. Whether they met again, though, you must ask him. Tomorrow, if you like: it's *la Fête des Rois*, and I know that he goes to the Epiphany Mass at the Cordeliers, for he lives nearby. Shall I see you there, and make you acquainted?"

The Convent of the Cordeliers! Tom opened his mouth and then closed it — for he knew of this church as a nest of the Duke of Guise's Catholic League. Did Hennert know in what sort of place his un-politic young friend worshipped?

Perhaps not, after all. On being thanked, the Fleming began to gather his belongings — the yellow gloves, the hat, the coat the apothecary's apprentice had hung up to dry — giving all the signs of being ready to leave. He looked less than pleased when Tom stopped his salutations and begged to ask another question.

"You misdoubt it was poison, but what if it were?" He motioned to the jars on the shelves all around. "Is there anything that could cause what you observed in Mr. Arundel?"

"Let's see…" Hennert paused with an arm in the sleeve. "I know there are all sorts of winter-tales about poisons — and here in Paris more than elsewhere — but in truth… Are you familiar with the working of poisons, *Monsieur* Abbot?"

More than I'd like. "Only with…" Lacking the French word for hemlock, Tom resorted to Latin. "*Cicuta.*"

"Well, *la ciguë* is something you won't find here, for it's an ill plant that can't be used to any good. But what I mean is that many remedies used in healing can become deadly if misused." He reached for one of the jars, bearing the name *Hyoscyamus Niger.* "Henbane is one such. It is good for pain, in the right measure; too much of it, though, will overheat the body, and cause ravings."

Henbane — the witch-herb, Tom's old nurse had called it — who had known more of these things than it was comfortable.

"What of the spots, though?"

At once Hennert pointed to another jar on the top shelf — far too quickly not to have thought of it before. "Belladonna — the one they call the Devil's Cherry. Too much of that would give the fever, the ravings and the spots — but it would be very difficult to make it last a week. It would take very, very careful dosing over several days, and still there would be a great risk of causing an early death."

"There's nothing to say the poisoner wanted it to last a full week. Once it was made to look like an ague…" Tom trailed off when he caught the confusion in the physician's eyes. "But let's say it wasn't belladonna. What else could it be?"

"What else, now?" Hennert looked around, not finding what he sought. "Ricinus — although one would have to swallow it for the fever, and touch it for the spots."

The scent of herbs and remedies grew cloying, and Tom swallowed hard. "All of them to be had for the asking and a few *sous*?" Lord, how frighteningly easy it was to poison a fellow man! "You say it would be difficult with belladonna… What of the other two, if it came to keep the fever burning for days?"

"*Ah, ça!*" The Fleming hummed. "Again, one large dose would kill much faster. It would take several smaller doses over the days — perhaps each stronger than the last — but perhaps, then, yes: Ricinus, especially, could be taken for an ague by an untrained eye. But, *Monsieur*, I can't credit that anyone would do it under the nose of three physicians."

Unless, of course, one or more of those physicians were responsible. And, of course, the physicians weren't always there.

"Did you ever see any visitor, besides Lyly and Sir Edward?"

The Fleming hadn't, but then he'd only visited three times.

"What of the servants?"

He'd only seen one. Faucon, or some such name… But certainly Jourdain would know. And with that, Hennert threw on his coat and donned his hat, and, promising to collect Tom from the Embassy on the morrow, took a rather hasty leave — much like one fearing that, with his own unwariness, he'd made trouble for himself.

There was brawling afoot on the Left Bank: shouting in the Rue St. Jacques, and black-gowned men running around in packs, hurling abuse at each other in French, Latin and German. They'd come to blows at the crossroads, or were on the point of doing so, and a clutch of sergeants stood by, for all the world as though they'd decided to let the ruffians break their own heads if they liked.

Tom found that he couldn't blame the red-coated men — but the double-chinned *bourgeoise* at his side had no such qualms.

"But look at them — they watch and do nothing!" she seethed, and turned a baleful eye on Tom. "Students are a plague — and the sergeants are worse!"

Which was rather unfair, for truly, what were the sergeants to do?

"They'd only make a greater row if they tried to apprehend them, *Madame* — and then the University would step in to claim jurisdiction…" Tom trailed off under the woman's sharpening gaze. Damn his accent.

"You're one of them!" she exclaimed, gripping her basket tighter, ready to do what the sergeants would not. "They should take all the English and kick them out of Paris!"

Also unfair — since there was no English to be heard in the commotion — but it was doubtful this termagant would listen to reason, and Tom was only spared a basket to the head when the turmoil surged towards the bridge, and spilled up the quay. At least the basket-wielding Amazon was lost in the rush — but, having no wish to reacquaint himself with the rabble, and perhaps be dropped into the Seine, Tom went the other way, bent on reaching Stafford's door circuitously, and rather wishing he'd set off on horseback.

Indeed it took some walking to skirt the mischief — and it was raining hard again by the time the Ambassador's house came into sight. Also, it was plain that the uproar had reached it, as the gate was newly spattered, and filth lay in heaps around it. Whatever had happened, it had passed by: the gate was shut, and the street deserted, but for one man who stood watching in dismay the remnants of disorder. A slender man in a dark green cape and a narrow-brimmed hat…

"Mr. Framlingham!" Tom called, as he crossed the street. "Won't they let you in?"

The youth whirled around, grimacing awkwardly as he recognised the newcomer. "Oh, Mr. Abbot!" he exclaimed. "I just arrived, and…" He gestured at the soiled gate. "Again!"

"If you can believe it, I just narrowly escaped being hit over the head by a righteous housewife — just for being English. This is what Paris has become, I fear."

Young Clement's hand went for the bandage still showing white under his hat. "Lord help us!" he murmured. Whatever he'd heard of Paris, growing up in his father's manor house, it hadn't been of riots in the streets.

"War will do that to a country — but come now: we'd better try the door." Tom made to take the boy by the elbow, and he flinched. What on earth…? "You need Maître Hennert again, perhaps? Your sister…?"

Another shake of the head, sharp enough to send raindrops flying from the hat's brim. "No — oh, no: my sister is well. And in fact…" A smile — a pitifully strained one. "I won't disturb the Ambassador, Mr. Abbot, because it's you that I sought."

Well now… "If I can be of any service…" And what was wrong with the boy that he must jump so?

"But you have been already, Sir. And I've been nothing but surly to you, and Anne too…" He took a breath. "Lord, but you'll think me a churl! What I'm saying, Mr. Abbot, is that you'd do my sister and myself the greatest honour if you'd partake of supper with us tonight."

It was said in a rush, like a schoolboy rehearsing his lesson. Poor Clement Framlingham — shaken to the marrow… And what a dismal supper it promised to be, with this fearful coney and his long-faced sister! If only it could be refused without appearing rude and ungracious past belief… But no — and much less because the youth wasn't done yet.

"You must let us repay what you did —"

"Mr. Framlingham!" Tom cut in. "There's no debt to repay, truly — but I'll very gladly accept your kind invitation. Now, won't you come in, out of the rain?"

He wasn't surprised when young Clement took a step back.

"No, thank you," he called, just above the hiss of the rain. "At six, if you please. The very end of Serpent Street, at the sign of the Three Ships." And with that he was gone in the pelting rain, his running steps raising twin plumes of dirty water.

Lord, what a fidgety fellow!

CHAPTER 5

Nick Skeres was displeased with Paris, with the Ambassador's folks, with the Ambassador himself, and with the whole of France — but, most of all, he was displeased with his master.

"Out all day in the rain, catching 'is death," he grumbled, once he'd dragged Tom into their small room, and out of his sodden cloak. "Trampling in the mud!" He shook the thing fiercely enough to send water flying all around, heedless of Tom's protests.

"Am I not wet enough?"

"One'd think not, seeing as you're going out again — to supper!" As though supper were some ill invention of the devil. "And what you think you'll wear for supper, the good Lord knows."

Which was true enough. Tom had packed no finery beyond a pair of decent sleeves and a couple of fine lawn collars, never expecting to need any under the guise of Abbot.

"Well, it will be hardly a Court soirée, and I'm only a lowly courier. They'll either take me in the brown sleeves, or have me sup with the servants."

"Ay, a drowned rat in brown sleeves!" There was more grumbling, and Skeres insisted on having the doublet too. "To brush, at least."

And who'd have thought, Tom considered as he undressed and bundled himself into a blanket, that the Minotaur would one day make a half-decent servant, thinking by himself to brush and dry clothes? Truly wonders never ceased — unless it was more a matter of the scullery girl's lures than his master's appearance.

Thinking of which… "Dolius, wait: have you learnt anything of the coachman?"

"Ay, the coachman." A fierce shake of the doublet. "A rare proper fellow, is Adkin Cavel. Sun rises and sets with 'im."

And behold, the Minotaur jealous! "You thought to ask anyone beside the scullion?"

There was a portentous snort as the cloak was again shaken with a noise like sails in the wind. "'Is brother, the cook, even the master and mistress, to 'ear 'Er Ladyship's woman — you'd think they all look to wed 'im."

"What of the old man — the steward or whatever he is?"

"Still in bed with a coldment or the like." Skeres threw the wet cloak over his arm, and snatched up the limp hat. "But 'e'll be all Adam this, and Adam that, too. I've 'ad my fill of Adam!" And see what a roll of the eyes…

"Good for Sally, then." Tom hid both a smile and a shiver in the depths of his blanket. "She could have chosen worse for herself."

There was a last grumble that Tom deserved no warm wine but would have it all the same — and Skeres's exit wasn't gentle on the door.

Come evening, Tom's clothes were dry enough to wear without disgrace, if without great comfort, and the brown sleeves cut a reputable enough figure. Having left indication of his whereabouts with Grimeston, and dispatched Skeres to procure a lantern, Tom was surprised to find Adam Cavel at the door, carrying a lantern, with a seething Minotaur at his side.

"Mr. Tom knows 'is way, and I can carry a light!" Skeres was protesting. Cavel as good as ignored him, bowing to Tom.

"Beg pardon, Master — 'tis just that your man here says he don't know the place. And yourself…" A grimace. "How long is it since you were here, Master? Things have changed something sad."

Which was all plausible enough — and yet so convenient. Stafford wanting to know whether supper with the Framlinghams was an excuse, and if so, for what? What would happen if the offer was refused?

"Thank you, but I won't impose on Sir Edward. I'm sure Skeres can manage well enough."

This had Skeres straighten most soldierly, and the coachman's face fall in wide-eyed earnestness.

"But bless you, Master — I have my orders. Haven't you seen the way it is, out there?"

And because it would seem suspicious to refuse… "Very well, then, Cavel: I thank you and your master both. No need for you to come along, Skeres."

Oh, the black scowl — all the fiercer in the lantern's uneven light! The Minotaur seethed and shuffled his feet as Cavel undid the bolts and, as the coachman leant out of the door to make sure of the street, grabbed a fold of Tom's cloak and held him back.

"What do you think, that he'll drown me in the Seine?" Tom scoffed.

At least Skeres made an attempt at quietness, and hissed instead of rumbling: "'E'll see where you go!"

"Yes — to Lady Gawdy's lodgings, just where I said I'd go — so let him." And with that, he followed Cavel out into the deserted street.

It was a less than cheerful walk — and, if truth be told, Tom found himself less than unhappy with the coachman's presence. The rain had ceased, leaving behind an icy dampness that would be frost by morning, and now coated everything in a dull gleam, and hovered in wisps of fog. Cavel, lantern held high and right hand gripping a dagger's hilt, set a brisk pace, and their steps splashed in the mud, and echoed against the shuttered houses. The law ordered lights to be kept burning at each street corner — and the order was obeyed with more zeal in Paris than in London, in the shape of the lamps at the numerous Virgin's shrines. Still, even those heretically pious flames achieved little enough, and a murky darkness filled the empty streets. Here and there light and laughter spilled out of some tavern's door, as cheerlessly raucous as though each place were the last of its kind left in a desolate city.

"You were right," Tom said after a while. "Things have changed. Paris was never very safe at night, but now..."

Never taking his eyes from the path ahead, Cavel shook his head. "Glum — that's what I call it. I came out here with His Honour back in eighty-three, and each year's been worse than the last... Lord save us all, for he alone knows why these French can't rub shoulders and make do, Papists and Protestants, like us back at home."

The coachman sounded so sad at this battle of faiths that, for a heartbeat, it set Tom musing. It was his life's work to hunt traitors, and not all Papists were traitors, nor were all traitors Papists, and they'd made do well enough back in England, but Cavel hadn't been there for a long time: wasn't it becoming harder and harder, by law and by practice? Few Catholics would have called it making do anymore.

There was a burst of shouting and a crack of broken wood, and Tom was jolted out of his musings as he walked into Cavel's outstretched arm.

The coachman was squinting up the street, peering through the thickening fog towards the noise. Tom observed that they stood in the shadows of a very tall church, and there were lights moving perhaps ten yards ahead.

"What is this place?" he asked softly. "I must confess, in this fog, I'm lost."

It wasn't especially reassuring that Cavel had lowered the lantern, hiding it with a fold of his livery cape. "This is the church of Saint-André," he explained. "I wanted to go that way, for the Rue de la Serpente is near, but… At the very end, you said? Then please you, Master, we turn that-a-way. It won't take long."

Shouts from the unseen fray rebounded eerily in the fog — and while what he caught sounded more like a matter of lust than doctrine, Tom was glad enough to follow his guide's lead down a quieter street. Quieter and even darker… *What do you think, that he'll drown me in the Seine?* he'd joked to Skeres — and yet his hand twitched for his rapier. It was only a foolish moment, and Tom hastened to cover it by conversing.

"You must do much of this service for Sir Edward's guests, surely?" he asked. "Beside driving the coach."

"Ah, there's little driving to do here, beside His Honour going to Court — for the place is a coney's warren. There's times like yesterday, that I fetched the guests, and drove them back — and it always takes twice the time it should — but most days 'tis walking." A shrug that made the lantern swing, and a pat to the hilt under the cape. "Not that I mind. 'Tis just a matter of being prick-eared and ready these days. But you'll know that, Master. Hob told me what happened the other day."

"Indeed. Your brother helped most valiantly."

It was a sad smile that tugged at the young giant's lips — and Tom found himself liking the fellow for it. "Ay, poor Hob: sometimes, in his head, he's still a corporal in Flanders. But look, Master." He raised the lantern. "That's the tail of your Serpent Street. What was the sign, you said?"

It was the matter of a moment to find the *Trois Barques* carved and painted over an architrave, and to knock.

At once the door was thrown open, and Clement Framlingham almost fell out of it.

"Oh, Mr. Abbot," he greeted a little breathlessly — and, to look at him, one would suspect the supper was as much of a chore to the host as it was to the guest.

There was, after all, much to be said for polite excuses, Tom thought, as he crossed the threshold and observed a narrow hall, and an even narrower staircase at its end, and a woman descending the stairs, too tall to be Lady Gawdy.

In fact, this person wore a grey kirtle so prim, and a widow's coif so austere, that Tom at first took her for a servant — but, as she drew nearer, he saw at once his mistake. There was nothing servant-like in the angular face and intent, pale eyes under flaxen brows, and in fact, it was not as a servant that Clement addressed her.

"Cousin Joyce, this is Mr. Abbot…"

Before he could introduce her, she walked up and performed that duty herself.

"I'm Joyce Blundell," she said. "The kinswoman for whom you spared Lady Gawdy and her brother."

This stiff utterance, the brisk, even voice, the brisker little curtsey... It wasn't often that Tom found himself at sea in gauging a person's station in life, but Joyce Blundell eluded him. He bowed back, on the safe side of things.

"I was fortunate in being where I was needed, Mistress," he greeted, while she appraised him with all the frankness in the world. Then, over his shoulder, she observed Cavel waiting on the steps.

"You can send your man home, Mr. Abbot. My servant will walk you back."

It was said flatly, as though by one accustomed to laying down the law. Tom wanted to laugh at the coachman's amazement, as he was dismissed with a vail, and the door closed in his face. And, as she gave her candle to Clement and drew the bolts herself, Tom scrutinised this disconcerting woman. A little older than his six-and-twenty, fair of complexion, lean as a boy, sharp in her movements... It was all he could discern before she gathered her skirts, took the candle from Clement, and led the way up the stairs.

"My Cousin Anne will be waiting to see you," Mistress Blundell said as they climbed up one storey and then two — for this was one of those tall and narrow Paris houses with room piling above room — and so Lady Gawdy was.

She'd been on her knees by the fire; the moment they entered the room, she bounded to her feet, eyes flashing golden, and curtsied deeper and slower than her cousin had.

Tom bowed back, and thanked her — and her cousin — for this most kind invitation. Most hostesses would smile at that; Anne Gawdy did not.

"It's a matter of what we owe you, Mr. Abbot."

Oh Lord, not that again. "As I said earlier to Mr. Framlingham, there's nothing owed, Madam."

For a long moment she just stood there, delicate hands folded at her waist, her honey-coloured hair and dark silks gleaming in the firelight, and observed him gravely.

"There is always some debt owed, Mr. Abbot," she murmured. "Great or small."

Pretty as a picture, but touched in the 'ead... Could the Minotaur be right in his estimation of Anne Gawdy?

It was rather a relief when, at Mistress Blundell's beckoning, a wiry manservant brought in the basin — a sign that they should wash their hands and sit at the table, which they all obediently did.

Tom suspected that this wasn't always a dining room, for they were seated at a board on trestles, rather than a table proper, and the far wall showed a row of paler squares, as though the high-backed chairs were normally arranged against it. It certainly wasn't cheerful, with its bare greenish walls and the silence that was only broken by the creak of the wooden floor under the servant's steps, until Joyce Blundell spoke.

"I hope you will forgive our plain fare, Mr. Abbot," she said. "We lead a simpler life than what you must see at the Ambassador's house."

Having yet to catch sight of the Ambassador's table, Tom had no trouble in assuring her that couriers led very simple lives — nor in complimenting the fine pie that was brought in, its crust made into a braided pattern.

Its bright colour, and the fragrance of cinnamon that wafted up when the crust was cut, brought a smile to young Clement's face, if a rueful one.

"It would be St. Stephen's day, back at home," he said, only for his cousin to click her tongue.

"I keep telling my cousins, Mr. Abbot, that there's nothing worse than to keep thinking what it would be like back at home. It won't take them back there, and it will keep them from being quite here. 'Tis Twelfth Night in Paris, Clement — not that we keep it."

How long had she striven to convince herself of this — and how far had she succeeded? Because, for sure, there was nothing approaching revelry in her house, but the chicken in the pie was cooked after the English manner, with cinnamon and sugar and verjuice, and there was salt fish after that, and remarkably good gingerbreads — and all the while Tom kept the conversation on Paris, and the commerce of tanned leather, when it turned out that Mistress Blundell had inherited her husband's business in that trade, and had much to say on the difficulties of it, all the greater as unrest grew in France.

Clement had endless questions about France and Paris, most of them rather innocent, asked with an eagerness that made him seem even younger. In all of this Anne said very little, picking at her food and watching Tom most intently.

He was asking Mistress Blundell how the English merchants in Paris were banding together against the present hardships, when Anne looked up from her plate with a flash of her large pupils.

"But you must know about it all yourself, Mr. Abbot, travelling to and fro."

Why a silence met this, Tom couldn't quite tell. It was, after all, a rather natural observation — although not one he cared to answer with the truth — and it was perhaps the unease of their companions that was jarring. Even the servant-boy who was gathering the plates faltered in perplexity.

Tom made himself smile. "I don't travel in these parts as much as I used to do," he said, which was quite true — and uninteresting, one would hope.

But Anne Gawdy, instead of being put off, gave the smallest toss of her head. "How like a man, to be able to travel, and yet to stay at home. Although some, it's true, have many preoccupations there —"

"Anne!" pleaded Clement, reaching for his sister's hand where it curled and uncurled around her goblet, and, at the same time, Mistress Blundell cut through it all.

"Don't be silly, child," she chided — if her sensible placidness could be called chiding. "What would Mr. Abbot know of these things, when he's no merchant? I'm glad that he asks, if he knows the Ambassador well enough to tell him…"

And for quite a while she laid out the English merchants' doles — and there were many of them, and Tom listened because it might be of some interest to Sir Francis — but no effort of Cousin Joyce could conceal the darkness in Lady Gawdy's eyes as she huddled in her chair, or the way young Clement never took his gaze off his sister.

When, as soon as it was decent to do so, Tom took his leave with a profusion of thanks, Mistress Blundell and young Framlingham saw him to the door, and their greetings were those of a final parting — and Fates be thanked for it.

As he followed the taciturn servant through the dark streets, Tom could only agree with Skeres: Anne Gawdy was not quite sane, much to her friends' distress.

He was most surprised, on reaching the Embassy, to find that Lady Stafford wanted to see him at once.

"You visited Lady Gawdy," she said, the moment he entered her parlour. Most severely she said it, most accusingly: a displeased goddess — but for the tapping slipper.

"So I did, Madam. Lady Gawdy and her brother, who came here earlier to extend an invitation."

"He came here? Hobelot says not."

Hobelot! Had she been asking the servants about him? "I stand corrected, Madam: I met Mr. Framlingham at the door. He invited me to have supper with him and his sister and, having done so, he never entered the house. Now I wish he had, since it seems that I need a witness."

It was a bold speech to make to the Baroness Sheffield, and in such vexation — but truly, that she should doubt his word, and question the servants as though he were an errant schoolboy!

And perhaps she saw it too, for it was plain in her tightened lips and flaring nostrils how it galled her to swallow a sharp retort — but swallow it she did.

"I'm not implying that you lied," she grated out, the viol's voice climbing down half an octave. "But, had I known of this invitation, I would have surely advised you against accepting it."

I wasn't aware I need Your Ladyship's permission... But if Lady Stafford could bite her tongue, so could Tom Walsingham. He counted in Latin, and by *quattuor* he was able to explain in a tone of reason: "Mr. Framlingham said this supper was meant to thank me for the assistance I offered the other day. Much as I said it was unneeded, I don't see how I could have refused with courtesy."

"Very proper of you," she snapped. "And if you thought this supper unneeded, I hope there will be no more such occasions."

Not that the lady met reason with any more favour than she had shown for boldness.

As though he'd sought or enjoyed *this one*! Which, even in thought, sounded peevish enough to call up the blood to Tom's cheeks — and it struck him that perhaps he was being a touchy fool, because most certainly Lady Stafford was not. He sought and held the disdainful black gaze. "But perhaps I should crave pardon for my hasty temper," he slowly said. "Surely Your Ladyship must have good reason for..." *For not minding Her Ladyship's own business.* "Please, Madam, if there's aught that I should know about Lady Gawdy and her brother..."

A fair request, after all — and still it sent Lady Stafford pacing, up and down, up and down, before she stopped in front of Tom, frowning at him as intently as Anne herself had done at supper, although her black eyes were steady and commanding. Tom frowned back and waited.

"Mr. Walsingham," she said, "I'd never met Anne Gawdy until you brought her here the other day, and what I know, I know from her. That she is unwell you've seen for yourself; her family sent her here in the hope that she may recover, away from her husband, for she's not happy in her marriage. And here, while she finds herself in danger and mortal fear, a comely young gentleman rides in and rescues her..." The fine black brows arched high. "You spoke of courtesy? Well, it would be courteous and prudent of you to stay well away from Anne Gawdy."

Tom gaped, speechless. "Madam!" he blurted out when he found his voice again. "What must you take me for? That you should think I'd thrust myself on a woman I've hardly met, unwell or not, and I on Mr. Secretary's business! That I'd woo a married woman under her brother's nose —" At this the thought stopped him like a blow: Frances.

Had he not wooed a married woman under her father's roof — a father who was his kinsman, his master and his mentor? And now playing the outraged Puritan — oh Lord!

Fates send Lady Stafford never saw how his mind was thrown a-whirl; let her think him dumb with indignation. Perhaps she was thinking so, and the narrowed glare was that of one who misliked being in the wrong?

When she said, "Then I'll trust that you will not," it rang more as admonition than trust.

Hope is a God-given virtue, Thomas, but seldom a guide for sensible judgment. Finding Sir Francis's voice in his head unusually dry, and Lady Stafford not overly pleasant company, Tom bowed stiffly, and tried not to retreat in too much haste.

As he crossed the chill darkness of the garden, Tom's mind began to clear of both the annoyance and the painful thoughts. By the time he reached the door to his cupboard, he could see that there was nothing in his love for Frances like what Lady Stafford had insinuated — and also that, whatever she thought of him, the interference of the Baroness remained quite strange.

A fissure of light showed under the door, so he began, even as he let himself in: "Now think, Skeres: why would a great lady intervene —"

And he went no further when Skeres, wild-eyed, bounced up from the pallet.

"Mr. Tom, ye're not drowned!" cried the Minotaur, seizing his master by the arm so fiercely Tom was half unfooted.

"Jove, Dolius!" he protested. "Should I be?"

The mighty harrumph was answer enough. "That Adkin coming back alone, and the row they made, and you not coming, and you'd said ... cuds-me!" He rubbed at his short curls. "What was I to tell 'Is 'Onour, eh? That I'd let you go out alone with Stafford's man?"

"Peace, you dolt!" Tom hissed, extricating himself from the dolt's grip. "What's this row they made? Was it when Her Ladyship found out?"

Skeres shrugged. "I know naught of 'Er Ladyship — but when Cavel came back, the cook told 'im off, for Sir Edward 'ad sent for 'im, and where 'ad 'e been..."

"Why, but..." *I have my orders*, the coachman had said. "Sir Edward sent for him? Are you sure that's what they said?"

"Am I sure! Such a fuss the cook made, I 'eard it from the scullery! So —" the lad tapped his nose most wisely — "'ere's a rat to smell, I tell myself, and skulk by the door, and listen — and you know what sweet Adkin says?" Oh, the triumph on the ruddy face! "That 'e'd been to see a neighbour's maid, 'e says. Sneaked out to 'ave a word with 'er! A word, ay!"

Tom sat down on his bed, his mind a-whirl. So Adam Cavel had his orders but not from Sir Edward, nor from his wife. "At least the Deacon isn't making up this one..."

And if he thought that Skeres was shaking his head over the prodigy of a truthful Gifford, he was much mistaken.

"Poor Sally," the lad sighed instead. "She cried something dreadful."

Ay — poor Sally, absconding in the scullery with Skeres in Adkin's absence! And, unlikely as it seemed... "You never thought to comfort her with the truth, did you?" Tom asked, and found some consolation in the lad's offended stare.

"What do you take me for, Master?" Offence gave way to a considering pout. "Besides, she's better off without 'im: neighbour's maid or no, 'e's a lying rapscallion, ain't 'e?"

"A lying rapscallion, yes." Tom began to undo his doublet's buttons. "And a spy to boot. Whose spy, I'd dearly like to know."

Yet another matter for Gilbert Gifford. If tangles kept cropping up this way, unknotting them would take a whole day with the fellow.

CHAPTER 6

Because Maître Hennert was prompt to a fault, and the Cordeliers' preacher wordy, they had to wait a good deal longer than Tom liked for the Mass to finish. The convent's church was large, with a rather unadorned front, and a columned porch — and under this porch Tom waited, half listening to the muffled singing from inside, half to the Fleming's apologies.

"It's just, *Monsieur*, that the Mass here is much attended," the man was saying for the dozenth time. "I'd say we repair to a *taverne*, but I'd be afraid to lose young Jourdain in the crowd, for there *will* be a crowd when they're finished…"

"It's hardly your fault, *mon Maître*," Tom murmured, also for the dozenth time, and his breath curdled into vapour. Why couldn't Gifford have waited for April to have himself arrested? At least it wasn't raining… There went Hennert again, tiptoeing to the door, listening and coming back again.

"It won't be long, I think," he whispered.

Wondering, not for the first time, whether the physician knew just what sort of Leaguer furnace this place was, Tom leant against the column farthest from the door, and idly watched the enclosed triangle of frost-eaten grass, with a single bare tree surrounded by hedges, and the city walls on one side. Three crows had taken up residence on the tree, two cawing as they fought for the highest perch, and a third watching. A fitting metaphor, if one was needed, for the state of Catholic Paris these days — with the King, the Guise with his League, and the English exiles…

And then the doors where flung open, startling the crows into flight as the first faithfuls began to trickle out.

Hennert hurried close. "Here they come," he said — as though Tom could fail to see it — and led him out of the porch, towards the gate to the street, where the huddled beggars were stirring and vying for position.

Again just like the crows, Tom thought — and began to scan the thickening stream of Mass-goers. Not that he'd know Jourdain on sight, but he watched for black coats with an ermine collar, although perhaps not all physicians here wore their profession's garb on feast days, like Hennert did. As he studied the little crowd, a figure caught his eye. A woman, tall and square-shouldered, head primly coiffed under a narrow-brimmed hat. He couldn't quite see her face, but her brisk movements, the tilt of her head as she spoke to a pair of finely dressed gentlemen... These two were tall and English-looking, one portly and one leaner, both sporting spade beards, and so like each other they could only be brothers. When the younger one gestured, the woman turned to peer past the gate, and there was no mistaking her: this was Joyce Blundell, who had just heard Mass at the Cordeliers!

She was a Catholic, then, this merchantess of tanned leathers — and so must be Anne Gawdy, entrusted into her care, and young Clement too, who had been neither reckless nor ignorant on arriving in Paris — only innocent enough to believe his faith would make him welcome, and shaken to find that he was not. And this explained Lady Stafford warning Tom away from the Framlinghams: she was a Howard by birth, after all, and rumoured to be a Catholic herself.

As Mistress Blundell and her grand companions drew closer, Tom moved away, lest she should know him — but not before he heard the portly one exclaim in English, "Why, but yes!" in a deep, gravelly voice — and, as he turned, he saw Hennert, beckoning from half a dozen steps away.

"Mr. Abbot, come!" the man called — Jove rain on him — but, by good chance, a quick glance backwards revealed only the back of Joyce Blundell, tripping out of the gate in her wooden pattens, oblivious to having been seen and known — and Fates be thanked. Tom let Hennert draw him towards the porch again, and introduce him to a young man who did wear a black coat, but lacked both the ermine and the yellow gloves.

"Maître Pierre Jourdain," said the Fleming, "and *Monsieur* Abbot, from England, who would ask about *Monsieur* Arundel."

Oh Jupiter! Could it be hoped that the Fleming's manner was more cautious at the bedside of his patients? As though it were the commonest thing in the world, Tom nodded at the startled Jourdain.

"I'm here, *mon Maître*, at the behest of Mr. Arundel's sister. She was distraught at the news of her brother's death, and wishes for some account of it."

Pierre Jourdain, the unpolitic fellow who worshiped at the Cordeliers, was a solid young man, whose full brown beard and moustache struck Tom as an effort to appear older. He squinted at the stranger from England through cold-reddened eyes, and it was with the greatest gravity that he bowed.

"It's a kind errand that you do, *Monsieur*," he said. "If I can be of service, beyond what Maître Hennert told you…"

Was there a colour of doubt to Jourdain's words? But perhaps not, because, when Tom observed that, as Mr. Arundel's physician, he must have seen more of him in his illness, he all but bounced on his toes.

"But yes, I was with him every day, although I must admit, I held out little hope of a recovery." He stepped aside to let pass two women in hooded cloaks, and bowed to them, and when he turned back, he wore a frown. "Such a fierce fever, wasn't it, Maître Hennert? Such delirium as I've seldom seen."

"And the spots," Hennert added.

"The spots, yes. A most remarkable quantity of them, especially large on his hands and forearms."

Ricinus. The name came back to Tom's mind from the apothecary's stock. The herb that would poison the skin when touched. Hennert looked troubled: had the thought occurred to him as well? Jourdain, Tom was surprised to see, was dabbing his watering eyes with gloved fingers. Surely he couldn't be moved to tears over a patient's death?

But no. "I must beg pardon," he apologised. "This wind… Would you object, *Monsieur*, if we were to converse in some warmer place?"

Tom would not — so they moved with the small crowd towards the gate, Jourdain exchanging greetings and bows with this and that person as they went.

They were close by the gate before Tom could resume his inquiries.

"You surely understand, *mon Maître*, that most of what you describe I can't report to my Lady Bevyle without distressing her. If you could just name the illness that killed her brother…"

"Purple ague," was the unhesitating answer. "Of a rare violence. There was naught we could have done to save him, was there, Maître Hennert?"

Hennert was all sympathy. "I'd held out some hope, at first, but such an acute bout could hardly fail to kill the patient. I must say I never saw the like."

What a curious man the Fleming was — one moment forging ahead with the subtlety of a regiment of pike, and the next offering Tom just the opening he needed.

For now it must sound quite natural that Abbot should seize on the statement. "You never saw the like? Then, I must ask your pardon, *mes Maîtres*, but Her Ladyship had a letter from an acquaintance, hinting at … well, at poison."

"Poison!" Jourdain stopped in his tracks to stare at Tom and then at Hennert. "Why, this is… Why would poor Mr. Arundel…?" He pulled at his beard. "I can't think of a poison that would kill in that manner. Surely, though, the purple ague would." The look he gave Hennert was nothing short of beseeching.

When the Fleming only tilted his head, he chose to take it as encouragement — because, of course, a patient poisoned under his nose would be a serious blow to a young medicus's ambitions.

See how he adjusted the coat around his shoulders, and lifted his chin. "But no, *Monsieur*," he said. "You can reassure *Madame*. The intensity of the symptoms may have been somewhat unusual, but there's no mistaking them: the fever, the spots, and most of all that madness-like delirium, they're all signs of the purple ague." He would have sounded more convincing without the reddened and watering eyes. How did this man make a living, looking so forlorn?

Anyone watching them would have imagined an exchange of the direst news, as Tom sadly shook his head and murmured, "Madness-like…" Lyly had been most insistent on Arundel's ravings, too. "Her Ladyship will be comforted to know there was no foul play, but still, madness!"

With all the air of one who felt on firmer ground, Jourdain resumed his step.

"Ah, yes!" A judicious nod. "You may mention delirium, as it often goes with fevers, after all. That of the purple ague, however, can be very distressing — and Mr. Arundel, well, sometimes he cried for the Lord's mercy, and sometimes he called for Sir Edward or his secretary. And then he'd grow confused, and cry out, now loud, now hoarse, now in English, now in French. This was especially at night. Nothing we did could abate his fever, and those cries... *Je dirai! Je dirai!* There are times when I still hear him in my mind."

Je dirai — *I'll tell.* Nothing like the protestations of loyalty in Stafford's story — which was no great surprise. But what was it that Arundel so wanted to tell? The very thing that had had him poisoned, as likely as not.

"A most pitiful end to witness." Jourdain shook his head. "I think poor *Monsieur* Lyly was very affected. To be alone with a friend dying in such terrible agony..."

"Alone?" Tom frowned at Hennert as they passed into the street, the beggars swarming up close, so shrill the Fleming didn't catch the word.

Jourdain did, for all that he was dropping copper *deniers* into the outstretched hands, and had to make himself heard above the furore of thanks and blessings. "Why, yes — alone but for myself and the servant — and the servant hadn't been with Mr. Arundel long. The one who'd travelled with him from England died late last summer, and then *Madame* herself found him this other Englishman, but of course..."

To all of this, Tom was only half listening. All this time he had assumed that Hennert must have been present at Arundel's end, because Lyly had been there — Lyly who swore he'd only ever visited Arundel to accompany the physician. So Grimeston was right, and Lyly lied — and there was something else that Jourdain had said.

"A friend, you said?" Tom cut through the man's chatter. "You called Lyly Mr. Arundel's friend?"

The physician blinked at being so brusquely interrupted, or was it in surprise at the question itself? "But yes," he said. "They were much attached to each other. Intimate, I'd say. It was in *Monsieur* Lyly's arms that *Monsieur* Arundel died —"

A sudden flurry of running steps and shouts cut him short, and a stone sailed their way and hit the gatepost — Lord smite all students! — and there was shoving, and pushing, and shrieks, and Tom found himself thrust backwards against Jourdain first, and then against Joyce Blundell's two fine gentlemen, catching himself by a handful of velvet cape and silver trim. Before he could beg pardon, he was pushed roughly aside, and the elder gentleman was drawing away the one who must be his brother. Even amidst the din of yelling and running, Tom caught the man's gravelly rumble, though the words were drowned out in the chaos.

But never mind those two. Tom whirled around, clutching his rapier's hilt, scanning the crowd for black gowns, finding none, seeking the two physicians... Oh Jupiter!

Pierre Jourdain lay crumpled against the convent's wall, Hennert crouched at his side in the mud — hatless and grim, his yellow gloves red to the wrist as he pressed his colleague's belly.

"*Monsieur* Abbot!" he called sharply.

Dragged out of his momentary stupor, Tom knelt by the two men, only to rise again as three grey friars came running out of the gate, sandals splashing in the puddles.

"What happened?" one wanted to know — a small fellow with a long, prophet-like grey beard and fierce eyes. "Who is this man? Let's bring him to our infirmary —" He stopped when his younger fellow drew a sharp breath, and went to stoop over the wounded man.

"Saint Francis help us, it's Maître Jourdain!" he cried, and at once began reciting the prayers for the dying.

This sent across the crowd a ripple of exclamations, and signs of the cross, and again the prophetical friar began to ask what had happened — and, because he stood over the two physicians, Tom was the one he asked.

"This man was stabbed," Tom said — not that he knew for sure, but no stone could draw that much blood.

Of course, on hearing the foreign colour to the answer, the friar stiffened. "You're not one of our flock," he said. "I'm sure I never saw you before." And the hard eyes travelled down Tom's person — and it was then that, following the unfriendly gaze, he observed a dark stain on his front, smeared downwards.

Slipping off one glove, he rubbed at it — and his fingers came away red. Good Lord... He swallowed hard, and looked up.

There the two friars stood in a grey clutch, for all the world like two brigands ready to pounce on him — but then, among all the sorts of Catholics he'd come across in his life, Tom had yet to meet a Franciscan who wasn't blunt and quarrelsome.

"He fell against me when he was hit," he said, although in truth he'd been shoved against poor Jourdain rather than the other way. Not that it mattered, for the friars didn't want to believe him anyway, and right then Hennert reached up to tug at Tom's sleeve.

"*Monsieur* Abbot," the Fleming called, low and urgent — and, turning his back on the friars and the crowd, Tom knelt again by poor, ashen Jourdain, who now lay on his back, with his head on someone's folded cape, breathing in shallow gasps, staring blankly upwards.

"He's dying," said Hennert, holding one bloodied hand in his own.

"Jourdain." Tom leant low over the poor fellow. "*Mon Maître*, did you see who stabbed you?"

There was no answer beside a gasp — nor could there be, for then a shudder shook Jourdain from head to toe, and, still staring fearfully, he fell back with the limpness of death.

The young friar crossed himself. "*Subvenite, Sancti Dei, occurrite, Angeli Domini…*" he intoned, and his brethren and the crowd all around joined in, asking the Lord's saints and angels to receive the dead man's soul.

Tom found himself shuddering as he sat back on his heels. "The devil!" he breathed, a good deal less piously.

At his side, Hennert blinked like one lost in a maze, and small blame to him. If he wondered at Thomas Abbot, twice caught up in violence in three days, he said nothing. Then there were calls to make way in the King's name, and three sergeants in faded red pushed through the little crowd.

"In the King's name — stand back!" their leader ordered, striding to stand over the dead body, wielding the verge with the King's *fleur-de-lys*. He was a thickset man, with the a fierce jutting jaw, and brown brows that gathered in a prodigious scowl when the friars moved as one to cross him, the grey-bearded prophet at their head.

"I don't know who sent for you, *Sergent*," this personage said. "Maître Jourdain was one of our parishioners, and was murdered on our threshold. It's a matter for the Bishop's courts."

Oh Jove! Tom swallowed a groan: the Bishop, who loved the English so! Now he'd be gaoled in the For-l'Évêque, in a cell next to Gifford's... But no: see how the sergeant affected to observe the body, pacing the short way between it and the gate, as if to measure it under the crowd's intent study. It was a quick thing, sooner done than said, and then he paced back to stand nose to nose with the Franciscan.

"That, *mon Père*," he said, pointing at the gate, "is your threshold. And here —" he moved his finger to point at the remains of Pierre Jourdain, sprawled in a puddle of mud and blood — "here lies your murdered parishioner — who also happens to be a subject of the King. If I were you, I'd go back inside the Bishop's jurisdiction — because you're out of it, here."

A cheer for this articulate and witty sergeant!

"Unless..." He raised his bush-like brows. "Unless you saw who did the murder?"

"No, they did not." Tom had been crouching by poor Jourdain with Hennert; now he rose to his feet. "The good brothers came running out of the gate after it had happened," he said, and there were murmurs and nods from all around, and a satisfied grunt from the sergeant.

"Thought so. Then, *mon Père*, I'll thank you for a couple of stout men and a litter. You'll have some place to keep the body. And you'll know where to find this poor man's family, I'm sure?"

For a moment the friar seethed so blackly that, when he raised a hand, Tom tensed, ready to ward off a blow. *I was arrested, Sir, for brawling with a friar in the street...* Instead the man sketched a sign of the cross in the air over poor Jourdain. "*Requiem æternam dona ei, Domine,*" he said and then turned, rather less fatherly, to the sergeant. "I'll advise the *Père Gardien*: he'll send someone to break the news to Maître Jourdain's sister — Lord comfort her! And you should know that this man —" he paused to point a most censorious forefinger at Tom — "this man is English."

"Is he? Thought he sounded like one. Eh, we're aswarm with them, these days," the sergeant said, crossing his arms as he waited for the friars to retreat. As soon as the convent's gate slammed shut behind them, he turned to Tom, eyes dark with suspicion.

"And now, *Monsieur l'Anglais*, I would see your papers, and hear why you're soaked in blood."

That the King's jurisdiction was better than the Bishop's, didn't make Tom happy to be held by the King's men, but, there being nothing for it, he showed his papers — not his courier's passport, but the other set he carried showing Thomas Abbot, of London, to be a lawyer travelling for certain transactions. As the sergeant perused them, Tom recounted the sudden commotion, the shouts, the stones, stumbling against poor Maître Jourdain…

"And that's how I came to be so stained, I reckon," he ended, rubbing his equally stained glove where the blood was drying and falling away in rust-coloured flakes.

The sergeant wanted to see Tom's parrying dagger, and even his rapier — pursing his lips when he found both clean, blade and hilt. He was studying the dagger when a pale-faced Hennert joined him.

"Believe me, *Sergent*," the physician said grimly, "the blade that killed Maître Jourdain will have a good deal of blood on it."

The officer sniffed, and scratched at his massive chin as he weighed the ermine collar against the dishevelled air and the foreign rasp of the speech. Was *Monsieur* English, too? he asked.

Flemish by birth, Hennert answered — but of Paris these last fifteen years — and a physician, like the dead man.

And had he seen the murder happen?

He had.

Had he seen who had stabbed his colleague?

No, Hennert said, sounding rattled of a sudden. Or rather, he'd seen several men run against them, and any one of them could have... He stopped short and swallowed. Poor Hennert — learned and discreet — how he must be regretting that he'd ever offered to help out Thomas Abbot!

Still, he stood by loyally, if a little fretfully, as the sergeant questioned the bystanders, whose numbers had dwindled with the approach of the dinner hour and the cold drizzle starting anew. A few persisted, keen as mice sniffing cheese from afar: the beggars, a few burgesses, a couple of soberly dressed women, a schoolboy holding a wide-eyed little sister by the hand. For the most part, they confirmed Tom's words — adding that the foreign gentleman and the physician had been talking with Maître Jourdain, and that the ruffians, some wearing black gowns and some not, had come from around the corner, shouting and then rushing Saint-Côme's way. What it was they'd been shouting, nobody could agree. Against the Huguenots, some said; against the friars, others swore; against the King (no, *for* him!), against the *Sainte Ligue* (no, *for* the *Ligue* and the Guise!), vengeance against the English — and this last no one gainsaid.

"*Et bien*," the officer said — raising his voice for the bystanders. "We've plenty of unruly folks who dislike good Catholics — and plenty of those who dislike the English." He looked over his shoulder at the body and crossed himself. "And sometimes, in the turmoil, death strikes undeserved."

Meaning, very plainly, that a dead Englishman would have earned whatever happened to him. As if to cinch this piece of gall, right then the gate swung open to let pass the young friar and two servants with a board. But for detailing one of his men to stay and assist, the sergeant ignored them.

He waved his verge at the small crowd instead. "Now go your way, good people," he called. "The King's justice will find the culprit." And then, knitting his brows most forbiddingly, he addressed Tom and Hennert. "And you, *Messieurs*, will be so good as to follow me."

Jove fulminate all officious constables. "Surely you're not arresting us?" Tom protested. "You heard those people: half a dozen men assaulted us!"

The fellow pushed back his hat to squint at the obnoxious Englishman. "Then I'm not arresting you — but you were still with the man who was killed. The *commissaire* will be keen on hearing you." Thrusting Tom's blades into his baldric, and the papers inside his sleeve, he motioned to his remaining men — and see Mr. Secretary Walsingham's man being marched through the streets of Paris with an escort of armed sergeants!

At least, for a mercy, it was a short way to the guardhouse. They called them *barrières*, these guardhouses they had scattered everywhere, all peopled with armed men — so thick one'd believe there was little trust between Paris and her citizens ... not that this arrangement had prevented black murder, had it?

Tom was quite out of charity with French justice by the time they reached the *barrière* by the church of Saint-Côme, and he and Hennert were left in a small, dank room to wait for the *commissaire*. So they sat on rickety stools at the rickety square table and waited — Hennert picking at the blood-stiffened leather of his discarded gloves, and Tom looking out of the barred window, as he turned things over in his mind.

Item: Jourdain had been stabbed to death while speaking to him.

Ergo: Stafford's talk of poison was no wild fancy, after all. Why kill the poor physician, otherwise? Why kill him just as he was speaking with the Englishman from the Embassy?

All answerless *quæstiones* — and here was another one: how did they know, whoever *they* were?

But no — this was descending into a disordered whirl, like a handful of coloured glass pieces thrown about. Tom took a deep breath, and began anew.

Item: The shouting rogues — some wearing black gowns, and some not.

Item: The two well-dressed Englishmen — Joyce Blundell's acquaintances — walking just behind them, and running so eagerly from the scene...

And only then did it occur to Tom that nobody in the crowd had remarked on the flight of those two, hence:

Quæstio: Who were they?

Quæstio: Should this be mentioned to the commissaire — if and when he bothered to appear?

Much better to inquire about these gentlemen alone — but of whom? Not of Mistress Blundell, and never of the friars, for all that they knew their flock sheep by sheep. Jourdain would have known, likely — but Jourdain was dead, murdered as he spoke to Tom of the servant, and of Lyly... Oh yes, that too:

Item: Madame had found an English servant for Arundel.

Item: Lyly had not seen it fit to mention at least one solitary visit to Arundel — never mind his friendship with the man.

Ergo: Either poor Jourdain had been much given to fancies, or people at the Embassy were lying through their teeth.

And then:

Quæstiones — *many of them: What had been on Arundel's feverish mind as he died, crying out* Je dirai? *What was he going to tell, and to whom? Was this about Stafford's wavering loyalties? But why promise, or threaten, and not tell? And why in French* —

"*Monsieur* Abbot, please, what do you think happened?"

The murmured words startled Tom, who turned to find a pale-faced Hennert staring at him from across the table — and who could blame him?

But what he thought had happened, Tom didn't want to discuss with the physician. "I wish I knew, *mon Maître*," he sighed. "In three days I've seen more unrest in the streets of Paris than in a month in London."

"Yes — but a murder?"

"You heard the sergeant."

"I heard him, yes, just as you did. And do you believe him?"

Oh Jove… Tom sat back against the damp wall. "Now, Maître Hennert —" he began, but the physician held up both palms to stop him, and leant across the table to whisper.

"I've changed my mind. Don't tell me. You come here — sent from *Monsieur* Arundel's sister, you say — and then begin to ask about poisons, and about the servant… What sister on this earth would want to know that? It strikes me that there are things you can't tell, and I don't want to know. But young Jourdain, *Monsieur*? Is he dead because of Mr. Arundel?"

Because of you? the Fleming didn't say, but it was there in his puckered brow and twisting lips — unless it was Tom's own uneasy conscience asking.

"I don't know that he is — or that he isn't," Tom whispered back. "But you're right in not wanting to know. Still, Maître Hennert, if I were you, I'd be careful for a while."

So swiftly did the Fleming draw back his hands from the table — it would have been comical at any other time. As it was… Tom leapt up, and went to pound on the door — and found that they were being guarded when, at once, a truculent voice asked from outside what was the matter.

"Are we to wait much longer?" Tom called irritably. "And, if we are, do you mean to starve us?"

"As long as you pay," muttered the voice on the other side. A minute later, some sort of inferior sergeant — or perhaps a servant, his ill-fitting coat patched enough to be someone else's cast-off — arrived carrying a trencher and a jug. A *sol* changed hands, the tidings were given that the *commissaire* would see them when he saw fit, and, once alone again, Tom and Hennert found themselves in possession of bread and wine, if nothing else.

But see how the Fleming gaped at this lofty treatment of the King's men! So appalled a gape it was, that Tom couldn't help a smile.

"I'd like to say it's my natural masterfulness," he said. "But, here as in London, these villains wait for naught but a prisoner willing to pay for his comforts — such as they are." He poured wine for them both, grimacing at the colour of it. "I'll take it you've little experience with all this, *mon Maître*? Then I should warn you not to expect much of the wine."

He raised his battered cup, and for a moment Hennert hesitated with raised brows — wondering perhaps just what experience Tom himself had of *all this*. It wasn't long, though, before the good-natured face unknotted a little, and the physician picked up his wine.

"*Votre santé, Monsieur*," he toasted. He took a sip and pulled a face. "How right you were!"

Atrociously watered down as it was, the wine loosened the Fleming's misgivings, and the bread, for a prodigy, was nothing worse than a little stale.

Everything's easier with a full belly, had been a maxim of Tom's old nurse — and she'd been more than right, to see how even such a paltry meal had evened Hennert's humours.

"I'm in your debt, *Monsieur*," he said, sitting back after washing down the last mouthful of bread — which was a very handsome sentiment from one who, but for Tom, would have been sitting at his own table in his own house at this point.

It was a sobering thought: but for Tom, the man would be neither here nor in danger. But for him, Jourdain would be alive... For which there was no remedy, naught to do but find the murderer. Because surely there was no doubt at this point? Just the act of sitting forward, of mustering the questions in his head felt like a clearing of cobwebs.

"In my debt? Hardly, but..." Tom poured more wine. "There are one or two things that Maître Jourdain said — things that trouble me."

The Fleming's face fell at once. "For reasons I don't want to know, eh?" He squared his shoulders. "Do ask, *Monsieur*. If I can, I'll help."

Good man. Tom waited while the bells outside struck three, their countless chimes filling the swollen sky above Paris. Among them must be the ones from that very Convent of the Cordeliers, where a life had just been cut short.

As soon as the peals thinned, Tom began. "Just before he was stabbed, Jourdain said that Lyly was very attached to Mr. Arundel."

"Did he?" Hennert fingered his clean-shaven chin. "I don't know *Monsieur* Lyly very well — too healthy a man for my profession, you see. When he accompanied me on my visits to Mr. Arundel, I found him to be quiet and serious."

"He accompanied you on all of them? How often did you go?"

"Every other day, in the course of that week. And I'm not sure I could tell you how attached they were. *Monsieur* Arundel was very ill already, and *Monsieur* Lyly rather restrained ... but perhaps poor Jourdain saw more of them together than I did."

Lyly gives the truth a good shaving, Grimeston had said. "At the very least, Lyly was there when Mr. Arundel died — and you were not." There and much distraught, unless Jourdain had lied — but why would he, on this of all things? And why was Hennert sucking his teeth so thoughtfully? "What is it, *mon Maître?*"

"The servant — Faucon, is it? He might know about *Monsieur* Lyly's visits, if you can find him."

It had seemed impossible — one Englishman in the whole of Paris — but now... "Did you know he's English?"

"Truly?"

"So said Maître Jourdain."

Hennert frowned, trying to remember. "I spoke little enough with Faucon, and never other than in French. It's not an English name, is it — Faucon? Still, now that you say so... I saw him once at Sir Edward's house — not that I knew him for *Monsieur* Arundel's man, back then — and he was talking to some servant or other, and perhaps ... yes, I think it was in English."

Which could mean little enough. "Do you remember which servant?"

No, the physician didn't. It had been a moment's observation, he said, and he wished that he could remember now. Did it matter much? And so crestfallen was he at his imperfect memory that Tom had to reassure him.

"It may yet come back to you," he soothed, which Hennert took most seriously. See how he sat hunched, with crossed arms and creased brow as he searched his mind... That this was the surest way not to remember, Tom didn't bother to observe. At least it kept Hennert occupied, while Tom himself considered this new knowledge.

It could mean little enough, or it could mean that the servant Faucon had friends at the Embassy.

They had to listen as the bells struck the hour once more, and to watch as twilight gathered past the window, and still they waited. Once again Tom pounded on the door, and was told through it that the *commissaire* had more important things to do than hear foreigners.

Hennert fretted. "Nobody can accuse him of not taking his time! Where on earth can he be, to make us wait so long? I am a physician! For all the man knows, my patients might be dying by the dozen!"

No, Maître Hennert definitely had no experience of this side of the law. "It may be the holiday, or he may be at the Cordeliers observing the body, if he's worth his salt — or both things," said Tom. "But I'm afraid that my being English doesn't help." *And while I could send word to the Ambassador, I won't.*

This earned a mirthless chuckle. "Oh, don't think that my being Flemish does! Fifteen years I've lived in Paris. I work hard, I hope I do some good, I married here, and my wife — Lord rest her! — was a Frenchwoman from a good family. And do you know what my own neighbours call me? Fifteen years — and still I'm *Le Flamand*!"

It was on the tip of Tom's tongue that being a Protestant must not help, either. "I suppose it's not very different in London," he said instead — and nothing more, because right then the bolts were drawn, and the servant entered with a light, to show in a young sergeant with his verge, a scrivener carrying a writing case and a bundle of papers, and a man in the long robes of a public official.

And glory be!

"My name is Guillaume Langlois," the main personage of this little cortege announced in a whitish drone. "*Commissaire* of the Châtelet. And you are Thomas Abbot, of London, and Reynard Hennert, Fleming."

"But of Paris…" the poor physician tried, earning no more than a supercilious glare.

He didn't look promising, this Guillaume Langlois, thin to the point of gauntness, with a mouth crooked in a line of distemper. Of course it could be ill humour at being dragged from his festive table, or a dislike of foreigners — but somehow it was hard to imagine the chinless face arranged in other than discontentment.

Not being especially happy himself, Tom didn't wait a moment longer. "Well, Maître Langlois, at long last!" he began — and see how the scrivener scrambled with pen and ink and paper to begin his minutes. "The sergeant who brought us here said we were not being arrested — as well we shouldn't, since we were mere witnesses to what happened, and not the only ones — and yet, we've been kept under lock and key for hours." At his elbow, he could hear Hennert shuffling his feet — thinking, no doubt, that the English madman would have them both in the Châtelet's darkest *oubliette*.

Caught in the act of sitting, Langlois stopped halfway, with the air of having expected broken French perhaps, and surely meekness. Slowly he sat down all the way.

"A lawyer, are you?" he asked, with the disgust of one who battled the legal profession every day of his life. He held out an impatient hand, and the scrivener shuffled his mound of documents, extracting and offering what Tom recognised as his papers. "No, you're not under arrest, *Monsieur* Abo'." He pronounced the name as French-wise as could be managed. "Not yet. And yes, there were many witnesses — as I took pains to find out while you sat here — and all of them say that the two of you were in the company of the murdered man."

And only the two of us you distrust on principle as foreigners and heretics, Tom didn't say. Nor did he ask how the *commissaire* had rounded up those many witnesses. Instead — surely to Hennert's relief — he took a deep breath and held his peace.

"You told my sergeant that half a dozen men rushed the people at the Cordeliers' gate. Now, these men —" the *commissaire* held up a forefinger like a schoolmaster at the play — "were they students?"

No, just the commonest of common ruffians... Tom bit down the answer. Sore as the temptation was to keep at least the Université out of the dance of jurisdictions, the witnesses had mentioned the black gowns to the sergeants. There was no reason to be too definite, though — in case Langlois also preferred to give the learned fellows a wide berth.

"I couldn't swear by it, it all happened so fast. We had the misfortune of stepping out just as those ruffians came running — Maître Jourdain, Maître Hennert, and myself. I was shoved hard, and when I regained my footing, poor Pierre Jourdain was on the ground, stabbed."

"The witnesses..." Langlois took another paper from the scrivener, and ran a fingertip down it. "They say you had your sword drawn."

"They are mistaken. I won't say I wasn't tempted — but the ruffians were gone before I could. Your sergeant took my rapier, and my dagger too: he — and everyone else, I'm sure — saw them both clean of blood."

Langlois's eyes travelled up and down Tom's stained front — and, again, Hennert fidgeted, fingers tight on the table's edge.

"Come now, *Commissaire*," Tom barely kept himself from snapping. "I'm sure you saw my rapier as well. Tell me there was a drop of blood on it, fresh or otherwise. Tell me I could have wiped it so thoroughly on my doublet without anyone noticing."

There was no other word for it: the *commissaire* sulked. He must have known all this from his men and from the witnesses — if he truly had heard any. What was he angling for? Again he shuffled the papers. "Well, this is neither here nor there!" he barked. "Nor does it tell me how you knew the dead man."

Ah, this now… This Tom had rather hoped to skirt, not wishing to have Arundel's death brought into it. "I didn't," he said — and stopped, also unwilling to drag the hapless Hennert into the discussion.

It is a melancholy fact that truth won't always serve as well as it should. That Tom did not know Jourdain happened to be true, and yet how weak it sounded to his own ears! Weak enough that Langlois caught the faintest whiff of hesitation.

"You didn't know him," he repeated, nostrils a-flare. "And yet you were with him?"

"He did not, *Monsieur*. And he was not with poor Jourdain. *I* was."

There! One might forget Hennert, at times, but that old Roman god, two-faced Janus, could have in himself no more surprises than the good Fleming did. Gone was the fretful stance, and Medicine itself was standing proud, side by side with English Law, in the face of the City of Paris.

"*Monsieur* Abbot is an acquaintance," Medicine lied with calm dignity. "He pays me a visit, sometimes, when his affairs bring him to Paris, and today he walked with me as I sought my young colleague over a professional matter. *Monsieur* Abbot didn't know poor Jourdain at all, until I introduced them today, and Jourdain — who, God rest him, had a lively and curious mind — started asking him about England."

There was a hum from the *commissaire.* "Which, if it's true, is just as well," he muttered. "For we've trouble enough with the English these days. But you, then, Maître Hennert? You did know your young colleague…"

Of all the idiotic things! Who had ever thought to make this petty half-wit an official? It was natural that the Fleming should bristle.

"Yes, *Monsieur!*" he cried. "I knew him well enough to like him, and to value his opinion, and I tried to save his life, which I would have done for the last lout on this earth —"

"As your many witnesses can't have failed to tell you, *Commissaire,*" Tom put in, before indignation carried Hennert too far. "Just as they told you that a rabble attacked those who were coming from the church. Come now, don't such turmoils happen every day here?"

"Words, yes, and stones — but a stabbing?"

"Would you say that it has never happened before in these disorders?"

"I wouldn't," Langlois conceded, with the air of one biting a sour quince. "But —"

"So, what's more likely: that either a stranger or a friend seized a sudden chance to murder Jourdain, or that one among many bursts of violence got out of hand?"

I told your father once that he should have sent you to the bar, Thomas…

And a poor barrister I would have made, Tom answered Sir Francis in his head, for there was a third possibility — that the chance might have been neither sudden nor unforeseen — the one Tom wanted to pursue for himself, without the Châtelet men underfoot, and he'd just as good as pointed it out, sitting for all to see between the horns of a false dilemma… But for a mercy nobody seized on it: the one who might have, Langlois himself, was gaping like a sturgeon, crimson with fury under the coney-like stare of his scrivener, and it was just as well that he couldn't see the quirk of the sergeant's mouth behind his back.

Oh, Fates be thanked for dull-witted inquirers — but it was also a poor barrister who made an enemy of a magistrate, no matter how puny. So Tom took a step back, palms spread.

"But, *Monsieur*, I tell you nothing you haven't already reasoned for yourself, do I?" he said, and made it as rueful as he knew. "I'm sure you've only too much experience with this unruliness."

Dull-witted Guillaume Langlois might be, but not too dull-witted to see when he was being offered an honourable way out. Not that he liked it, and when he took it, it was with the worst grace.

"But yes," he ground out, and motioned so brusquely for the scrivener to write, he nearly upended the man's ink-pot. "I won't deny that the streets of Paris are unchancy. Full of resentment towards the English…" He waved as though Tom had protested — which he had not. "Yes, yes: not just the English. While you'll forgive me for saying that English people had better stay in England at such a time, it must be said that some of our religious factions are just as troublesome. As you yourself say…" A clearing of the throat, and he began again, in a more formal manner. "Having seen the body of the deceased Pierre Jourdain, and having heard the witnesses, it's my opinion that the fray in the Rue des Cordeliers was yet another instance of the deplorable violence that we observe daily. While no attacker could be apprehended, the said fray is all too likely to have been the work of Protestant fanatics, attacking the good people coming from the Mass, and the said Pierre Jourdain, physician, of the *Quartier* de la Harpe, was slain accidentally in the tumult. *Sergent!*"

The guard stepped forward to release the witnesses, and Langlois was already at the door, with the scrivener on his heels, when Tom called to him.

"If I could have my papers, *Monsieur le Commissaire?* And my blades."

They must all have been burning to get rid of them, because the papers were unearthed from the scrivener's bundle and handed back in a flurry, while rapier and dagger were fetched at once, and Tom and Hennert were as good as shoved out of the guardhouse.

"Well!" Tom huffed, as he drew his cloak tighter around himself against the cold, wishing that he could hide the bloodstains — not that it would matter much, once they left the halo of the *barrière*'s lanterns, for the street was quite dark by then. "Lord smite all self-important, witless ass-heads! What did he think, that the *Lieutenant Criminel* would thank him for a groundless charge against an Englishman, at this of all times?" Having been cursing in English, he stopped at the sight of the Fleming, who stood shivering at his shoulder, and shifted to French. "Your pardon, Maître Hennert, I must sound very callous to you. Truly, I can't begin to say how sorry I am that you were caught up in this matter."

Hennert shook his head as he peered this way and that along the dark Rue de la Harpe.

"I thought Sir Edward wouldn't want to be dragged into this, and you'd want it even less. With the bad blood between

Catholics and Protestants being what it is… I hope I didn't do wrong, *Monsieur*?"

Poor fellow, how haggard he looked in the yellow light, all his round-cheeked benignity lost. "Why, you did very well, *mon Maître*. I am thankful."

This earned a very grave, very steady gaze. "You are thankful that I helped you turn the Châtelet's attention from the truth of poor Jourdain's death. You didn't ask it of me. I did so of my own will, trusting that you won't let the matter lie, and the murderer go unpunished. Or was I wrong, when I chose to lie to the *commissaire* for your sake?"

You didn't quite lie… It was not for my own sake… You were right earlier, in not wanting to know… Answer after answer rose to Tom's mind, and one after the other he discarded, as he held the physician's troubled eyes.

"Other than that neither you nor I killed him, I don't know the truth of Jourdain's death. I have suspicions — of why it was done, not yet of who did it — and these are such that I can promise you two things. One, that the Châtelet meddling in this matter would help nothing and harm much; and two, that I will not let the matter lie."

As for the murderer not going unpunished… Too many times Tom had seen it happen, no matter how he tried — out of his own inability, of policy, of necessity — too many times to make promises.

If Hennert was waiting for more, it didn't take him long to see he wouldn't have it.

"Thank you, *Monsieur* Abbot," he said. "I reckon it's as much reassurance as you can offer."

Precious little it was, and Tom, chilled in the cold draught that whistled down the street, felt rather helpless. But there was one thing he could do, considering the Fleming's unarmed and dishevelled state. "It's very dark. Let me walk you... But no, you live outside the walls, don't you? The gates will be closed by now — damn Langlois once more! Well then, we'll go back to the Embassy: surely Sir Edward will provide you with shelter."

It wasn't very flattering, the haste with which the offer was declined. "But no, no, thank you. My wife's nephew lives quite near, you see?" Hennert pointed. "Close by the Convent of the Mathurins. It won't be the first time he takes me in for the night."

Not very flattering, but understandable — whether the poor man had had enough of Tom for the day, or wasn't anxious to meet Stafford just at the moment... Either way, since the convent was no great detour, Tom insisted on seeing Hennert to his nephew's house, and waited until a servant answered the door. They exchanged greetings then, and Tom renewed his warning, and the physician, a foot already across the threshold, hesitated.

"Now it will be you walking alone and without light, *Monsieur*. I'm uneasy to send you away like this..."

Truly a good man, and kind — after such a day! Tom hitched his cloak aside to show his rapier. "I'm well armed."

But worry the Fleming did, and wasn't happy until he borrowed a lantern from the servant, and lit it for Tom to carry.

"You don't want the men of the night Guet to catch you lightless, and fine you."

The Guet, Paris's ill-famed night watch — all Tom lacked now! As he took the lantern, he nodded at Hennert. "I won't lose my way, you have my word on it."

And let him make of it what he liked best.

CHAPTER 7

It had been unreasonable, perhaps, to hope of slipping inside the Embassy quietly. Not only was Hobelot manning the door with great anxiety, but Skeres was with him — and that, too, was to be expected.

As it was that both should exclaim at the sight of his bloodied cloak.

"Sworn to make me old before me time, 'ave you?" the Minotaur hiccupped, patting his master's front, seeking wounds that weren't there.

"If it were my blood, Dolius, I wouldn't be walking," Tom protested wearily. Unharmed he might be, but of a sudden he found himself so fatigued and cold that he made no protest when he was pushed to sit on a bench by the door. In fact, he was thankful to lean back against the wall for a moment, and rub at his face, trying not to think of Pierre Jourdain, alive and conversing one moment, and the next bleeding to death in the mud… His eyes flew open, and he was startled to find Hobelot hovering nearby, nibbling at his knuckles, watching the bloodstained cloak with pupils that gleamed black in the one candle's sickly light.

Sometimes, in his head, he's still a corporal in Flanders, his brother had said.

"Hobelot, my good man, it's nothing to worry about." Tom dragged up a smile, drawing the folds together to hide the stain — and noticed an absence. "What have you done with Skeres?"

To Tom's great relief, the shadows cleared from Hobelot's countenance. "He's gone to fetch you some wine, Master," he said. "We've all been worried about you."

Had they? Not for his own sake, perhaps — but wondering how they were going to explain to Mr. Secretary his kinsman's disappearance. It was easy enough to imagine, when the chaplain arrived at a solicitous half-run.

"Lord be thanked, Mr. Abbot!" the man cried. "Sir Edward was beside himself with worry!"

"Was he? There was no need whatsoever."

But Hakluyt *had* worried. "No need? We didn't know what had become of you — not even your servant. Now he says you met with a mischance — oh, Lord deliver us, you're hurt!" He stepped forward, hands outstretched, as one ready to catch a collapsing man.

Feeling a little light-headed, Tom brushed his fingers down the stiff, dark smear (his wretched new cloak!) and, again, explained that no, the blood wasn't his — until Skeres's noisy arrival put a merciful end to it.

"'Ere." The lad all but elbowed aside the chaplain, and thrust into Tom's hands a warm pot, from which rose a vapour of wine, cinnamon, and sugar. "I 'ad Sally make it."

Bless the Minotaur, ordering about the Ambassador's servants. Tom sipped gratefully, and over the pot's rim caught sight of Hakluyt moving away.

Oh yes, Hakluyt with his blithe vouching! "Mr. Hakluyt, please wait," he called, and mustn't have concealed his vexation too well, because the chaplain's manner grew wary.

"I must advise Sir Edward —"

"He'll know, by now — and it's but a word. If you please."

For once, Tom felt inclined to thank Stafford's loose tongue: plain Abbot Hakluyt might have disregarded, but a

Walsingham… With every sign of unwillingness, the chaplain stopped. "Well, then…"

Hesitation being as good as consent, Tom abandoned his pot to the protesting Skeres, and pushed to his feet. "I'll walk with you," he said — only to stop them both as soon as they'd passed the threshold, out of the servants' hearing. All the same, he lowered his voice to a sharp whisper.

"You said that Lyly hardly knew Arundel."

"Did I? I may well have said it, because it's true…"

"It's not. He went to see Arundel often, for they were close friends."

Hakluyt stared, and one would think him honestly surprised, even flustered. "Close friends? I never heard of this, I assure you — from Mr. Lyly or anyone else."

"Are you sure? Lyly must have spoken of Mr. Arundel, of his death?"

Another shake of the head. "He was a little quiet when the poor gentleman died — but seemed to feel no more than any good Christian would feel for a fellow creature."

Any good Christian! And yet the man was no fool… Could one be too taken with faraway lands and their inhabitants to observe those living shoulder to shoulder with him? Or was this still the uneasy juggling of Conscience and Convenience? As Tom formed these spleenful thoughts, the chaplain's eyes had wandered to the bloodstains again.

"But I must say that I don't see…" Tearing his gaze away, he gathered himself into severity. "What if they were friends? Why are you asking? You claim to want to exculpate Lyly, but do you? I wish I knew what it is that you truly seek."

And here was Conscience gaining the upper hand! But then, Tom knew how to use severity too. "What I seek is justice, Reverend — and yet you will not help me."

Hakluyt backed away a step, his whisper growing harsh. "Justice on the conscience of men! Papist Spain uses its priests as inquisitors — but we —"

He stopped short when Tom grasped him by the sleeve. "Justice for a death — for two! Didn't Sir Edward tell you that Mr. Arundel was murdered?"

He had not, it was plain: the confusion and dismay on the chaplain's face could not be feigned, surely? "Lord spare us," he murmured. "How?"

"Poison. And then this morning Arundel's physician was stabbed before my eyes." Tom touched the stain. "This is his blood."

The grey eyes went round. "But you never suspect Mr. Lyly?"

And Stafford, even more, and Her Ladyship perhaps — all lambs of this man's flock. "As you once said, Sir, I must winnow truth from falsehood." Tom didn't even try to stop the bitter sigh. "It becomes difficult when all lie or keep things from me."

For the longest moment Hakluyt stared at Tom's bloodstained cloak — brows knitted, lips pursed — and, when he looked up, his gaze was troubled.

"Can you promise me it's justice that you seek?" he asked. "Justice — and not your master's advantage?"

Could he? It struck him that perhaps he had misjudged the chaplain: the battle was raging indeed — but perhaps Convenience had nothing to do with it. And such earnestness deserved honesty, surely? Or, at least, would respond better to it...

"I serve Mr. Secretary and, through him, Her Highness. But I would think that Truth and Justice must be everyone's advantage?"

Only a measure of honesty, after all — at least where Stafford was concerned — but it was enough that Hakluyt nodded minutely several times.

That he was still unhappy was plain in the way he began: "But, Mr. Walsingham, of Lyly and Mr. Arundel I truly don't know —" only to stop when he caught sight of something behind Tom.

The something proved to be Skeres, hovering and watching just past the door — and, on being observed, choosing to regard himself as summoned.

Ignoring his servant, Tom held the chaplain's gaze. "Mr. Hakluyt, you were going to advise Sir Edward? I'd be grateful if you could beg of him to see me, as soon as possible. As for Mr. Lyly..."

After Hennert, here was another who found himself knowing more than he liked — though for a different reason. "I'll regard what you said as a confidence," the chaplain murmured. "And leave you to deal with it."

And, there being no other word for it, he fled — not reassured, surely, by the Minotaur's mighty snort.

"Skeres!" Tom scolded, but took the pot that was held out to him, still lukewarm, and sipped again, savouring the sugar and the cinnamon and the unwatered wine ... until it came to him that, since breaking his fast in the morning, he'd had naught but a piece of half-stale bread. With a sigh, he gave back the pot.

"I'll need a clear head for Stafford, Dolius," he murmured, and wearily began to unbutton his ill-used cloak — only to find that some of the blood had seeped through, leaving a smaller mark on the doublet. He needed to change — but into what? Was he going to have to borrow clothes — from Lyly, perhaps? The irony!

Skeres was fingering the cloak with great displeasure. "A pain to clean, it'll be — and I'd just sponged it!"

And leave it to Skeres to grouse! "Next time I meet a murderer, I'll tell him —"

"Abbot!"

Oh, devil take it! There, down the staircase, Stafford himself was descending like a Jove in octavo, haloed in the glow of the chaplain's candle right behind him.

"Back, at last," he called, face knotted in displeasure. "And loitering! Now you'll oblige me with an account of what happened."

"Most certainly, Sir." Tom motioned to his stains. "As soon as I'm —"

"You think I give a straw if you wear half the blood in Paris? Come and be quick, man!" And, waiting for no answer, he stalked upstairs again.

Ah, well — there went any hope, or need, of changing. Tom threw the cloak at Skeres. "Do what you can — if I'm still whole to wear it, after I'm told off."

But, as he caught the garment with an awkward lurch, the lad leant close, tapping his nose — the Minotaur signalling secrecy. "Wrote 'ome today, 'e did," he rumbled, and held up two fingers. "Two letters — one to 'Is 'Onour, and the other…" He raised a shoulder, miming a hump. The Cecils.

How Skeres had learnt of Stafford's correspondence was a matter that could wait. Tom climbed up the white stairs, to find Hakluyt waiting at the top, looking unhappy.

"Don't tarry, Mr. Abbot," he urged. "Sir Edward's already displeased."

And wait until he hears my story, Tom thought, as the chaplain led him through the empty secretaries' room, and knocked on the door to the study.

"Come, come!" sounded the vexed summons, and there was a grimace crinkling Hakluyt's face, as Tom entered the bear's den alone.

The bear awaited — equally alone — pacing the den's width, brow creased in utmost severity.

"I half thought you'd run back to London!" he growled, stopping before Tom, peevish rather than severe. "What's this of a physician? What other mischief have you been doing?"

Because, of course, it *had* to be Tom's fault! In no mood to seek a gentle way to break the tiding, he squared his shoulders and announced, "Mr. Arundel's physician was murdered."

There. The air went out of Edward Stafford — and surely it was unchristian to find satisfaction in the way he gaped once, then twice, before croaking, "You must be mad!"

"You had the right of it from the first, Sir: Mr. Arundel was murdered, and now Maître Jourdain has been silenced because he may have seen it done — or even had a part in it."

"Good Lord have mercy!" The Ambassador threw himself into his chair, so vehemently he made the candles on the table quiver. "How...?"

And, for what felt like the dozenth time that day, Tom told the tale of Jourdain's death. It was strange how, with each retelling, it felt stiffer, and more solid, as though it were being carved in stone. Was this how history was formed? Lord, but he must be tired, waxing philosophical before Stafford of all men.

Not that Stafford was in the right mind to notice anyone's fancies: huddled in the chair, he stared at the flames crackling in the fireplace, and nibbled at his lower lip. It was a while before he said, "The Pagets' men, surely...?" When he received no answer, he twisted around, hitting both palms on the tapestried table. "It *must* have been the Pagets! Who else...?"

Now would a murderer, one capable of slowly poisoning a friend, even try such a clumsy diversion? But then, *Je dirai...* But even supposing Stafford was innocent... "If Mr. Arundel was truly helping you, Sir —" Tom held up a hand to forestall protest. "If you were bringing him back to Her Majesty's service, then there must be those, on the other side, who deemed him a traitor."

"Yes — yes, the Pagets, I tell you!"

Or the Guise, or King Henri, or the King's mother, or, to hear Gifford, Mendoza, or more than one of these... "And this means one thing alone: your dealings with him were known."

The Ambassador's small burst of laughter could have been many things: disbelief, outrage, desperation, bitterness... "Gifford's doing, you see? *You see?*"

That Gifford had painted Arundel as a traitor to England, Tom didn't bother to point out. "What I see, Sir, is that Mr. Secretary must be advised."

Which Stafford must have been expecting, at least since hearing of Jourdain, for at once he was all solicitude. "Yes, yes — of course. I'll write. And if you wish to send a letter of your own, of course, I'll attach it."

Not an objection — and, most of all, not a mention of the packet he'd just sent. *An excess of promptness, Thomas, is as revealing as any hesitation.* And so was an omission.

"Thank you, Sir." Tom half-bowed. "And, if you're right about Gifford, surely it grows even more imperative that I should meet the man."

Edward Stafford must have been thoroughly fed up with being told he was right, and also quite fed up with Tom.

"Well, it doesn't grow easier to accomplish, though. Besides —" Stafford rose to his feet, dismissal plain in the gesture —

"you saw what happened when you insisted on speaking to the physician. Perhaps you'll listen now, when I counsel prudence."

And trust Sir Edward Stafford to blame all but himself. When Tom answered, it was with more sharpness than was seemly: "What happened, Sir, is that we had your suspicions confirmed, that murder is afoot. I'll bid you good night."

With a brisk bow, he left — and let the man think him a good deal more ruthless than he felt, and to believe himself safe for now.

"Baggage!" was Nick Skeres's pronouncement, once they were ensconced in their cupboard, and he'd heard the whole tale. Poor Jourdain's death he'd taken philosophically, and that Stafford or Lyly might be guilty seemed to afford him a certain glee. When it came to Stafford's reproof and Tom's own qualms, that was when he scoffed.

"If that fellow knew aught, they were going to do 'im in, with or without you."

Clad in his spare shirt and a blanket, Tom was eating half-heartedly from a trencher of bread and cold meat his servant had procured. "And it's by chance that he was killed just as he talked with me?"

A scowl fixed on the sleeves he was detaching from Tom's doublet, the lad raised his shoulder. "Chance me foot! They didn't want 'im to tell what 'e knew, and that's plain. All I say is, they didn't want 'im to tell a soul, not just you."

The Minotaur logical... Tom sat back against the damp wall, and yelped on finding in his way a sloping beam — damn this low-ceilinged pigeonhole!

"Still," he grumbled, rubbing the back of his skull, "if you're right, then they were wrong, for Jourdain was very firm: no poison, he said."

"That 'e's dead don't make 'im 'onest when 'e was alive. Or sharp of wits."

"Not of necessity, no — but he could have been innocent and frightened, and I could have warned him, and —"

A mighty grunt, as Skeres tussled with a tighter knot. "And if 'e was that frighted, maybe 'e wasn't innocent, and what use was a warning then, *and*..." He looked up. "Feeling sorry for yourself won't bring 'im back."

Well, that was true enough — all of it. Tom gestured at the doublet. "Is that all that's left of my clothes? What of my poor cloak?"

"Sally's washed out the worst, and I'm giving 'er this one, too. All put out by the blood, she was, poor chuck." And see how sweetly the Minotaur beamed.

When Tom teased that Sally must be in want of some consoling, the smile waxed larger. And then there was the well-filled trencher...

"Cavel is still in disgrace, I take it?"

"Very much!" And then the triumph gave way to consideration. "Keeps to 'imself, these days — even with 'is brother. And keeps to 'is tale, which makes Sally mad. And keeps to the 'ouse. I'd thought to follow 'im, see where 'e went..."

"Well thought!" Tom said, and the lad hitched his shoulder.

"Ay, well — but 'e goes nowhere. Not of 'is own notion, and not even ordered. 'Tis 'Obelot as runs errands these past days, or the stable lad, and even Sally once — poor Sally. Well!" Having undone the last of the points, he set aside the sleeves. "These she don't 'ave to wash."

And when Tom moaned that it would never dry overnight, and he'd have to borrow, the lad shook his head.

"Not from Lyly, for 'e's away," he said. "And it takes two of you to fill Mr. Grimeston's clothes... And, by the by, 'twas 'im as told me of the letter. Seeks me out, says where's me master, and whispers in me ear —"

"What do you mean, Lyly's away?" Tom cut in. "Stafford never sent him to London?"

"No," Skeres began and then stopped, pursing his lips. "I don't think. There was another fellow came and went, one as don't live 'ere — like you didn't live 'ere, back when you rode courier. Where Lyly is, though, Lord knows. You think —" the lad gawped — "you think 'e scuttled?"

Did he? Tom chewed a piece of meat as he thought. "Well, he's lied about Arundel," he said slowly.

"'E would, that one." Skeres nodded sagely. "Never looks you in the eye."

"Besides, he used to be in Mary Stuart's pay: now that she's dead, who pays for his fine lace collars?"

Skeres laughed, and flicked at the threadbare bedding on his pallet. "Never Stafford, that's for sure!"

But was it? *Lord forfend Sir Edward should risk young Lyly going into the lion's den...* And Lyly standing stoutly at the Ambassador's side... But did the Ambassador know of Lyly's closeness to Arundel? Tom pushed away the trencher, and gathered the blanket tighter around his shoulders.

"Oh, I don't know, Dolius, I don't know. Can you really believe that whoever had Jourdain killed is getting rid of all those who might know about Arundel's death?"

"Why not?" Skeres eyed the discarded trencher, where a few scraps of meat remained. "Ain't you eating that?"

"Because it's near on a fortnight since Arundel died, and nobody else died — until I began asking questions."

"Nobody else that you've been told. For all you know, there may 'ave been a score. Ain't you eating —"

"Jove, you've the stomach of a horse — go ahead!" Tom waved impatiently. "Lyly's alive, and so is Stafford…"

"Ay, well — they would be, if it's them as did the murthers."

"Either of them or both, yes. Then there's Hennert, also alive — and the other physician, Duret. And there's Arundel's servant, Faucon… That one I must find. He's an Englishman, and has friends here among the servants. I want you to find out tomorrow."

There was, for an answer, a full-mouthed grunt.

"But suppose he's alive. Suppose they're all alive — except Jourdain. Then perhaps whoever had him killed knew just what I'm up to…"

Skeres chewed thoughtfully. "Mr. Ambassador knows. And little Lyly."

"And Grimeston, in truth — and Hakluyt —"

"The Reverend?" A snort. "'E near swooned just for seein' the blood on you."

And he'd seemed much surprised to hear of Arundel, but still… "We can't know what he said to whom — even in all innocence. And then there's Lady Stafford."

Skeres, who was busy picking the last crumbs of bread and meat from the trencher with a wet finger, stopped short to stare. "Come now, Mr. Tom! She never 'ad 'er own cousin murthered!"

"You didn't say so of her husband. But no, I don't think she ordered it. It's like Hakluyt: whom does she talk to? Worse than Hakluyt, though, for she's a Howard, a Catholic most likely, a friend to the Queen Mother, to Simier — who is the

King's man — and, most of all, she lied." Pushing off the bed, Tom paced to the window that looked out onto the sleeping garden, white and black under the sliver of moon that shone from among the ragged clouds. Across it, in the main house, candlelight flickered behind one glazed window. "Like everybody in this cursed place, she lied. That servant of Arundel she hardly noticed? Well, Jourdain said it was she who found him for her cousin."

"And you take 'is word over 'ers?"

"Oh, I mean to find out — but I'm not much minded to believe her."

It never failed to amuse and vex Tom in equal parts, when Skeres dusted off that chivalrous corner of his soul that now made him pout so fiercely in Lady Stafford's defence. "Now, that's just because you feel bad that Jourdain died…"

"And because she's so keen to keep me away from the Framlinghams — and perhaps it's not them at all. Perhaps it's that Joyce Blundell —"

"Who's that — the cousin?"

"The cousin, yes — who knows that I'm attached to the Embassy, and is a Catholic, with gentlemen friends at the Cordeliers…"

"And 'ow does *she* know just what you're up to? Attached to the Embassy's one thing; nosing around's another."

"I know, I know." Tom exhaled, long and slow, and rubbed at his face. "But I've half a dozen people who could have wanted Arundel dead, or informed on him, or been ordered to silence him — for being a traitor, for knowing too much, for wanting to tell…"

"Running in circles, that's what you're doing. Running in circles, all bedevilled."

Tom couldn't help a huff of cheerless laughter. "Yes, Dolius. It bedevils me that I never truly believed Arundel had been murdered — still wouldn't believe it, were it just Stafford's word."

"Which 'e took back in 'aste."

"Yes, the moment he found Walsingham's hound at his door. I much doubt he'd counted on that."

A snort. "Did the lack-wit think 'Is 'Onour would 'ear *murther* and let it rest?"

Not so much a lack-wit as one who steered his ship by sight — which made him more of a danger, rather than less, both in the immediate moment, and to Sir Francis's designs.

Tom sighed — it was a day of many sighs. "I may have to send you back to London, if I want to write safely — and I do, very much."

This Skeres didn't like a whit. "Back, 'e says!" he grumbled, tugging savagely at the wretched doublet's lining. "And if I ride back, who's to make sure you don't end up gutted like the Frenchman, eh? If I were them, I'd get rid of the one who's asking questions."

"Or of the messenger on his way, for that matter. Well, we'll both have to take our chances, if it comes to that."

Even Minotaurs knew when they'd run out of objections, and Skeres subsided into black-browed silence.

Across the garden, the windows had all gone dark and the tracing of the climbing plant showed black like a maze of fissures, as though the whole house were about to crumble at a touch.

CHAPTER 8

Contrary to expectations, Tom's cloak and doublet were returned to him at first light. They were still damp, and wrinkled, and reeked of smoke and herrings and grey soap, and the cloak still showed a ghostly trace of the mishap, while the doublet had a scorch mark where it had been held too close to the fire — but they could be worn. Barely.

Tom was fastening the doublet when a flash of brightness in the garden caught his eye, and through the window he spied Lady Stafford pacing in her green cloak, her woman at her heels.

Well, this time she wouldn't have the safety of her warm parlour! Followed by Skeres's expostulations, Tom made for the servants' wooden stairs — little better than a ladder — and hurried downstairs and through the kitchen.

At the gallery's door he ran into Grimeston.

"Beg pardon," Tom hastily called, as he recovered his footing, and would have gone, but the secretary caught him by the arm, brows raised. Oh, yes, Stafford's letter.

"Later, Mr. Grimeston." Tom glanced through the door to the gallery, and past it to the garden, where his quarry paced.

Grimeston peered too. "Her Ladyship —"

"Doesn't like to be bothered early, I know," Tom said, and nonetheless disentangled himself and strode out to meet the Baroness.

She liked it very little. See how she stiffened at the sound of steps; what queenly displeasure she turned on the intruder — Juno in green velvet!

Tom stopped half a dozen steps away, the frozen gravel crunching under his shoes, and swallowed an urge to apologise. He was Mr. Secretary's man, and the lady had lied to him. Setting his jaw, he bowed, as coldly as he knew.

She stood very straight and still — Juno displeased. "It's very early, Mr. ... Abbot," she said, the small pause a reproof in its own right.

"Your Ladyship will forgive me, I hope — considering what happened yesterday."

For a moment they faced each other in the cold morning light. The night's wind had thinned the clouds enough that the winter sky showed pale through them, and a light frost had settled. Lady Stafford called her maid, who shivered patiently five steps behind.

"Fetch me the muff," she ordered. "The zibet one."

As soon as the young woman was out of earshot, she said, "I don't own a zibet muff. And Avison isn't quick-witted. You have until she returns in a fluster."

Pinch the woman! But it was more time than Tom would have without Mr. Secretary's weight behind him, so he stepped close. "Then, Madam, I'll waste no time with compliments and apologies: Your Ladyship was less than forthcoming the other day."

One perfect brow rose. "No time wasted, indeed," she murmured, and see if she didn't look — of all things in this world — amused. "Was I?"

"Your Ladyship knows very well that Mr. Arundel had an English servant — why, it was you who found him for your kinsman. And I'd wager, Madam, that you know where the man is now."

"Oh, you're a very, very vexing man!" The Baroness tossed her green-hooded head, fixing her glare on the bare climbing rose. "Yes, I know of John Faulkes. I know that he's English, because, on my cousin's death, he came to the one relation he knew his master had had in Paris."

For a moment, it seemed she would say no more. She stood glaring at the door through which she expected the maid to reappear. Tom waited, shoulders and jaw stiff against the cold that bit through the damp doublet. Fools didn't stop to snatch up their cloaks.

"And he begged for help again?" he prodded after a while.

"He begged for help for the first time. He hoped to work here, and he even managed somehow to interest Mr. Lyly in his case — but we had no need of another servant. Still, because he'd been my cousin's man, I found him work elsewhere." And who would have thought that the Baroness could take a mulish air when annoyed? "This is all I know of Faulkes — and I don't know why you must think otherwise, but I didn't find him for poor Charles, as you put it."

And yet, *Madame herself found him*, Jourdain had said. He couldn't have meant any other than Lady Stafford, surely? "I'm tempted to think otherwise, Madam, because at the very least you lied about not knowing where he is now — and are still keeping it from me."

Even in the shadow of her hood, it was plain when the Baroness went white with anger. At the boldness of this Walsingham satellite? At having been caught in a lie? At both things, most likely, and at having to put up with it all.

"Faulkes is in a French household now," she said, gloved hands clenched together, nostrils flaring. "One where you won't go stirring trouble. Doesn't it seem to you that Mr. Secretary's men have done my husband harm enough?"

The thought flitted across Tom's mind that he must now tell a baroness, a Howard, and a friend to queens that she couldn't order him about. "And what must it seem to Mr. Secretary, Madam, if you hinder my inquiries on this matter?" he asked, before he could dwell too much on his own forwardness — made all the worse by his unspoken meaning: *Is what this Faulkes knows worth defying Mr. Secretary?*

The image of the hourglass in the Ambassador's study painted itself in Tom's mind, the red sand softly falling while Lady Douglas Stafford, Baroness Sheffield, answered in her mind the unvoiced question. Weighing perhaps the dangers of her husband's guilt at worst — or perhaps just the bounds and the price of Lord Burleigh's protection. Was she aware of the compromise between the Treasurer and Sir Francis? Some said she still hated the Earl of Leicester so bitterly, there was little she wouldn't do to spite him — and Leicester was Sir Francis's ally of a sort. But perhaps being this volatile personage's mistress had taught her to pick her battles, for...

"He's at the Hôtel d'Hercule," she said at last. "House-servant to *Madame* de Nantouillet."

And how the lovely viol's voice grated when its owner was angered!

"Thank you, Madam." Tom bowed. "And it strikes me that whatever tidings I seek, indeed, my seeking tidings at all would appear less strange if I had a letter for Faulkes. One in which Your Ladyship describes Thomas Abbot as sent by Mr. Arundel's sister, to learn of her brother's death."

Lady Stafford gave a huff of scornful laughter. "Is this how you disguise yourself — as Jane Bevyle's man? I warn you: she never cared much for her brother."

Not even enough to want to know if her brother was murdered? Not that it mattered. "With any luck, Faulkes won't know that."

This earned a slow, tight-lipped half-smile. "Walsingham's wolfhound, my husband calls you," the lady said, just this side of a sneer. "I would say a terrier — unearthing, and nosing, and —"

And, considering, Tom was thankful that right then the maid tripped out of the door in a fluster, as her mistress had foreseen, curtseying as she went, and babbling of muffs that weren't, that couldn't, that didn't...

"Don't be foolish!" Lady Stafford snapped. "Fetch me paper and pen, instead." And she turned to go, sharply enough to make the green cloak billow around her, and called over her shoulder, "Come then, Mr. Abbot, if you want your letter."

A little light-headed from the encounter, Tom hastened to follow, wondering if the Baroness had yielded too easily — and if he'd find the servant Faulkes alive.

John Faulkes was alive, after all, and as colourless a fellow as could be — of thirty years of age perhaps, smallish, soft-spoken, with a balding head and a mousey face that sat ill with the red and azure livery. Perhaps he was also short-sighted, for he took his time reading Lady Stafford's letter, squinting at it, and angling it this way and that to catch the grey light from the window in the servants' parlour.

It had been a good notion, this letter — for it had carried Tom past a haughty porter and an even haughtier *majordome*, and now, hopefully, it would convince Faulkes to answer this stranger's questions.

Having very little trust in Lady Stafford, Tom had not only observed the writing of the letter, but also rushed with it to the Hôtel d'Hercule, lest the Baroness should send someone ahead — not to murder, but to warn Faulkes. And in truth, what he suspected from a league between mistress and servant, he didn't quite know; nothing, perhaps, had it not been for that reluctance to reveal the fellow's whereabouts.

"Please you, Master —" having finished his reading, Faulkes went to stand before Tom where he sat, and put the folded letter in front of him on the table — "I hadn't been long with Mr. Arundel, God rest his soul, but I'll answer as I know."

A careful speech, carefully delivered... But then the man's whole demeanour was as careful as a mouse's.

Tom motioned to the chair before him. "Sit then, Faulkes. You are English?"

"Thank you, Master, but it's not liked here that a servant should sit before a gentleman. I'll stand, please you. And yes, I'm English, Surrey born and bred — though I've been in France these past eleven years."

"Long enough that they call you Faucon, I hear."

That Hennert and Jourdain had done so, Tom wasn't going to say — but both the porter and the *majordome* had.

"Jean Faucon, yes." Faulkes raised his shoulder. "You know what these French are like, Master."

"You must have liked it, to serve an English gentleman for a while."

"Mr. Arundel was very good to me," said Faulkes.

Had the mild gaze gone a tad blanker? "It must have been a sad day, to see him die — and you alone with him..."

"Oh — but no, Master. I wasn't alone with him."

"Lady Bevyle had a letter from an acquaintance, saying that her poor brother would have died alone but for the goodness of one servant... And that must have been you."

The fellow shifted his weight from foot to foot. "I'll say naught of my goodness, for it was just my Christian duty to tend to my master — but he wasn't alone. His young friend was there with him to the last, that's a Mr. Lyly, and there was

Maître Jourdain, the physician — and another, who was sent by my lord the Duke himself, had been there for a while. No, you can assure Her Ladyship that Mr. Arundel wasn't alone."

Tom nodded gravely. "She'll be much consoled. I'll have to speak to the physician. Jourdain, you said? And then this Mr. Linley...?"

"Lyly, Master," Faulkes corrected. "He brought the English Ambassador's physician, who is a Fleming, I think."

"Yet another physician? Then Mr. Arundel was very well attended on his deathbed."

"It served little enough." The servant shook his head. "But neither the Ambassador's physician nor the Duke's man were there the day my master died."

"But this Mr. Lyly was? I thought you said..."

"He came alone, too. Every day since my master took ill."

"Lyly, yes. Now I remember — the Ambassador's man, is he? I've yet to meet him, but I didn't know he was such a close friend of Mr. Arundel's."

"Well now..." Head tilted, forefinger to his lips, Faulkes thought. "In fair truth, I'd only seen him once or twice before — but when my master took ill, Mr. Lyly was always there. He visited with the Ambassador, and with the physician, and alone ... and in the end, oh, he was so distraught, poor gentleman. It was very sad to see." A shake of the head.

"Her Ladyship would learn something of it, for the letter said very little..."

"The purple ague it was, Master. A fever fit to burn a man, worse and worse with every day. And such spots — like rotting meat they were — and he raved ... and nothing helped!" He glanced at Tom. "Were I to die like that, Master, I wouldn't want my sister to know."

It was more than Tom could help, to think of his own sisters. Would Barbara send to inquire, if he died abroad? Would Mary? Yes, Mary perhaps. Frances would want to know, but then Frances was not his sister. "I'll be discreet with Her Ladyship. Only... You say that Mr. Arundel raved. Did he call for her? Did he ... did he pray?"

Faulkes dithered at that, reckoning in his mind, no doubt, what would give offence. Was this sister also Catholic? What would this man who asked on her behalf want to hear? The servant watched Tom's reaction as he chose each word: "I think that he hardly knew what was what in the end, Master. He had a priest, on the last morning but one, but after that... He'd call for Sir Edward — that's the Ambassador, isn't it? — and for William, that's Mr. Lyly, when they were there, and when they weren't. Mostly, though, he'd cry things of no meaning, in English or in French."

"In French?"

"*Je dirai.*" Faulkes stared at nothing, like one haunted. "*Je dirai* ... again and again and again. Ah, Master, it was a most terrible thing. I won't blame Mr. Lyly for weeping, for I wept too."

So, again, the distraught Lyly. And, again, not a syllable of deathbed repentance, nor of dying protestations of fealty... Not a great marvel, perhaps. And instead that strange cry in French... Although it sounded different coming from an English mouth, more like *The dearie.* And yet Faulkes's French was quite good — good enough to have understood the physicians consulting among themselves, perhaps...

"And the physicians ... they all called it the purple ague?"

"Why, yes." Faulkes blinked.

It was like watching the carp in the moat back at Scadbury — the shrewd ones that grew to be old and big — coming to the surface for breadcrumbs, and then dropping down again at the slightest sign of danger, at the shadow of an angling rod. *They know*, Tom's brother Guildford had been fond of saying. *They know.* And just what did John Faulkes know, to drop back under the surface of blank mildness? Time to dangle some bait before him, or before his masters — or some warning, if he was innocent.

"It's just that my Lady Bevyle's friends... Well, you're proving them less than well informed — but..." Tom watched the servant carefully. "The letter hinted at poison."

"Holy Virgin watch me!" Faulkes's hand shot up in a sign of the cross. "But, Master... Not a soul called it anything but the purple ague. You never think...?"

Not that they would before a servant, so it meant little enough, even if it was true. If it was not, all this discomposure could as well be dismay as fear — or fine play-acting, for that matter. Now it remained to be seen who, if anyone, would receive Faulkes's report.

"That Mr. Arundel was poisoned? In truth I don't, but Her Ladyship wanted me to inquire." Tom stood, and passed the man a *double.* "I believe that now I can reassure her, though."

And, as the man bowed low and scurried to open the door for Tom, he asked, as though it were an afterthought, "Oh, one last thing: how were you taken into Mr. Arundel's service?"

The carp-like wariness again, the mild mouse's smile... The man was a whole vivary!

"Didn't Her Ladyship tell you, Master?" he asked. "She doesn't like to have her generosity bandied about — but it was through her own goodness."

"Lady Stafford?"

"A most generous lady, Master. And because I'd served her kinsman well, she also found this situation for me."

And once he was outside in the Rue des Augustins, Tom stopped under the shadow of an ornate turret, frowning at the Hôtel d'Hercule's eponymous half-god — who brooded above the lintel, leaning on his club — and at the fretful comings and goings at the crossroads. Only then did it occur to him how close lay the Rue de la Serpente... Again and again all the threads of this tangle kept knotting together in this corner of the Left Bank. The joints and flexures of the affair, Sir Francis would have called them — and indeed many threads joined together here: Joyce Blundell's house, the fateful church of the Cordeliers, and now this mouse of a man. A lying mouse, though? Not about Lyly, unless poor Jourdain had lied too. About Lady Stafford? Because someone was lying: Her Ladyship or John Faulkes? And why? It rather struck Tom that, had the Baroness truly placed Faulkes with her cousin the way she'd placed him at the Hôtel d'Hercule, they'd have agreed on the same story. Ergo, it stood to reason that Faulkes must be the liar — on this, if not on Lyly — but why? And if he was, then who was Jourdain's *Madame*? Or had Jourdain lied about Lyly, and about Faulkes's patroness? Of course, he might also have said what he thought was the truth — and, lying, honest or foolish, who had wanted him dead? Stafford? Or Lyly? *He'd call for Sir Edward and for William*, Faulkes had said. Call for, or threaten? And was this murderer going to spill more blood?

"Mine, for instance?" Tom muttered to himself. "Now that I've put the nature of my suspicions in plain sight, perhaps the murderer will betray himself?"

There was no answer from the stone Hercules, unless one counted that less than sharp-eyed lower.

Ay, well, Tom thought, as he made his way back to the Embassy: a fine state of things, when the knot was so entangled that he must hope for the murderer's blade to undo it!

Tom was still considering the likelihood of his own assassination as he climbed up the ladder from the kitchen, and stopped short before the door, gripping the hilt of his rapier. Was it a step he'd heard inside? A soft tread, most un-Minotaurish?

But they'd been quick, devil seize them... And yes: there! There came a rustle again.

And just how would they be here already? cold reason scoffed. *Sneaking unseen past the kitchen servants to do murder under the Ambassador's own roof when Paris had no lack of deserted alleys?*

All of it solidly true — and yet, there being thieves in this world as well as murderers, and, more importantly, spies, Tom drew his blade with a soft rasp, leapt for the door, and flung it open.

There was a gasp inside, and stumbling steps, and a crash as Grimeston toppled backwards onto Skeres's pallet.

Oh, Lord give patience! "Grimeston!" Tom sheathed his blade, and pushed the door closed behind his back. "If you wanted to get yourself skewered..."

Purple-faced and winded, the man waved him silent, even as he scrambled to his knees. "Thank God it's you!" he hissed, hoarsely. "I've but a moment. I saw you from the window, and..." He caught Tom's proffered arm, hauled himself upright, and slipped out of a sleeve a folded piece of paper. "Here. From Gifford."

Tom unfolded it, to find a few scant words in Lyly's hand. *PhilVI* was heavily crossed out, then *Fat*, and half a dozen numbers. "What on earth...? Is this code?" he asked, only to have the thing snatched from his fingers and turned over.

"It's just a note of the letter," Grimeston choked. "All I managed — but the gist is all there."

"Gifford's letter? You saw him?"

"Not an hour ago — and I left nothing with him this time, I swear to you, no matter how he pressed. And when I came back, I found Sir Edward in high dudgeon. He's had tidings — I don't know how — that Gifford has told the French where his ten crowns came from, and now..." He tilted his head at the scrap of paper.

Oh, bless all fools with hot water! "Did Sir Edward — did *you* believe he wouldn't?"

A helpless shake of the head. "I must go, before I'm wanted. But please — please, Mr. Walsingham, I never told you!"

He disappeared at a run through the door, before Tom could ask about Lyly. Following, he caught the man on the landing, opening a door, panelled so it almost disappeared into the wall... So that was how Grimeston had arrived, and not through the kitchen.

"What's through there?" Tom asked.

The secretary waved vaguely. "Rooms above the gallery, all the way to the house proper. I and Mr. Hakluyt lodge there, and Lyly, and the lesser guests — but truly, I must —"

"Yes — only tell me: where's Lyly?"

"Lyly?"

"He was away, yesterday. Has he come back?"

"Oh. No, he hasn't — but then, Sir Edward's errands at the Louvre take a good deal of waiting." The thick lips stretched into a sour line. "Not that I know, mind: going to Court is work for young William."

And then, remembering discretion of a sudden, the secretary fled without another word.

Ah well — Fates be thanked for jealousy, and for Stafford playing favourites, if it made Grimeston eager to gain Sir Francis's favour.

With a shake of his head, Tom went back to his cupboard, and smoothed the secretary's clandestine copy on the windowsill. A brief enough note, as Grimeston had promised, of Gifford's missive, scrawled in haste and full of abbreviations.

Trusts that what speeches his enemies have given forth of his behaviour towards H. Lordship, they will not cause H. L. to break with him.

The Deacon guarding against the hour when Stafford would hear of his loose tongue.

His cause brought to that pass that for 30 crowns he'll have his liberty; but not knowing where to find 30 sous is forced to fly to H. L. for succour.

The gall of the man!

Sends herewith letter and bill to his father in London, who'll repay it presently, were it 300£.

And did the Deacon truly expect Stafford to fall for it again? He must be counting on squeezing out the money before the rumour reached the Ambassador's ear. Well, it was too late for that — Simier's work again, no doubt — and Tom now found himself itching to discuss once more his own visit to the For-l'Évêque with Stafford, whose arguments against it must be wearing rather thin.

Committing the few lines to memory, he crumpled the note, and, climbing down to the kitchen, went to throw it in the fire. As he watched the flames consume Grimeston's work, he found the cook and a freckled young woman, who must be Skeres's friend Sally, staring at him.

"Are you well, Master?" the cook asked.

Of course, they would have heard the door slammed, and Grimeston falling, and nobody but Tom himself coming down… Still, they were bound to know of the other access from the house proper. What these two were thinking, only the devil knew: thieving? A tryst gone wrong? A fit of madness? Spies at work? Oh, what a fine cautionary tale on the art of secrecy — if Grimeston only knew!

"Quite well, thank you," Tom said, affecting the mildest surprise — and went in search of the Ambassador.

He found Stafford reclining in a well-padded — if a little faded — chair by the window in his room, having his beard trimmed by a barber.

"Are you done?" Stafford growled in French at this personage — and, on receiving a soft-spoken protest, barked, "Well, you'll have to wait. We have great urgencies."

This last was said with much ill grace, and a scowl directed at Tom, who waited while the barber retreated with the dignity of an offended bishop, and Stafford wriggled out of a number of white towels, revealing himself in his shirt-sleeves, and collarless.

He strode to the four-poster and snatched up a fur-lined gown that was spread out on it. As he thrust his arms into one sleeve and then the other, he snarled, "So, what is it that you want now?"

Sometimes Tom feared he must have a petty disposition. How else was he to explain the satisfaction he found in facing the ill humour with undaunted calm?

"Have you made progress with Gifford, Sir?"

A tug at the fur collar. "I never want to hear that man's name again."

"Nobody would blame you for it, Sir. The sooner we can have him out of prison and back to London, the sooner you'll have your wish."

Stafford laughed bitterly. "Out of prison, you say? Ah, but there's nothing easier!" A *portefeuille* of worked leather also sat on the bed. The Ambassador picked a letter from it, and all but flung it at Tom. "See for yourself!"

What Tom saw was that Grimeston, in his effort, hadn't done justice to the Deacon's prose — two thickly written pages of protestations, promises, injured innocence, humility, and begging, all woven into a display of the most barefaced impudence.

There was no need, when he reached the end, to affect a disbelieving chuckle. "He's always had a certain flair for self-apology."

This the Ambassador met with the utmost disgust. "The brazen scoundrel! To think…"

To think of ten more crowns, given on the same pretext, and gone Lord knew where.

"Brazen indeed, to ask you of all men! But then… You're thinking to pay, Sir?"

"God above, man — how many times must I tell you? I want no ties traced to the Embassy!"

See the red-faced outrage, the palm hit against the bedpost. Well, here was Gifford's match for brazenness.

"But if it will get him out of the Bishop's claws?" Tom reasoned in his most innocent manner — the one his friend Watson had used to call just this side of dim-wittedness. "After all, you already have Mr. Grimeston posing as his procurer;

surely there's a way to convey the money? I'm sure even Gifford can be trusted to keep quiet about such —"

"Trusted!" The gown had a row of very bright enamelled buttons. They caught the firelight, glinting as Stafford fastened them one by one. "The worst knave in this world — and you talk of trust! I'm astonished that Mr. Secretary will let Phelippes make use of him. That Phelippes should set him on me, then... I refuse to believe that it was at your master's behest!"

"I've told you how the matter stands, Sir. The question now is whether this money can buy Gifford's freedom."

Of course it wouldn't. And how Stafford had thought that ten crowns — or thirty, for that matter — would buy free an English spy... Not for the first time Tom marvelled at Lord Burleigh's choice of an ambassador, as Stafford wandered to the fireplace and leant an arm against the mantelpiece.

"It won't," he said at length.

With such glumness, he said it, with such slumping of the shoulders! Here was a confession coming...

"How can you tell so surely, Sir? Neither French justice nor Church justice are immune to bribes. And, unless Mr. Grimeston is somehow under doubt, you have the means to do it in a way the French won't suspect —"

"The French already know, damn it!" Stafford roared, whirling around. "They know — and I can tell so surely because, before these thirty crowns, the knave asked for ten, saying they would get him his freedom, and, like a fool, I sent them — and not only is he still the Bishop's guest, but now I've tidings that he told his gaolers where the ten crowns came from!"

The Ambassador choked to a halt. Tom let the silence stretch — watched as Stafford seethed, affecting the disbelief he might have felt, had it not been for Grimeston.

"I see," he murmured at length. "Or, in truth, I wonder if I do..."

It was a great impertinence, of course. Stafford stalked forward like a bull charging. "Don't you dare, you presuming pup!" he shouted. "I've weathered alone this storm you meddling fools in London made! I'd have spared nothing to help that snake out of the For-l'Évêque, but he refused everything I offered, for surely he thinks to gain favour with the French, and there's naught he wouldn't confess to save himself — and you wonder if you see!"

For the first time, Tom almost felt sorry for the man, facing Gifford's disaster, and all that shrewder minds than his could make of it. "No, I see well how difficult it is, Sir — but it can still be set to right, by whisking Gifford back to England —" he forged through the beginning of a protest — "I may have arguments that you have not, and I'll use every caution." Not that it was needed anymore, the French knowing all there was to know of Gilbert Gifford and the English Embassy. Or, perhaps, not quite all. "Did Gifford also uncover Mr. Grimeston as your man?"

Bewildered and frowning, Stafford swept the barber's towels off the chair, and lowered himself into it. "There was no word of Grimeston that I've heard. And he was not the only one I used as messenger... Certainly not the only one to visit Gifford."

"Good, then." Tom held up the letter. "It's plain the Deacon still hopes to gain money from you, if nothing else. He wouldn't compromise his means to receive it. Now, it's only natural that you'd want to discuss his request — for this rigmarole of his father is baggage... But instead of Mr. Grimeston, I'll go this time."

Here was a glimpse of how the Baroness governed her husband: finding himself short of objections, the bluster gone as though it had never been, the Ambassador became eager, even pleading — although perhaps he thought he was giving orders.

"But mind," he said, twisting the rings on his fingers in a way that, Tom was sure, would have made his wife grit her teeth. "You must not believe a word he says! He'll still try to turn you against me, like the lying scoundrel he is. Remember there's nothing he wouldn't say or do to save himself." He looked up sharply. "Why, I wouldn't be surprised if he'd poisoned poor Arundel!"

Oh, for goodness' sake! "I thought that Gifford was in the Bishop's dungeons before Arundel even fell ill?"

This was briskly waved away. "Some poisons are slow to act."

And some were not. *There are all sorts of winter tales about poisons*, Hennert had said. Was it worth explaining about repeated dosing? And that, all else apart, Gifford surely hadn't been at the Cordeliers to stab Jourdain? And yet, see how taken Stafford was with the notion — how anxious to seize on it — and to have Tom do the same. A sign of guilt, on the face of it — and yet could this voluble blunderer, snatching at this straw and that, possess the boldness and calculation of Arundel's murderer?

Having been on the point of asking why Gifford would want Arundel dead, Tom stopped.

"I'll be on my guard, Sir," he said instead. "And see what our good Deacon knows about Mr. Arundel."

165

The Ambassador made to speak, and then didn't — and, when he did, Tom could have sworn it was not to say what he'd had in mind. A slightly more gracious dismissal, in fact, and a prayer to send in Grimeston — so suddenly courteous, that it could only be meant to conceal distrust.

Ah well, Tom thought as he took his bow, the feeling was entirely mutual.

CHAPTER 9

"The Deacon?" Skeres all but squeaked. "Ye never think —?"

Tom shushed him. Perhaps a bookshop wasn't the best place to discuss things with the Minotaur — much less because, like them, several people had taken shelter in there from a sudden squall. "I'm not sure that I don't, but Stafford does — or so he says. What I didn't expect was to find you believing the fellow innocent."

"Oh, I don't know." The lad fingered the gilt-brass figurine of a crouching lion that weighed down a small pile of ballad sheets. "As nasty a weasel as you please, but murther? I'm thinking of the murtherers you've caught — the ones as meant it, not as were paid to do it."

"And?" Tom prodded, rather fascinated than not.

"And I don't know: there 'ave been wolves, and snakes, and rabid dogs, foxes and vixens. Weasels, though? Not even one of them."

Thinking back to the years he'd spent uncovering killers for Sir Francis, Tom couldn't deny it. "But, as you say, there are also the hired ones."

A hum, and Skeres weighed the brass lion in his palm, making the chiselled mane catch the light. "If I wanted a murtherer, I don't know that I'd 'ire that one."

"Neither do I — besides, Gifford was in gaol by the time Arundel began to help the Ambassador in earnest."

Another hum. "Unless…" Checking himself, Skeres leant close to whisper. "Unless the Deacon smelt a rat, poisoned Arundel, then the French pinched 'im… But no." The round face fell. "The Fleming says there's no poison as would kill after a week, don't 'e?" And was that a covert glance, angled at the bookseller's watchful apprentice?

Oh Jove...

Tom snatched the lion from the lad, and slapped it back on the table. "*No*, Dolius — and *think*: with Jourdain's death, the chance of murder grows harder to discount, so Stafford tries to blame it on the man nobody will believe."

One triumphant forefinger rose. "Because it's 'imself as did in Arundel, and 'e don't want you to nose about too much!"

But was it? Stafford, blustering, clumsy, and resentful, and so convinced of his own subtlety... "I don't know," Tom sighed.

"Why not? The Deacon calls 'im a traitor, and Arundel was going to buy 'is own pardon by denouncing 'im. *Dearie dearie*, and whatnot."

All of it true enough, and yet... "You said it yourself, Dolius. Think of how these murders were done: is Stafford the right sort of beast?"

Skeres scratched his head, and chewed his cheeks, and tilted his head this way and that, as though he were contemplating the Ambassador, until... "Cuds-me," he huffed. "But then who's done away with the physician?"

A handsome Seneca in-folio had pride of place on a draped table. Hadn't this Roman philosopher written that diligent research would unearth things hidden? Tom leafed through the book — but what he came across was how future lies in uncertainty, and man always squanders his allotted time. What a cheerful fellow! "Perhaps we'll get an inkling soon enough, if Faulkes's true master — or mistress — will just take fright enough." And Tom told the tale of the man who wasn't, after all, Jean Faucon, and found it met with nothing less than consternation.

"'E asked 'im of the poison!" Skeres slapped his thigh: *witness, o Lord, what a reckless blockhead of a master I am burdened with!*

There was no saying what the Lord witnessed, but several customers and the gimlet-eyed apprentice stared at the outburst. Grabbing the Minotaur, Tom marched to the door, tugging harder when Skeres regretfully eyed the brass lion.

Once they were in the Rue Saint-Jacques again — and in the rain — Skeres went back to his grievance. "Bless ye, Mr. Tom, for all your Latin and your thinking, you lack the sense God gave the little sparrows! Next you'll hang a placard round your neck: *I'm 'unting down the villain as poisoned Arundel; murtherers, come 'ither!*"

This startled Tom into a huff of laughter, but he sobered soon enough. "After the Cordeliers, I'd say they know already. Faulkes was a stone thrown in the water; let's see the waves he makes. And speaking of that, did you find out what friends he has at the Embassy?"

"Ah, that." Skeres turned thoughtful. "I've asked Sally, and 'Obelot, and the groom-lad in the stable… They've all seen 'im, Mr. Arundel's man — but not particular, not to say that they were friends. Sally don't even know 'im by name."

This last said most earnestly — not that Tom had truly suspected Sally the scullion of being a spy. Ah well, it had been worth a try.

The chill rain was loosening the mud in the runnels, and had chased most Parisians from the streets — and small blame to them. Unwilling to risk another shop, Tom dragged his servant under an awning, his mind still on John Faulkes at the Embassy.

"A pity that Faulkes doesn't strike me as the sort to play dice in the stables," he mused, and see how Skeres flushed! "But never mind Faulkes — *you* do! Is that where you disappear, when you're not making love to the scullion?"

The Minotaur had the gall to splutter. "You want me to make friends, 'ow am I to make them talk?"

"I don't even want to know — just do me a favour: don't cheat, will you? All we lack is you brawling with Sir Edward's people —"

"Master, look!" Skeres cut across him.

He was pointing at a tall, ginger-haired figure hastening up the street. Speaking of Stafford's people, there went Adam Cavel — catching sight of Tom, and wading through the mud to duck under the awning. There were no smiles this time, as the coachman doffed his soft cap and bowed. He was so tall, he could only stoop in the confined space.

"You're wanted, Master," he said. "That is, His Honour asks, would you attend him at once, please you. I'm to tell you it's a matter of importance." And all the time he kept his eyes low. Waiting, Tom could have sworn, to be called to task about the other night.

I know where you were when your master sought you — and it wasn't where you said. Out of the corner of his eye, Tom could see Skeres waggling his brows. A sideways glare put paid to that — or so Tom hoped, for, if the fellow was allowed out of the house again, he could be followed, provided he didn't think himself suspected.

"Thank you, Cavel," he said. "Lead on."

And they dove out under the rain, in the ankle-high rush of filthy water, mud and ordure.

"Tonight, at the church of the Mathurins. You know the place? It's on the Rue Saint-Jacques. The exiles meet there, and never to any good."

Stafford was pacing before his writing desk — three steps one way, three steps the other, while the returned Lyly kept silent watch by the door to the secretaries' room.

Of course Tom knew of the Mathurins. "You wrote about it more than once, Sir," he tried, and was waved quiet.

"And now the Pagets are meeting someone there." Stafford stopped in front of the fire. "A man from Rheims, from Allen!"

It should come as no great marvel, perhaps. Cardinal Allen wove his own treasonous web in Rheims, training young exiles for priesthood with money from Rome. Not much of it, admittedly, but still the man was dangerous — as Tom had once found out for himself — and yet another beacon to the worst of English Catholics. That he was no great friend to his Paris cohorts was something of a blessing; that he should want to meddle in the affairs here was no great portent — but...

"Why?" Tom asked.

"*Why?*" The Ambassador made a show of disbelief, raising his voice as though for a dim-witted child. "Gifford is one of his own priests, one of his spies, perhaps — besides being yours!"

"And he's been in gaol these three weeks."

"Poor Charles Arundel's death..."

"Arundel's death was a fortnight ago. Why would Allen send a man now? Or were there more before?"

"This we don't know," Stafford huffed in irritation. "But you've seen how tidings barely trickle out, even here: it will be even more difficult to learn things from Rheims. Or perhaps

they've heard of a man from London making inquiries…
Surely, Gifford wasn't Allen's only man here."

"Some of them, no doubt, ensconced close to Bishop
Gondi's people," Tom said — and didn't add that smelling
them out should have been the Ambassador's task, instead of
blaming the man from London. "But still, Sir, if I may ask:
how did you come to know of this meeting?"

A perfectly sensible request, and yet it made Stafford flare.

"Now, Walsingham, hear me well. Measures were taken here,
under my orders: pretences were established, and had to be
sustained. I'll wager you, too, must have worn false colours
once or twice."

Did he know of Tom's brief stint at Allen's *Collège Anglais* a
few years earlier, under the guise of a Papist from Kent? Not
that it mattered, not when Stafford had just given himself
away.

"Measures … such as Gifford described to the French, and
— begging your pardon, Sir — such as you denied ever
using?"

"Don't you presume!" The Ambassador's face had the
colour of apoplexy. "I never initiated this pretence or any
other, but Lyly was approached… Was I to let such a chance
slip? With Her Highness's enemies giving themselves into my
hands, must I shy away? Even *you* would be given that much
leeway, I'm sure!"

Which seemed to be the man's one argument, and in truth
was neither here nor there — and half a dozen answers lined
themselves, each one enough to discomfit Stafford's watery
logic. However, being of a mind to see where this was going,
Tom quenched his debating instincts.

"I won't hold against Mr. Lyly what I'm going to hear," he said instead. *Or against you.*

Stafford's snort might have been impatience, or disbelief, or both. "William, if you please."

Arms locked behind his back, Lyly took a grim step forward, eyes fixed ahead like a soldier reporting. "It's through me that Sir Edward heard of Allen's man," he said. "And I had it from a Catholic friend."

There was not a single Protestant subject of the Queen who didn't number one Catholic at least among friends and relations. But it was another matter — though not at all uncommon — when this friend was an exiled traitor and a plotter. Tom let it pass.

"And what is it that you had? Not just the time and place, I'll reckon?"

Or perhaps he hadn't let it pass as much as he thought, for Lyly stiffened.

"Mr. Arundel's death has caused alarm in Rheims," he ground out, hooded eyes fixed on the floor. "And Gilbert Gifford was a Rheims man, after all."

And more besides, surely, for the question still stood: why now? And, even more to the point, why was Tom being told at all? Why not just have Lyly quietly go?

"This friend summoned you to attend, I take it?" Tom asked — and Stafford beat his secretary to the answer.

"No, he did not!" He waved a testy hand. "You never had the misfortune of a Gifford to ruin you, I'm sure. Gifford's letters paint poor Lyly now as a traitor to England, now as a snake in the breast of the exiles — and God knows what else he's made up. So now the exiles don't know what to make of him anymore!"

This time Tom did nothing to hide his disbelief. "And yet they advise him of this meeting?" He looked from one man to the other.

"They don't advise — they threaten!" Stafford snarled — but Lyly shook his head.

"They don't, in truth — or at least..." He raked a hand through his fair hair. "The man who warned me — and I won't tell you his name — this man only warned me for the sake of friendship, with much strain on his conscience, for he believes that my case will be discussed, among many other things."

"And is it likely that he'll advise you afterwards?"

"He already risked much to warn me, and..." Lyly drew in a breath and let it go. "And he's not so sure he truly believes in my innocence and good faith."

One would believe him stricken in earnest! With such a player's gift, Lyly must have made a fine would-be martyr among the exiles and conspirators. Unless... Tom's memory provided a picture of those he'd liked in Rheims, much against his better judgment. Unless the man's qualms were honest — and then how naive of Stafford to shake his head and protest!

"I wish I'd never had him join their ranks!" he said. "Now he's bound to be in peril at those murdering scoundrels' hands."

But was he? "Hardly in more peril now than he was already, Sir," Tom pointed out. "No more so than yourself or Mr. Grimeston — from the moment Gifford's letters were read."

And, if the Ambassador scoffed at this remark, it was a surprise that Lyly took Tom's side.

"They waited for no messenger from Rheims to kill before," he said.

So they did know there had been no others, after all. Tom wished he knew how these two chose what lies to tell and what truth — if there was any truth told at all. For one thing, again: why tell Sir Francis's man of the messenger from Rheims?

If it was true, though… "If this nameless friend won't talk, is there any other way to know what is to be discussed tonight? Because, forgive me, Mr. Lyly, but I misdoubt all Allen wants is to discuss you."

Again, the secretary nodded. "There's a way to abscond in the church, and listen in —"

"No." Stafford strode to Lyly, and caught him by the arm. "If you were discovered, you'd be lucky to be imprisoned… Why, it could even be a trap!"

Thoughts of Skeres's list of murdering animals stirred in Tom's mind.

"Would those who stabbed Jourdain in the street resort to such hugger-mugger now?" he asked.

But this was the sort of thinking that came of seeing too many murders done, and it was little wonder that the Ambassador should scoff. "Hardly the same, was it?" he asked. "Your Jourdain was never supposed to be one of them!"

Or had he been? How did Stafford know for certain? Tom swallowed the retort, for there was nothing to gain from it now. "Not that I know, Sir, no. And there will be people at the Mathurins who know Mr. Lyly. Perhaps Mr. Grimeston had better go."

"A very fine notion, if Grimeston were here!" Stafford exploded. "Not an hour ago I sent him out of Paris with some letters. Now, if he can be back before the gates are closed…"

They all looked at the windows. The rain had gone, leaving behind a dark sky, and already the twilight closed in.

"But after Vespers, the church will be locked for the night," Lyly said. "Then there will be no way to enter the convent unobserved."

"Perhaps Grimeston will be back in time," Stafford said, but it was plain such good fortune could not be relied upon, and it struck Tom that only one course remained open.

Yes, one and one alone — and so plain it was, so squarely convenient... The familiar, well-loved sensation of glass pieces falling into place invaded the back of Tom's mind.

"I'm going," he said. "If you'll just explain where I'm to hide."

To this they made a pretence of objecting — oh, so earnestly! Tom would never find the place alone, the secretary said, for the convent was a maze. What, asked Stafford, if he blundered where he must not?

"Sir," said Lyly, looking pleadingly at Stafford. "There's naught for it. Even Grimeston doesn't know. Whoever goes, I'll have to show him."

Yes, a good pretend-martyr. "Won't that put you in danger? If you're discovered, it will matter little whether you're spying or showing me the way."

"Not if we go to Vespers. It's always crowded enough that I can show you the way from the church, and you can slip inside to the cloister from there, and hide. I'll wait for you outside."

Sensible enough, on the face of it — as sensible as such a plan could ever be. And see how Stafford reconciled himself to it; how he all but ordered that Tom should bring his man as well.

"You've seen for yourself what the streets are like," he urged. "And while I pray you'll have no need for help..."

Oh, true enough, and most sensible, if one had to traipse around by night on secret errands. Or if the Ambassador wanted Mr. Secretary's men out of the way — both of them.

There is more danger, Thomas, in suspecting too little than in suspecting too much.

And although this was more than a suspicion, it was with Sir Francis's maxim in mind that Tom bowed.

"If we're to catch Vespers," he said, "then we'd better be on our way."

CHAPTER 10

It was a short way to the Convent of the Mathurins, just off the Rue Saint-Jacques — for, once again, all happened in that one corner of the Left Bank. Huddled against the chill, armed with nothing but daggers hidden under their cloaks, they walked at a fast pace, Lyly with an arm threaded through Tom's, and a glowering Skeres on their heels.

"Prepare yourself for a long wait," Lyly instructed, not for the first time. "They won't meet until later. Besides, I attended this sort of thing, back when I was in favour, and one thing I can tell you is that the Pagets never show up early."

"Not even this time, out of regard for Allen's messenger?"

Lyly chuckled. "Oh, it's likelier that the messenger will arrive even later. They can be very petty, these Catholics. The more important they think themselves, the pettier." And there was a mocking bitterness to the words that Tom hadn't expected. But then, Lyly was nervous, walking all hunched, eyes darting this way and that in the gloom. When they passed the *barrière* in the Place Maubert, he gripped Tom's wrist, and stiffened so that it was a miracle the sergeant loitering on the door didn't become suspicious.

"Stop that!" Tom hissed. "What ails you?" He wasn't even the one going into the lion's den. Of course, to have them all arrested and spending the night at the Châtelet would keep Tom away from the Embassy more surely than most things.

But Lyly only picked up his step, all but dragging Tom into the Rue du Plâtre. The street was winding, and so narrow that the houses seemed to lean together, like conspirators bent on keeping daylight away — not that there was much of it left.

Through this gloaming they advanced in hurried silence, but for Skeres who grumbled in the rear-guard, until Tom lost patience.

"Well, tell me more of the place, of those who will be there," he prodded, and caught Lyly studying him askance. At once the secretary looked away, but it hadn't been a friendly gaze, not even one of plain curiosity. Never the gaze of one ruminating on murder, surely?

Whatever his purpose, Lyly must not be at ease with it.

"What more must I tell you?" he fretted. "Of the passage from the sacristy you know as much as I do — for I never used it, although it was shown to us, once. And I know only of the Pagets."

And of how many more friends whose names he wouldn't tell? The man was lucky there were many things Tom was ready to let pass, at that moment. "Mr. Arundel would have been there, were he alive?"

"But he's not," Lyly snapped — only to check himself. "But yes — yes, he'd be there, most likely. Lord Paget, if not his brother, would have wanted him to hear... Not that they'd agree on what they heard."

Which you'd know from Arundel himself... Tom bit back the challenge. Better to let the fellow think himself safe from suspicion for tonight. Better to watch him, and wait.

They took the Rue Saint-Jacques just as the bells began to chime for Vespers — Saint-Yves looming just overhead with its twin turrets and, across the street, Saint-Severin on one side, the apse of the Mathurins on the other. In that direction they crossed, and Lyly had been right: there were many others making their hurried way to the church for the evening prayer. When they entered the narrow street that led to the churchyard, Tom beckoned Skeres abreast with him.

"You wait outside," he ordered, and at once the lad looked mutinous. "One man can skulk better than two, and I'd rather have you outside if I'm taken — which I won't be, will I, Lyly?"

The secretary was taken aback. "Why, no," he stuttered, just as a black-browed Skeres caught Tom by the sleeve, and it was in the most natural way that they became separated among the faithful: Lyly ahead, Tom behind enough to hiss for Skeres alone:

"If you wait outside, so will he — for he must make sure neither of us goes back."

Skeres gaped at Lyly's tall figure a dozen steps ahead, and then back. "Why … then there's no man from Rheims? No meeting?"

"Something there must be, if they hope I'll remain here long enough."

"Long enough for what?"

From the churchyard's corner, Lyly was beckoning. Tom nodded to him.

"I mean to find out."

"And 'ow, seeing as you're in there?"

Stopping with a small bow, Tom gave way to an old lady with a companion. "That I'm going in now doesn't mean I'll stay. See that you keep Lyly out here," he said.

"Ay, and if you get into trouble?"

"I'll whistle if I need you. Three times."

And, before the Minotaur could point out the uselessness of whistling beyond barred doors, Tom hastened to join Lyly. And see the secretary's vexation! Had Tom still doubted, it would have been enough to make him certain.

"It would be wise to take your servant, you know," Lyly muttered as they entered the dimly lit church.

Dipping his fingers in the marble font to cross himself, Tom shook his head. "If the worst comes to the worst, I'd rather have help outside than a fellow prisoner. Where's this sacristy of yours?"

The battle was plain on Lyly's face: insist, and he'd raise Tom's suspicions... In the end he gave a brisk nod. "You'll know what you're doing. This way."

The church was rather narrow, with a row of shallow chapels on each side. Most were dark at this hour, but in the ones closer to the altar the candlelight reached to touch painted statues and rich reliquaries and to strike gleams from those gilt baubles Papists liked to give the saints in thanks for some granted prayer — dozens and dozens of *ex-voto*, winking from each chapel's walls. A crucifix hung over the altar that shone with wax candles and gold; around the altar stood a fretted screen with seats of carved oak, each occupied by a friar in the black and white of the Trinitarian order: the Mathurins themselves.

As Tom and Lyly took their place at the left of the nave, another friar, wearing a green chasuble over his robes, entered through a door between the first chapel and the chancel arch, attended by two youths in white surplices, each carrying a tall candle.

"There's your door," whispered Lyly, as the friars started singing a hymn in Latin, and the little crowd murmured in the same tongue.

Bowing his head, as though in prayer, Tom spent the hour that followed studying the chapels from under lowered eyelids, while at his side Lyly answered the celebration with every appearance of quiet fervour.

Not half as false a Catholic as he would have us think, Gifford had written once — confirmed by the spy Rogers. Lord send he wasn't thinking to buy himself into the exiles' favour again by offering them Secretary Walsingham's kinsman. But no — that was a foolish notion: how could Lyly — and, more, how could Stafford — have explained away such a capture?

By the time the Vespers ended, Tom had chosen his hiding place. Not the sacristy — not yet, for the friars were bound to loiter there, but one of the lesser chapels, far enough from the altar that it was in shadow, and deep enough for a man to hide. Lingering at the back of the retreating flock, he slipped into the chapel — hopefully unseen even by Lyly, and crouched behind a dark marble sarcophagus. From his dark corner Tom caught a glimpse of the secretary's tall figure dithering a moment on the threshold, and then disappearing past the door.

Well, here he was — once more inside the lion's den. Ulysses in the Cyclops' lair, he'd thought himself, back in Rheims. Oh, he'd been young, that Tom Walsingham of three-and-twenty, who saw all things through the words of ancient poets. It would be easier work, now, for there was no Allen to convince, and Tom had no ancient tale for the patience and the stealth this night's work would require — unless it was that ugly fellow, what was his name, the one the Trojans sent to spy on the Greek ships, disguised in a wolf's pelt. But no: that particular spy had been caught and killed, hadn't he? On the whole, Tom decided, he'd do without poetry this time.

Drawing up his knees, he squeezed himself between the damp wall and the chill marble of the sarcophagus, and waited. After the last of the worshippers had gone, the sacristan closed the postern in the great door — the bolts rasping into their cleats, the crossbar hefted into place — then began a round of the church, muttering to himself as he went from chapel to chapel putting out the candles, and making the gloom denser. No light was burning in Tom's chapel, but still he pressed deeper into his hiding hole, his dagger's hilt digging into his side, and held his breath, listening to the sacristan's progress. The man passed him by, and made his way to the altar, where he lingered a long time — until a boy's treble resounded from the sacristy, and then another, raised in a squabble.

"Bons anges, aidez-moi!" the sacristan exclaimed. There was a flurry of hurried steps, and a brief burst of light, as a door opened and closed.

After that, for a short time, voices rose and fell in the sacristy, and then faded away. Tom waited a little longer and, when the quiet continued undisturbed, he unwedged himself from his corner.

He had to feel his way out of the chapel, for the church was dark now, but for the red glimmer of the chancel lamp hanging from the arch. He waited, straining his ears. There was another, louder commotion, but it came from outside — a burst of shouts, and raucous laughter... Fates send that Skeres and Lyly didn't find trouble out there — nor he, for that matter, for he had no intention of staying for the long wait that had been promised him. Not all of it, at least.

Even guided only by that small ruddy pinprick, it wasn't hard to find the sacristy door and open it; harder to feel his way around the black room. Once he hit his knee against the hard corner of a cabinet, and felt something totter atop it. Reaching out blindly, he just managed to grab some tall object — a candlestick — before it fell. Something small toppled, though, and rolled to the floor. Cursing under his breath, Tom went down onto his hands and knees, feeling the flagstones until he found it: a candle-end, cracked by the fall, but still holding together.

He crouched for a moment, listening, and, when no sound of alarm reached him, he rose with his prize. Taking Skeres's little tinderbox, he tried to light it. It took some fumbling in the darkness, but at last a spark was struck, and the candle lit, and by its flame Tom had a good look at the sacristy, a square place, with a tall, white vaulted ceiling over a row of dark cupboards, wainscoted all around, with a small altar on one side. There were two obvious doors, one to the church, the other likely to the convent, but the one Tom wanted was hidden.

It's in the panelling, Lyly had explained. *Under a painting of the Virgin Mary.*

And there the painting hung, with the blue-cloaked Virgin in prayer. The panel beneath looked no different from its neighbours, carved with a pattern of fruit and branches. *But there's a catch in the frame.* A secret way, built during one of those bursts of violence that again and again tore France apart, or a means for priors — or whatever they called them — to spy on their friars? Whatever the thing was, Tom had no intention of using it — not yet. Oh, let Lyly think he was in there, haunting the passage like a ghost, waiting to hear English spoken beyond one or the other of the secret doors along it, while whatever he was not meant to see happened at the Embassy!

But it stood to reason that, if the passage led to the sacristy, there also had to be a way outside — from there, or from the church, one that Lyly hadn't bothered to mention.

Armed with his candle stump, shielding the flame with his hand, Tom returned to the church and began to search. It wasn't hard to find a small door in the apse, tucked into the curving ambulatory around the choir. A small door that the novices used for unsanctioned excursions, Tom suspected, for the one bolt was well-oiled, and outside, in the narrow walled space that hugged the apse, a gangly shape stood propped against the wall. Just what it was, Tom didn't have time to see, for, the moment he stepped outside, a draught blew out his candle — but the flame's last flare was enough to show the way. Drawing the door closed behind him, and abandoning the now useless stump, he felt his way to the wall, and wasn't too surprised to find by touch a broken tall-backed chair. He smiled to himself in the darkness: Lord be thanked for unruly boys... Although perhaps this way out wasn't meant for a grown man, and once or twice it seemed the rickety support would crumble under the weight of one. It didn't, though, and soon enough Tom was perched atop the wall, looking down on a corner of the Rue Saint-Jacques. It was full dark by now, and the shrine at the corner just beneath him, where some zealous soul had lit a lamp, shone right into his eyes and was little help in surveying the street, while it would show him plainly to anyone who passed. Flattening himself on the wall top, he scampered away from the puddle of yellow light, and waited. A late cart creaked past, and then a gentleman with no less than two light bearers ... and then, as soon as the street was empty, Tom dropped down to the mud-covered paving. How he'd climb back he'd worry about later, he decided, as he made his way back to Stafford's house.

Soon enough Tom was back on the Rue des Bernardins, hidden in the shade of a carriage gate across from the Embassy, his collar up, hat tilted low over his face like a murderer at the play, and silently calling himself names.

What had he expected to accomplish, coming back in secret like this? He'd known he couldn't enter the house, and of course there was nothing to see from the outside — but for the two lighted windows he could glimpse over the garden wall, where a weak glow showed through the not-quite-drawn curtains. He could have sworn they were the windows of

Stafford's study ... and yet, what did that prove? That the Ambassador worked late, as likely as not — or that his mysterious visitor, if there had been one, had come and gone, and now Stafford dithered in his study, pacing and bemoaning his lot. Or else that the visitors had yet to come, and wouldn't do so for hours yet.

It was damnably cold, with an unpleasant little wind, and there was nothing for it but to huddle against the gate and wait, for Tom didn't dare to pace, or even to move more than to rub his arms now and then, lest a passer-by or anyone peering from a window should notice a man lurking in the shadows and raise an alarm ... but Jupiter, such cold! A long wait he'd been promised, and a long wait he was going to have — but at least the Mathurins' secret passage would have been warmer, surely? The only good thing was, he ran no risk of dozing off.

It's an art, that of thinking your plans through, Frances had used to say, when playing chess — and of the two of them, she had been best at following her father's maxim.

If I had the art, love, I wouldn't be here now, catching my death and —

A rasp of drawn bolts from across the street startled Tom out of his thoughts, and sent him back deeper into the shadows, ears strained.

First came muffled speech, and the light of a lantern. Then the soft thud of a door closed with caution, the bolts again, and quiet, unhurried steps — two sets of them, perhaps three — and the yellow light lapping closer and closer... Then a young voice spoke — foreign, low, but not so low that Tom couldn't catch the words.

"*Solo piensa en su venganza —*"

"*Silence!*" another, older voice ordered in French — but it was too late.

All the breath rushed out of Tom's lungs, and he squeezed against the weather-beaten gate, watching as two shadows walked past in stiff, high-collared capes and tall hats, one leaning heavily on the other's arm, who carried the lantern. And no matter how they whispered now, Secretary Walsingham's man had heard enough: Spaniards walking out of Stafford's house at night, commenting on how the man only had mind for his own vengeance!

The moment the two Spaniards were out of sight, Tom made for the Rue Saint-Jacques in a rush. He would have run had he not feared to attract attention, or to stumble in the darkness. Besides, what need had he to run?

He'd discovered more than he'd come to Paris to find.

Or had he? Stafford was a traitor — and not in league with the English Catholics, either, nor with the French, but with Spain! Of course, it could all be a charade to trick Mendoza, courting the Spaniard's trust to obtain knowledge — or so Stafford would claim, if he were confronted, for he'd always been eager to try such stratagems, and had always been roundly forbidden. But receiving nightly visits from Mendoza's men — devil take the Spanish Ambassador for an intriguing spider! — discussing vengeance with them until even they reckoned him mad... Vengeance against Sir Francis, most likely, for Stafford saw wrongs against himself in every word and act of Mr. Secretary, and had never had qualms about sharing his grievances, or so it would be believed.

So it could well be true.

All the dark and windy way back to the Rue Saint-Jacques, Tom sifted through his discoveries — glass pieces, tossing and tinkling, and refusing to settle in a pattern that made much sense: one faction of the exiles through Arundel; the other through Lyly; the Queen Mother's party through the Baroness; and now Spain... What cursed sort of game did Stafford think he was playing?

Before he knew it, he was standing again at the foot of the wall behind the Mathurins' church — and for the first time he observed that the drop from outside was not as high as it was inside, the church ground being lower than the street. Still, it was some ado to jump high enough to grab the wall's edge. He failed once, his gloved fingers slipping, and he failed twice bare-handed, and cursed far too loudly — and all of it in the light from the shrine, that sputtered and flared in the growing wind. Tom eyed resentfully the painted Virgin Mary... But then, night after night the Papists burnt their candles before her: she couldn't be expected to smile on the efforts of a Protestant spy, could she?

A foolish thought, and time wasted, for sooner or later someone was bound to come down the street, or look out of a window... Again Tom jumped, and this time grabbed the edge soundly enough to hold. For a few long moments he dangled there, scrabbling for a foothold. Why hadn't he thought to try from the other, darker street?

A moment later he thanked the Fates he hadn't — for from that very direction came the sound of steps and voices. The Guet? Surely it must be, for they had a guardhouse just down that little street — Jove fulminate all watchmen, and all the careless fools who forgot them! With one breathless heave, Tom hauled himself atop the wall, and found that he could see nothing in the darkness beyond it — not the ground, not the broken chair — but he could hear the steps nearing the corner, and another noise that could well be a window being unshuttered...

Cursing, he slid off on the other side, dangling in the darkness by his fingertips, with teeth gritted and ears that strained to listen.

Beyond the wall, the steps rounded the corner. A man called, and was answered by muffled laughter. A cheery lot, this Guet — and idle! It felt like an age before the steps passed by, and a wooden clatter from above announced that whoever had peered out had had enough of it. Only then did Tom let his cramping hands release their hold, praying he wouldn't crash onto the chair... He didn't, for a mercy, if only by a whisker, though he hit an elbow against it. Had he made too much noise? For a moment he crouched where he had dropped, rubbing his bruised elbow, but there were no raised calls, no returning steps.

Picking himself up, he made his way back inside the apse, and, by the light of the chancel lamp, to the sacristy.

Lighting the candle stump he'd recovered, he found the panel again, and began to feel the carved moulding for the catch, thinking of another passage such as this he'd come across in the past. It had taken a joiner, then, to open it — but Tom had paid attention, and he remembered the way the man had searched and pressed, and perhaps the French cabinet-maker who had devised this door had been less secretive in intent, for it wasn't long before a carved leaf moved under Tom's fingertips and, with a soft click, the panel creaked open, revealing a narrow black hole.

The candle flickered in a breath of dusty chill and mouse droppings, and the weak light revealed, together with the shape of a door not far ahead, no lack of cobwebs. The floor was covered in dust, enough of it to see that no one had stepped this way in a long time, but for the mice. A strange, sigh-like noise came from the black depths: did this open on the outside at its far end, that the wind found its way inside it? Stuffing one of his gloves between panel and jamb so it couldn't close completely and seal him inside, Tom drew the secret door behind him. After a moment's hesitation, he blew out the candle — for he needed no light to listen, and there was no telling who might glimpse it through another door — and made his quiet way in the darkness, shoulders hunched, steadying the dagger against his hip, and feeling for the doors.

He hadn't gone a long way before he became aware of a feeble glow and a faint buzz of speaking. Not far ahead, someone was speaking in one of the rooms, and light spilled through a fissure above the door. Tom pressed an eye to this fissure, but it was too thin to see anything but the flicker of the light, and a shadow moving across it. When he tried to listen, the words were muffled, but there was no mistaking that whoever was in the room was speaking in English.

So Lyly hadn't lied, after all — not entirely, at least, though he'd have been a fool to do so, and risk Tom returning to the Embassy too early if he found no meeting at all — but it was soon clear that the passage must be an escape route, and not especially meant for spying, for it was hard to hear what was being said.

The names of Arundel and Gifford were made several times, and one particular man had a high-pitched, carrying voice that was easier to catch. When this fellow began to insist that word be sent to Allen, he was obliging enough to become vexed, and to grow loud.

"I'll say it again, the Cardinal may know of Gifford," he exclaimed. "But we don't know what his mind is."

There was an answering rumble, indecipherable — and ayes, and nays, and then the angry fellow again:

"You always say so, and I say: let's ask His Eminence. A messenger can be with him tomorrow night —"

An argument rehashed, by the sound of it — but one thing was plain: no man from Rheims was there, had been there, or was expected to be tonight or in the near future.

On and on they went, and if they spoke of Arundel, it was to lament his loss.

"In spite of all, his death must grieve us," someone said at one point, bitterly enough that there must be little accord on this — and yet, if they had thoughts of poison or murder, nobody said so aloud. Nor did Tom hear about an over-prying man from London... Not that he could be sure, and he would have given much to understand that low rumble that always seemed to turn the tide or argument, much to the loud man's vexation.

Lyly was dismissed quickly. There was no knowing whether they'd discussed him earlier, but the mention of him excited none of the clear-worded passion that Allen, Arundel or Gifford's names had warranted. Nothing else did after that, and Tom found himself unable to catch more than a word here or there — among them, several times the name of England, and London once. If these were plans for invasion, they were going about it with remarkable placidity. Or were they rather exchanging news of the homes they must all miss? Tom couldn't help the thought: how many of those who left England dreamt of going back borne on the strength of French arms, and how many instead only longed for the home they might well never see again? And while he let his mind wander in these idle thoughts, the exiles reached the end of their meeting. There were farewells, and one burst of laughter, and the rumble raised in reproach, and then a door was closed, and the fissure went dark.

Tom made his way back. How pleased with themselves Stafford and Lyly must feel, thinking they'd fooled him into wasting half a night while the Spaniards made their visit.

And then, when he was a dozen steps away from the passage's end, Tom stopped short. The gloom was no longer unrelieved, and the silence was broken. He squinted and listened, and for a heartbeat he had the strangest sense that time had gone back. There he was, standing in the dusty passage, hearing a quiet buzz of men speaking, and a line of weak light was slicing the darkness. Only, this time, the line was vertical, and the words French.

Someone was in the sacristy ... seeking him? How had they known? Lyly, curse him?

But no. There was no urgency in the voices, one placidly giving what sounded like instructions, and others murmuring. But what were they up to, this late?

Of course!

A memory from Rheims lit up in Tom's mind, and he could have slapped himself: the Hours, and the nightly office that friars kept. Was it already late enough for ... what was it called — Vigil? Matins? Surely not. But then, different orders perhaps prayed at different times?

No matter, though: the fact remained that the friars were there, blocking the way out — curse their zealous ways!

Thoughts of the passage's other end were soon discarded: what if it opened into the prior's own bedchamber? The other doors, though... Tom quietly felt his way back to the first one, and spent a useless while trying to pry it open by touch alone in the darkness: if there was a way to do it from this side, he couldn't find it.

In disgust, he padded back towards the sacristy. Perhaps, once the friars were at their prayers in the church, he could try the other door? But no, for it soon became clear that the good brothers, having no appetite for winter rigours, held their night-time devotions in the smaller, warmer sacristy — pinch them all and their idle ways!

There was nothing for it but to sit down and wait. He stopped in the act of leaning against the wall. Hadn't his new cloak suffered enough these past days, without gathering all the dirt and cobwebs of friarly neglect? So he stood and waited, listening to piece after piece of sung Latin, always hoping that each would be the last. He waited, sifting through what little he'd heard from the exiles' bickering — a scant prize, if it hadn't been for his secret walk back to the Embassy. And at last the friars were done and went away, eager for their beds — and Fates be thanked! Now let them just...

But no, for the light wasn't put out, and it became clear that someone lingered, and, the moment the steps faded away, there sounded a testy muttering.

"There were two in the candlesticks, I tell you. I left them there after Vespers, ready to light — and when we came back, there was only one!"

Tom didn't catch the reply, but he had a shrewd notion of what these two were missing: the candle stump. The one he'd meant to replace, had there been time, and instead was lying just inside the hidden door...

"I'm not mistaken!" the friar — the sacristan? — protested. "It was there, and then it wasn't, and I'll be blamed for it."

A soothing whisper earned a snort. "One'd think you don't know *Frère* Guillaume!"

And then they began to search the sacristy, judging by the moving light.

Oh Jove — they were bound to notice that the secret panel wasn't quite shut. Did these two even know about it? But even if they didn't, they couldn't fail to observe it… And all the while they were working their way closer. Hand on hilt, Tom began to retreat into the depths of the passage — not that it would help much, for they would find the glove, and —

"What are you doing here?" a new voice demanded and there was silence.

It was easy to picture the two men straightening up, exchanging glances, and then:

"Tidying up, *mon Frère*," the sacristan said, all testiness lost. "*Frère* Jean was helping me."

Another short silence. "Well, it's tidy now. Let us not idle about."

And, bless all stern exacters, the two searchers went meekly, and the sacristy was left empty and dark.

If only that crisply-spoken friar knew how his discipline had saved an English spy! But the laugh that bubbled in Tom's throat died an early death when he heard the clack of a key turning in its lock — once and twice.

No, no, no, no… Tom waited in ear-straining silence for returning steps and, when there were none, he opened the panel and leapt out of the passage and into the smell of burnt wax and incense. During this adventure, the wind had risen; it sang outside the one tall window, and enough moonlight shone through the parted clouds to show Tom his way to the door that should lead him to the main cloister.

And once the friars are abed, Lyly had said, *you'll find your way to the garden, and climb out over the wall.*

Oh yes — unless some ill-tempered friar locked the door from the outside! Even before he tried, Tom knew there was no use in pushing. That laugh he'd swallowed made itself felt again — only it was bitter this time, and he heaped no blessings on the stern friar's head *in absentia*.

Tom's mother had used to call such mishaps the good Lord's punishment for the multitude of his smaller sins — although, surely, never in her life would Lady Dorothie have imagined her youngest son locked inside a Papist sacristy in Paris at night...

Only, he wasn't quite locked inside, was he?

It was just that he misliked to reveal the existence of another way out than the one Lyly had provided. Would he suspect? Would Stafford? Well, thanks to the cursed *Frère* Guillaume, there was nothing for it. Pausing only to recover his glove and the candle stump, push the panel shut, and hide the candle under the vestment spread on the table, Tom hastened to the church, where the chancel lamp still burnt and winked above the altar. He slipped out into the apse, and made for the little door. With any luck, the friars would blame the undrawn bolt on their fractious novices, surely? And if they didn't, it was the last of Tom's troubles, after all...

And then, as he was about to draw the bolt, the sacristy door opened again, and someone entered with hushed steps. For a heartbeat Tom gaped in the darkness. Truly, must the good Lord make him pay for *all* his smaller sins this night?

Whoever had come in carried a light — a lantern, perhaps, for it shone more steadily than a free flame — and held it now higher and now lower, as he moved around between the door and the altar, throwing a dance of shadows that billowed and shrank up the pillars. The sacristan, Tom was ready to swear, still seeking his damned piece of candle!

Cursing silently, Tom moved away from the little door, pressing against the choir's screen. Surely the fellow never thought a piece of candle could have gone from the sacristy to the apse on its own? But perhaps he did, for the yellow light and its attendant shadows were gliding closer around the choir.

Had the man heard Tom move? The steps sounded too unhurried, the brief mutterings more vexed than alarmed — unless...

Unless he knew of the boys' secret, and suspected his candle had gone that way... Oh, Hades and Hell! Tom backed away, around the curved screen, quiet and hunched low, step by careful step while the sacristan advanced on the other side, his light swelling before him like a golden tide on the apse's wall. And of a sudden there was something against Tom's back, something tall that swayed. Spinning around, he barely caught a pillar of carved wood, taller than he was, and heavy. Teeth gritted, he held on to the thing, not daring to right it lest its feet made a noise hitting the floor.

By the time he'd steadied the cursed thing, the light had stopped and lowered. The sacristan must have put the lantern on the floor.

Tom held his breath. Even over the wind, he heard a bolt rattled and then drawn. Oh, the sacristan knew his novices — but not the winter wind. When a sudden gust slammed the door shut, it must have caught his hand, for, hissing in pain, he moved away — and froze at the sight of an intruder.

Jove rain on the man — gaping, slack-jawed, clutching at the front of his cowl. "*Sainte Vièrge, aidez moi!*" he blurted and, instead of running for help, what must he do but lower his head and charge!

Being still unarmed — not that he wanted to run through the fool — Tom toppled the candelabrum, sending it to catch the friar full in the chest. With a muffled cry, the man staggered, and fell backwards under its weight.

So much for slipping out unobserved! Tom bounded around the friar, who sprawled gaping like a grounded carp, but wasn't too winded to reach out and grab the edge of Tom's cloak.

Damn the stubborn churl — weren't these friars supposed to be men of peace? Tom kicked backwards, hitting flesh — and bounded for the door.

And see, the man squirmed out from under the candelabrum, grabbed the lantern and hurled it at the intruder. It sailed far off the mark, hitting the wall with a great clatter, enough to wake the whole convent.

Not lingering to find out if it did, Tom ran through the door and slammed it shut, rushing to clamber up the lame chair. It broke under him this time, but not before he managed to catch the wall, and all but vault over it. Ah, but pursuit gave a man wings! Not very good ones, though, and not for long: landing awkwardly in the mud of the Rue Saint-Jacques, he rolled to his feet again and dove into the nearest alley, where, Fates willing, Skeres and Lyly should be, waiting for him to climb over a different wall...

There was no need to seek them out, no need to whistle, for at once the Minotaur trotted up, with Lyly on his heels — and a good thing it was, for Tom was finding himself shorter of breath than he cared to admit as he leant back against the wall.

"Master, are you 'urt?" Skeres asked, just as Lyly exclaimed:

"What have you been doing? They came out a good while ago —"

Tom waved them both quiet. "Let's go," he ordered, for now light filled the apse windows, and calls sounded from the garden inside, and it wouldn't be long before the Guet was called.

They crossed the Rue Saint-Jacques at a sedate pace and, once in the shadows of an alley, ran in the angry wind.

"And what if they'd caught you for that piece of imprudence?" Stafford demanded — and, truly, the man's gall!

Having been sent on a fool's errand, climbed more walls than he had since boyhood, discovered the Ambassador dealing in secret with the Spaniards, and evaded capture by a whisker, Tom was in no mood for being chided.

"Well, they didn't!" He glared at the secretary. "No thanks to Mr. Lyly's information!"

They were all crowding around a smoking fire, hastily lit in the little parlour — three seething figures of copper and black, conferring in testy whispers — and Lyly didn't like to be called to task.

"How was I to know they'd lock you inside the sacristy?" he groused.

"Oh, you weren't. Nor that I'd hear precious little from that passage of yours —"

"I was shown the thing once — should we ever be surprised, they said. I never —"

"That's as may be," Tom cut him off. "But I'd say you've greater worries: whether the Pagets were there I can't swear, for no names were named — but for sure no Rheims messenger showed up at all, nor was he expected. Your tender-conscienced friend lied."

Faces were always harder to read by firelight, what with the flickering shadows and the odd glinting of the eyes — but there was no mistaking that both Lyly and Stafford weren't half as discomfited as they should have been.

"A trap," the Ambassador pronounced. "And now they'll wonder who was so nearly caught in it." There went the reproach again, just this side of gloating. *Walsingham's men again a-blunder…*

Oh, let him gloat! Let the man believe himself successful in his ruse, and safe in his dealing with Philip of Spain. *A spy revealed, Thomas, is a petty satisfaction; a spy uncovered in secret, however, is a most precious tool.*

And here, perhaps, were even the weights and counterweights reset in the game with Lord Burleigh...

Tom did his best to affect glumness, but one thing could be put to good use at once.

"Still, I wasn't caught," he said, in his best stubborn manner, "and there's one thing I learnt: they put great store by what Gifford knows, will tell, and won't. So you see, don't you, Sir, that I *must* speak to Gilbert Gifford? Tomorrow, I think."

Oh, how Stafford stopped in his tracks! How he clasped and unclasped his hands, glowering at Tom askance. Perhaps he knew otherwise, but saying so would reveal his game, or perhaps he did not, and was cursing himself for gifting Tom with this advantage. Either way, there was little he could do.

"Yes, Walsingham," he growled low in his throat. "Yes. I had in mind to send Grimeston tomorrow — but yes: you will go instead."

At his master's elbow, Lyly has lost all his smugness — and, whatever Sir Francis might have thought, Tom felt there was something to be said for even the pettiest satisfactions.

CHAPTER 11

The For-l'Évêque, prison and tribunal for the Bishop's jurisdiction, sat across the Seine, glowering at itself in the mirror of the water. It had a desolate courtyard that was entered through a great, looming arch. Tom couldn't help thinking it would make those who preferred to be judged by canon law question the wisdom of their choice.

Inside was bleaker still. First a low-ceilinged cubicle, where a gaoler, under guise of inspecting Tom's basket of food, accepted a round of cheese and a vail for not inspecting too closely. Then a maze of corridors and dank rooms of strange shape, its cold grey gloom unrelieved, its stench putrid. It was to one such room, tucked somehow into an elbow of those endless corridors, that — after disbursing a few more vails — Tom was shown, to find the prisoner slumped on a stool, and watching the winter sky through the one barred window — a picture of despondency if ever there was one.

He did not stir until the door was noisily locked again — then he turned, heaving a great sigh at the sight of a stranger. "Now who…?"

But, of course, Tom was no stranger. Recognition flared in Gifford's eyes, and then disbelief as he gaped in silence.

Prison was kind to no one, and why should Gifford be an exception? Three weeks of the Bishop's hospitality had made him gaunt, unkempt, and older than his eight-and-twenty years, bringing every bone to relief in the triangular face. Only the black eyes, sunken as they were, burnt as malevolent as ever.

When he found his voice again, it was to blurt, "I think you must be a devil!"

Not that Tom had expected a welcome. He switched to accented French, as his guise wanted, as the Fleming scrivener to Gifford's French *promoteur*. "Why, thank you, Deacon —"

"Father," Gifford snapped. "It's Father Gifford now. And you *must* be a devil: whenever I'm in trouble, you turn up like … like…" At a loss for a comparison that was bad enough, the man threw up both hands with a wordless exclamation that turned into a fit of coughing.

"Fair and soft," Tom ordered quietly — and, for a wonder, found himself obeyed. "Now, *mon Père*, my master is unwell, so I've come in his stead."

"And does he think I lack trouble, that he must send you?"

"I'm sure you can imagine that the choice wasn't his." Tom put the half-empty basket on the table. There was another stool, and he went to sit on it, right in front of the prisoner. "Now there are matters that we must discuss, and in your place, I'd be as helpful as can be."

Resentful, malicious, sullen, arrogant, frightened — through their encounters Tom had seen Gilbert Gifford in many ways, and never once smiling, either in jest or irony. If he was trying to do so now, he only managed a sour grimace. "Why, of course, Roper. Discuss to your heart's content."

Roper — Tom's assumed identity back in Rheims… "You didn't catch it right, *Père*. My name is Tessel." Hitching his stool closer, and turning his back to the door, Tom leant both elbows on his knees, so that he was close enough to whisper. "First of all, and in truth: how did you come to be arrested?"

Stinking ill and unwashed, Gifford leant closer still, earnest of a sudden. "Arundel," he said. "Arundel must have betrayed me."

Which came as no great wonder. "Is this certainty or conjecture?"

"Who else could it have been?"

"You've been spying on half the English in Paris."

"Yes, but that one…" Gifford reined himself in — a most unusual sight. "He always was a two-faced knave, and hated me because I saw through him."

"You know he's dead?"

"Grimeston told me."

"And did he also say it was poison? But perhaps not, for Stafford calls it your doing."

Having expected an explosion of outrage, Tom was surprised that Gifford only stared, as one hurt by a piece of unfairness.

"Mine?" There was even a hitch in his voice. "But why on earth would I…?"

"Because he was a two-faced knave and hated you?"

A fierce shake of the head. "You don't believe that. Charles Arundel was alive when I was caught. I tell you, he revealed me to the French, because I was reporting on his friend Stafford to your uncle!"

Cousin. "Which would still have given you reason to poison him."

"You don't believe that!" Gifford repeated — but this time he sounded hoarse.

Was the Deacon losing heart? Not the Deacon — not anymore… It would take a while to get used to calling him Father Gifford.

"Oh, I don't know." Tom raised his shoulder. "For now, the one thing I don't believe is that you stabbed Arundel's physician."

"Stabbed!"

"At the Cordeliers, two days ago, when you were in here. We were talking, and someone stabbed him —"

"He was talking to *you!*" Gifford sprang up from his stool with enough force to topple it. "How is it you're always around when people die?"

There were steps, and then a call of *"Monsieur?"* A pockmarked face appeared at the peephole. "Is he giving you trouble?"

Tom reassured the gaoler, and the hole emptied again, but Gifford stood for a long time squinting at it, hunched and stiff-shouldered. He coughed when he bent to pick up the stool and sank down onto it again, with his head in his hands. "Oh God!" he gasped. "Two men murdered — and you want me out of here!"

"Not particularly, unless it's to get you back home."

Gifford gave a sour little laugh. "Ay, *home*, where your uncle will want my hide!"

Would he? Tom found himself unsure of what Sir Francis would want to do with this untrustworthy fellow — not that he was going to tell. "Of one thing you can be certain," he said instead. "If Mr. Secretary sends you to the gallows, it won't be on Stafford's word alone."

Another bitter laugh, a wildness glittering in the black pupils. "What of Lord Burleigh, then? Mr. Secretary I've served faithfully, but Stafford is a Cecil man, and I know such things — *such things!*" He began to rise again. "You think they'd ever let me —"

"Be quiet!" Tom tugged him back to sit, fingers tight on the grubby sleeve. "Now heed me well. If you truly have so much to fear from Stafford, and unless you want to remain at the Bishop's tender mercies — don't you think you'd be better off under my cousin's protection? Come back willingly, and you'll be shown mercy."

"Even as a murderer and a traitor?" The attempt to pull free was weak. "You don't believe me, and neither will His Honour."

"Oh, I don't know about that." Tom released the trembling wrist. "You can't have stabbed the physician, that's for certain — and I have trouble believing that two men who knew each other can have been murdered within a fortnight of each other, by different people, for unrelated reasons. Now, it's true that the same person could have had you poison Arundel, and someone else kill the physician, but..." He held up a silencing forefinger. "Let's say, for argument's sake, that it wasn't so. Let's say that you're innocent — of this, if not of much else."

There had been a time when Tom had found Gilbert Gifford's face harder to read than most, beyond the opaque mask of resentment. Now, however, be it priesthood, be it one change of heart too many, or this soul-wearing life of always being on guard, the man had grown what Sir Francis called a transparent face: the reckoning of danger and advantage was plain to see, and, with it, the misliking. "Let us say I'm innocent," he said at length. "So what?"

"So, if you didn't kill Arundel and his physician, who did?"

The black eyes darted towards the peephole, and Gifford bent double to mouth soundlessly: "Stafford!"

And this, too, was little wonder, after all. Gifford had called the Ambassador a traitor... Why not a murderer too?

Still, the lack of surprise must have looked like disbelief, for Gifford nodded like one in a frenzy, and switched from French to Latin. "It is either the Hiberians or him," he breathlessly muttered. "He talks to the Hiberian Legate. He takes the Hiberian King's gold."

Well, after last night, this was easy to believe. "And it never crossed your mind to let us know?" Tom scolded in the same language — little as it mattered, for they were speaking too softly for anyone but the most fox-eared of listeners.

"I'm telling you now!" Gifford hissed. "And it was going to be in my next letter, for I thought I could show that Arundel was Mendoza's man — and lo! I was arrested for an English spy!"

"The French had been waylaying your letters long before that."

"But they lacked the cypher! They found it with my papers — together with the letter on Mendoza and Stafford. And Arundel…"

He reported poor Charles Arundel as the rankest traitor, sent to haunt me by the Spanish Ambassador, Stafford had complained.

"So this you didn't write to Phelippes — and yet you told the French." Which wasn't quite true — and had Gifford protesting.

"I didn't —"

"Oh, you did. It's come to Stafford's ears, and he told me, when he could have kept it to himself."

The briefest hesitation. "I told the French that *Arundel* was in Mendoza's pay. The rest was for your master."

Had it been, truly? Not in the letters, at all events. Tom hummed. "Still, why didn't Arundel have you killed instead? Paris is a dangerous place, these days, and you don't lead a choirboy's life. Why, if they'd thrown you in the Seine…"

"Everyone would have thought I'd run — but who knows? Perhaps Arundel had a conscience." Gifford coughed, and when he spoke again, it was in a hoarse murmur. "Or else he thought nobody would believe me, and I'd be discredited on both sides."

Which was likely enough, and this latest play at Papist zeal would hardly have helped. "Did he know what was in the letters?"

"Not quite, but he suspected enough that..." Gifford halted and lowered his gaze. "You'll know they found me with a woman."

"And with a man, from what I hear."

"Yes!" Gifford's face twisted. "Because the moment we heard the sergeants on the stairs, Nell went to open the door. To see, she said — and this fellow burst in, and right on his heels, in marched the King's Law, and seized us all. But I'll swear to you: in that moment before the sergeants trampled in, that man made for my trunk. He was an Englishman."

Stafford had mentioned this in his letter. "He calls himself a servant of the Earl of Essex. And a friend of your woman."

A shrug. "He calls himself what he likes, I'm sure. But Essex — what would he want with my letters?"

Rumour had it that the young Earl, Lord Leicester's stepson and his successor in the Queen's favour, very much wanted intelligencers of his own. Still, wanting was one thing; knowing enough to take interest in the letters of this disgraced priest was quite another.

"Then say that Arundel paid this pair to snatch your letters — a very chancy plan — but they failed ... so he had to try and recover them himself?" It seemed to Tom that the tale was becoming more and more knotted, and Gifford must have caught his doubt, for he nodded wildly again.

"In truth, there wasn't much in the papers, for I was loath to put it down in writing yet, but Arundel must have thought that I had proof, and it was too late, for now the Gauls knew, and it was bound to leak out sooner or later. So he took fear, was going to confess to your uncle, and make his peace with the

Regina at Stafford's expense, and —" He broke off, startled, when Tom rose and began to pace.

Oh, it was plausible enough — and it explained why Stafford had brought up the matter of Spain when he had. As likely as not Mr. Ambassador regretted it, now that he knew what was in the letters, and what wasn't. And he also knew who else might well know more about it — but this Tom wasn't going to point out.

"Suppose — and I'm not half convinced — but suppose that Stafford did murder," he said. "There's this matter of Spain — and I can't begin to imagine why you'd have held back on this. Still, if you have any way to prove it, now is the moment."

With a moan, Gifford hunched still lower on his stool, pulling at his greasy hair, and switched back to French. "Lord, you're thick-headed for the name you bear! How must I tell you? I can prove nothing — that's why I couldn't write to Phelippes yet! And yet I know for certain, just as one other knew, and now that other's dead!" He looked up, eyes burning in the haggard face. "Who else could it have been?"

"You said it yourself: Mendoza. Or perhaps you're wrong, and it was the purple ague. Or else, there was no love lost between Arundel and the Pagets."

The first two suggestions Gifford might as well not have heard; it was the third that dragged a high-pitched laugh from him. "The Pagets! You really think they count for much?"

"Perhaps they'll count for more now."

"And you Mr. Secretary's kin! Think of Arundel's physician, killed while he talked to you: who was better placed to know of the physician *and* of you talking to him — the Pagets, or Stafford?"

And this there was no gainsaying — why, Tom had thought of it for himself.

Finding himself not rebuked, Gifford pressed his advantage.

"When I was taken, Stafford took fright. Why do you think I refuse his help in getting out of here?"

"His help, but not his money."

"Oh, that. I was rather hoping he'd refuse, and drag things along. The ten crowns he sent, so I asked for thirty…"

"I've convinced him to send those too, for all that he was furious when you told the French about the first ten."

"They forced it out of me!"

"Not on the rack, by the look of you."

"They already knew!"

So someone was talking to the French. Simier, most likely. Hardly Lady Stafford, no matter how close a friend she was to the Queen Mother.

"Or else, they tried a shot in the dark, and you obliged. Well, it's done now. You'll have your thirty crowns soon enough — through the *promoteur*, not through me nor Grimeston."

"My father —"

"Don't be a fool. There are too many people in this tangle already. Here." Tom took from his sleeve a note folded into a small square.

Gifford snatched it quickly, twisting around so no one observing through the peephole could see what he was doing. Tom knew the contents — a few lines written by Grimeston — and thought it hardly a matter for hilarity. Still, Gifford's shoulders shook.

"I must not tarry in here, he says." A breathless laugh. "I must make all haste to get out — not that he'll help. The wolf calling to the lamb!"

Such a likely lamb! "In truth he will, but we both know thirty crowns won't buy your freedom, *mon Père*."

And, who would believe it, Gifford gaped. "Why not? They've nothing. No man in all of Paris can witness anything dangerous against me."

Tom couldn't help a huff of startled laughter. "Nothing but your letters, your cyphers, and all that you told them — and now they know for certain that you're in league with the English ambassador." Tom reached for the letter, and it was past belief that Gifford still dithered.

"I could have it hidden. Securely."

"As securely as you hid the first one? Come, come. You have your orders."

The sour twist of the lips again. "The gentleman will be angry, if I don't send it back. There will be no money... Oh, but you know already. I'll wager you wrote it yourself."

When there was no answer, he surrendered the scrap of paper. "Can I write, at least?"

He eyed longingly the remaining cheese and the fine pie, as Tom unearthed from the basket a blank sheet, a quill, and a small ink-horn.

"He always sends food, and I never touch it — much as I'd need it, for I'm unwell. It always goes to the gaolers."

"And they're all dead?"

A rush of colour rose in Gifford's cheeks, come and gone in a heartbeat, though the twist of his lips remained. The paper spread on his knees, he scratched a line and paused.

"Never think you don't have it easy, *Tessel* — with the name you bear, and your folk so sure of you!"

I never betrayed anyone, I... Tom swallowed the retort, thoughts of Frances flickering in his mind — and then, less uncomfortably, the pretence that his great debts made him open to the Cecil's machinations. A pretence it was, and nothing else, but it wasn't politic that, should this snake

Gifford ever hear of Robert Cecil's pressures, he should even doubt the matter.

"*You* they'll never drag this way and that, until you hardly know yourself," the snake rasped. "Until each and all will call you a turncoat, and your own blood will watch their speech before you."

And so hoarse were the words, so white the knuckles tight around the quill, that Tom could almost find it in himself to pity the fellow.

"Write what you must," he ordered.

With a sigh, Gifford dipped his quill again, and hunched lower over the paper — and at that moment there was a rap on the door.

"Are you done, *mon Maître?*" the gaoler called. "There's a gentleman to see *le Père* Gifford with *Monsieur le Vicaire*, and they won't wait."

"One moment," Tom called back, brows raised at Gifford, who shook his head. Whatever weakness had seized the man's heart a moment, it was gone, replaced by the usual liar's calculation.

It's dangerous to allow oneself compassion, Thomas — Sir Francis warned in Tom's head — which, as he gathered quill and ink-horn, reminded him of something else.

"What of Adam Cavel?" he asked under his breath, making Gifford pause in the act of shaking his note.

"The coachman? A chatty fellow."

He hastily folded his note, and Tom pocketed it together with Grimeston's letter a wink before the door opened, and the gaoler appeared.

"A fine day, eh, *mon Père?*" The Bishop's man grinned at the half-empty basket that would soon be his.

"Well, *mon Père*," Tom said to Gifford in his best Flemish rasp. "I'll tell my master. What he can do, he'll do." And he let himself be shown out, where another, older gaoler waited to bring Gifford to the Judicial Vicar's room.

Fierce scowls ran between these two gaol-lions, neither eager to walk away from the spoils — and could it be that there went a chance?

A chance to know who this gentleman visitor was, and to hear what Gifford told him.

"Well, fellow," Tom groused. "I'll leave, if it isn't too much bother."

The man grunted, looking from the door to the troublesome visitor and back again. "You've stayed enough for confession, lad. You can wait a tad longer."

Inside, the other gaoler was taking his time.

"Ay, long enough to get a fine snub from my master, thanks to the good *Père*. Stay, if you like. I've no need to be shown out." And Tom took the corridor at a clip.

Now let Greed be stronger than Duty… Feeling the gaoler's eyes on his back, Tom rounded the inexplicable bend — and no call came, nor when, a dozen yards ahead, he dove into a branching passage. Greed victorious — and mother to Chance!

There was a moral, in this, and Tom's mind was so formed it couldn't help trying to dress it in Latin meter, and never went past observing *cupiditas*, most fittingly, was good for both Greed and Gluttony — as he peered around the corner. Finding the corridor deserted, he scampered back to the bend, just in time to see both gaolers, the younger one carrying the basket, hurrying Gifford ahead, and up a flight of stairs. And, since the Fates seemed well-disposed today, let them smile a little longer.

It seemed to Tom that he did little but eavesdrop, these days. Hardly a gentleman's work, if he were to be punctilious. But it was a long-ingrained maxim that a good measure of scruple was among the sacrifices one offered in the cause of Queen and England — and, in fair truth, Tom had done worse in his Service days than hide under the stairs, and strain his ears to catch what was being said behind a closed door.

Not that he heard that much, either, for the Judicial Vicar's room had a thick door. Still, something filtered — such as Gifford demanding to know, in English, whether His Lordship came as a judge or as a friend.

"As a friend," His Lordship answered. "A friend, dismayed that you should ask!"

In such a pained voice, he said so! Pained, deep, rich, gravelly... Could this be...?

"It's a strange manner of coming as a friend, my lord!" Gifford again — and none too humble. "Yet, if there's anything you wish to say, I'll listen — little good as I fear it will do me."

A third man spoke in French then, half in entreaty, half in reproach. The Vicar exhorting the prisoner to meekness?

"No, *Monsieur le Vicaire*," His Lordship said in French. "I'm sure Father Gifford has..." The rest couldn't be heard — but even the wordless rumble was enough to banish all question: this was the man Tom had heard at the Cordeliers, just before Jourdain's death.

Oh Jove! Who was this, present at the murder, and now visiting Gifford? Caution be damned, Tom sneaked out of his hiding place — and this, too, he'd been doing too often of late — and sidled closer to the door, just in time to hear Gifford's next explosion.

"It was by your own friends' consent! The Cardinal himself knew, and Your Lordship's own brother with his friend Morgan, they all knew what I was doing! And I was not alone in that. Mr. Arundel himself —"

He broke off, coughing, and when His Lordship answered, very little could be discerned: *Loyalties... Brother...* and then, most alarmingly, *Walsingham...*

Oh Lord. Was this where Gifford made a clean breast of it all, to this man whose brother was a friend of Mary Stuart's foremost agent? One name alone came to mind...

In the Vicar's room there was the shortest silence — Gifford reckoning his chances, for sure — and then...

"*Never man came so near to cheating me as Gifford,* that's what Walsingham thinks of it. And he threatened that I'd pay for it. He himself told someone, whose friends told me, and if you don't believe me, my lord, you'll have no trouble finding someone to confirm it!"

The shameless liar! The breath Tom hadn't known he was holding hitched out of him in a silent laugh, at the thought of Sir Francis cheated by Gilbert Gifford. His Lordship must not have credited it, either, for the priest burst out:

"Ay, return into the country, and I'd be received with mercy. I know Walsingham's mercy!" A fit of coughing stopped him, together with a sharp answer.

"You know it, yes — only not at first hand." His Lordship must have risen and come to stand close to the door, for his words sounded clear. "You saw it used on Anthony Babington."

Oh, the cursed letters again, and Phelippes's indiscreet quill — although, how did this man know that Babington had expected mercy?

A chair scraped on the floor.

"And Your Lordship calls himself a friend!" Gifford always became shrill in anger. Now he was also hoarse with coughing. "*Monsieur le Vicaire*, return me to my cell."

"You'll go when I say so, Gifford," barked His Lordship, and the Vicar raised his voice for the first time.

"*Messieurs!*" he called. "*Milord* Paget, *Père!* Is this the way…?"

And the rest Tom didn't hear, for the noise of feet mounting the stairs tore him from the door, and sent him scurrying back into his hole, with every last doubt set to rest: Lord Paget had been at the Cordeliers, he'd talked to Joyce Blundell, and now he was here! And, Tom would wager, he'd also been at the Mathurins last night. He squeezed unmoving in his corner as a clerk and a guard hurried by, talking in whispers. By the time he tiptoed to the door again, the argument inside had died down, and Lord Paget's rumble had the colour of gentle pleading. It went on a while, with the Vicar adding his weight now and then.

Once they were done there was a short silence, and, when Gifford spoke, he sounded steadier.

"I've already confessed, my lord," he said, each word slow and careful. "If you won't believe me, then don't — but the Lord knows the truth of it: my dealings with those in England began the year before last, around Easter, with consent of the Cardinal, your brother, Morgan and others. I swear that I never wrote to London anything that I wasn't certain had come to their ears before, and I've done nothing for which I had not the consent of the Cardinal himself."

Oh, it was done well. Sounding so very earnest — just a little too earnest for the Bishop's man and Paget to be sure whether they should believe it. Just enough that the French wouldn't like to let the man out of the For-l'Évêque. And, for a mercy, not a syllable of Tom's visit.

Not that this happy state of things could be trusted to last — but, for now, Gifford feared Sir Francis less than he feared Stafford. And with this Tom had to be content for, hearing chairs being moved, he slipped back to the stairs, and hastened down them.

It was most fortunate that, when Tom arrived back at the Embassy, Grimeston was working alone in the secretaries' room. Sir Edward, he explained, was closeted in his study together with Lyly, leaving orders that he shouldn't be disturbed. And, if he didn't look happy in the first place, when Tom gestured for quiet and beckoned to him, he grimaced like one with toothache.

Extricating his bulk from the writing table, he drew Tom as far away from the Ambassador's door as the small room allowed.

"Mr. Walsingham, I'm very ill at ease..." He stopped, shaking his head, the very picture of helplessness. He brightened for a heartbeat when Tom gave him the two letters. Gifford's answer he set aside at once, and checked carefully his own returned note.

"Did he make trouble?" he asked, putting both in a portefeuille. "He always does."

Having yet to meet a soul who didn't dislike Gilbert Gifford, Tom huffed. "He tried — not very hard."

"And..." the secretary peeked over his shoulder at the closed door. *And what did he say of Arundel? Did he denounce the Ambassador? Did he denounce me?* "Was he helpful?"

As helpful as anyone who could not be believed. "He was talkative, which isn't necessarily the same. But there's one thing he told me, and I hope you'll know more about it."

"Mr. Walsingham, I don't —"

Tom ignored the squirming. "There was a woman arrested together with Gifford — a creature of scant virtue by the name of Nell."

"I don't know her name, but yes: an Englishwoman. And an Englishman, too — one Colton, or Cotton, claiming to be Lord Essex's man."

"Do you know where he is now? Or the woman?"

Had Tom asked for the whereabouts of the mythical Laestrygones, Grimeston couldn't have been more flustered. "But I don't know! It was assumed that you in London would sound out the matter of Lord Essex. Other than that..."

And had they in London sounded it out? Phelippes might have — for all that the cypherer was greatly unsettled by his disgrace. Well, this would have to be asked about in Tom's next letter. Meanwhile... "Whoever this Cotton is, something must have been done with him. Was he released or thrown into the King's gaols? The Bishop can't have claimed a foreign layman."

Again Grimeston shook his head.

"What of the Ambassador's friends — those who smuggle letters to him?" Tom insisted. "Come, surely they'll have kept an eye on those two?"

"I'm not saying they didn't, but I've no way to know. Sir Edward tells me very little, and I can't ask, for my place here is not one of trust. Why, you've seen for yourself: I'm hardly allowed in the study alone!"

Not for the first time it struck Tom as odd that Grimeston should be chosen to deal with Gifford on the one hand, and on the other... "Is it not strange to keep a secretary out of the study where the papers are?"

"Sir Edward grew suspicious, after I came back from England." A sickly smile. "Not that he's wrong, is he?"

Grimeston shook himself from this cogitation. "But do you think there would be aught about those two? In writing?"

Hardly, in truth. It seemed like the sort of tidings that would be passed by word of mouth. "It would be best to make inquiries at the Châtelet."

The secretary's eyes widened. "But I —"

"Not you. Have the French promotor do it. It will be most natural, and nobody will think twice about it." And, because Grimeston still fretted, unconvinced and unsoothed, Tom added with little patience, "Stafford will never hear of it, I promise you."

Grimeston darted another glance at the closed door, and lowered his voice to the point where it was hard to hear. "But I fear he knows already that I spoke to you! Yesterday he sent me away of a sudden —"

"To carry letters — I know."

A frantic nod. "Notes of no importance, compliments that would have held a day, or a week, for that matter. But I was sent in haste, and late enough that I'd never be back in time before curfew."

"And he sent me away, and my servant, and Lyly —"

The secretary's brow creased. "Lyly also?"

"I mean…" Tom's breath caught, as one small piece of coloured glass shifted inside his mind: just how far in Stafford's confidence was Lyly, truly? He was — or had been at least — Paget's man, after all, and a close friend of Arundel. "Lyly, yes. More the working of a guilty conscience than of grounded suspicion, wouldn't you say?"

This Grimeston considered, nibbling on his thumb. "It's hard to believe. Sir Edward trusts young Lyly very much. The boy as good as has the freedom of the study, has the key to that cabinet…"

"It doesn't mean there aren't secrets beyond Lyly's reach. Back in my day there were all sorts of stories about Ambassador Cobham's hiding places. Stories that even we lowly couriers knew. Canterbury tales, for the most part, but…"

And, had Tom still doubted, Grimeston's wince would have been enough to betray knowledge — a wince that, instead of fleeting by as most winces do, moulded itself in the man's features as he walked away, and went to lean against the windowsill.

And see how he startled when the sound of steps was heard from the next room, and spun about, gaping at the door like a hunted hare. There came a murmuring, more steps, then all went quiet again.

"So?" Tom prodded.

A great sigh. "So there's a place. A secret drawer, perhaps — but I don't know. I only overheard Sir Edward mentioning it to Her Ladyship once."

"In the study? That inlaid cabinet? The table?"

"I don't remember what he said, other than that none but himself knew, and even Her Ladyship would never find it. She laughed, though. It could have been in jest."

The thought of the formidable Baroness laughing with her husband somehow didn't paint a picture of loving familiarity. "You never tried to search for it?"

A gape, a twisting of hands. "At the of risk being caught?"

"And are you sure it's in the study? Not, say, in Sir Edward's bedroom?"

The secretary looked up like a startled coney. "You're never thinking…? I shouldn't have told you!"

"You didn't tell — I asked. And, whatever I have in mind, the more you can tell me, the less likely it is that I'll come to mischief." *And you with me.*

It might have been a hitch of laughter or a sob half swallowed — Tom couldn't have said. How did the saying go? Caught between the devil and the sea, poor fellow.

"I'm a translator, Mr. Walsingham." A forlorn shake of the head. "My gratitude knew no bounds when Sir Edward offered me this post in Paris... For the sake of my studies, you understand. But yes, you do understand, for someone, back in London, told me that you're a man of learning —"

Oh Jove — *captatio benevolentiae!* "That someone was too good — but it's all very much beside the point. You know that there are accusations against you in Gifford's papers?"

A halting nod. "Sir Edward told me."

"Well then, now I'm giving you a chance to counter those suspicions."

Cold as the room was, Grimeston wiped a hand down his sweating face. "All my life I've striven to be a good Christian, and a good subject to the Queen." He held up a hand, as he warmed to his argument. "Is it right, I ask you, that now I must fear Mr. Secretary on one side, and on the other Sir Edward, who is my Lord Burleigh's man? Is it right that there should be no way out of this dilemma?"

And Tom might have been more touched, but for the rhetoric flourish. "You do have a way out," he said. "A very easy one, to begin with: the study or some other place?"

Poor fellow, how the purple cheeks fell! Speechless before such callousness, no doubt.

"The study," he said at length. "They never said so in as many words — but it's of the study that they were talking."

On being ordered to go and buy a dark lantern, Nick Skeres snorted. Nose and round cheeks scoured red by the wind, as they stood halfway down the ill-kept flight of steps leading to the river, the lad wasn't happy at all.

"You spend 'alf the night in that convent," he groused. "Only you weren't there, were you? And then you meet Deacon Gifford, and all you 'ave to say is, buy a dark lantern?"

"Father, Dolius." Tom never turned from his contemplation of the empty steps, all the way to the roiling grey water, and the spire of Notre-Dame across the river's arm. "I met *Father* Gifford, for he's a full priest now. And I was at the convent — only not all the time. By the way, this is another thing you'll do, while you procure my lantern. Go to some place around the Mathurins — a shop, a tavern, whatever you like — and find out whether there was mayhem at the convent last night."

Another snort. "You know there was: you made it yourself!"

"Yes, and I want to hear what it is they say about it."

"And if they say it was an English madman?"

"Then you'll shake your head mournfully, and bemoan what the world has become."

Skeres bent to pick up a bit of crumbling stone, and threw it down towards the river. It fell short, rolled down a step — and stopped there. "Cuds-me, a priest, Gifford! Can't picture it."

"Priesthood doesn't agree with him — or else it's life in gaol — but other than that he's very much the way he was as a deacon, just as charming and honest. He calls Stafford Mendoza's man — and also a murderer."

Skeres just shrugged one shoulder, and picked up another stone. "Like you 'adn't thought of it for yourself!" he said, and grunted as he threw harder, almost overbalancing as he did. This time his missile made it to the water — barely.

"I'm not fishing you out if you take a plunge," Tom warned — which Skeres ignored, in favour of expounding:

"You've worked out about the murtherings, I mean. And about Mendoza, too."

Tom picked up a stone of his own. "For now, all I have are two Spaniards walking out of the Embassy at night."

"And Gifford's word."

"Which there's no believing."

"And that 'e sent you on a sleeveless errand last night."

"Yes, but confront him with it, and he'll say he's pretending to have dealings with Mendoza so he can spy on him, and he had to get me out of the way because Mr. Secretary mislikes initiative that's not his own."

Skeres burst out laughing — loud enough for all Paris to hear — and, when Tom ordered him to be quiet, he had the cheek to wave at the deserted steps. "Takes more than Mr. Ambassador to cozen old Mendoza!"

"This being why Sir Francis never wanted Stafford to play games. And thinking himself greatly offended, either Stafford thought he'd prove his mettle against orders, or he saw no reason to shun Spanish gold."

Eyeing Tom's stone sideways, the lad went to pick up another, hissing when he found it covered in bird droppings. "I'll eat a cat — raw and unskinned — if 'e knows who plays and who's played," he grumbled, rubbing his fingers on his breeches.

"And if I were a cat, I'd feel quite safe — but a disobedient fool and a traitor are two very different beasts."

"One as unchancy as the other, if you ask me. And that's without counting if 'e's a murtherer."

"Still, Mr. Secretary will want something sounder than Gifford's spite and two Spaniards out after curfew." Tom threw his stone. It hit a step, and only after bouncing twice did it disappear into the muddy water — plainly not a good throw, by Skeres's amused reckoning.

"And for that something, you need some thieves' trick, eh?" The lad chuckled, good cheer restored. "You know they put you in gaol for 'aving a dark lantern?"

"I'm not sure they do here," Tom said. "Still, see to it that you're not observed, and think what irons you may need — because tonight, Dolius, we're going to break into Stafford's study."

"And you, Mr. Tom, looking so innocent!" Skeres shook with mirth, hands pressed to his belly. The Minotaur diverted.

CHAPTER 12

Come night, Tom supped at the *Plat d'Étain* with Skeres, and heard how there were all sorts of tall tales about the ado at the Mathurins — of thieves, brigands, murderers, German mercenaries, and Huguenots — none of them worrying in the least. He was careful to return to the Embassy only after the study windows went dark, and an unusually long-faced Hobelot let them in.

So long-faced, in fact, as to make one wonder if anything had happened in the last couple of hours.

When asked, poor Hobelot twisted his face in unhappiness.

"'Tis Adkin, Master," he said. "With what he's done... He says maybe we'll have to leave."

There had been little to see of Adam Cavel these past few days. *Keeps to 'imself ... keeps to the 'ouse*, as Skeres had put it. Perhaps Stafford was reconsidering Gifford's accusations against the coachman. "The Ambassador's never turning you out?" Tom asked.

This hadn't occurred to Hobelot, whose large face scrunched up. "Why, no, Master! 'Tis that Adkin has deserted his post. 'Tis a bad thing, Master, to desert one's post." A heavy burden for what remained of a soldier's mind — and, surely, a good explanation to offer to such a brother, if a man meant to walk out of harm's way.

"Sometimes even the finest soldier must do bad things for a good reason." Tom felt like the blackest of cads when a half-smile cleared the shadows from poor, innocent Hobelot's face. It was only the relief of a moment, though, and the doorman sobered again.

"You're kind, Master — but … a girl? He never told me he was sweet on a girl besides Sally." A glance at Skeres. "Now Sally goes away when Adkin's in the kitchen. But, Master, that he should never tell me…?"

Tom patted the poor, betrayed fellow's arm.

"Who knows, Hobelot? Perhaps it will still turn out for the better."

"God send, Master, for Adkin's a good lad," the man said, and went to draw his bolts and bars.

As he did, Tom and Skeres went to the hall. They made a pretence of letting themselves out into the garden and, closing the door again, hastened back to hide in the shadows behind the white marble staircase, where they sat on the floor, waiting, with the blind lantern Skeres had brought hidden under his cape. It wasn't long before Hobelot arrived to bar the garden door, and then walked away most forlornly, with shoulders hunched and head low.

"Poor fellow," Tom murmured, when the light of his candle had disappeared.

There was a sniff from Skeres. "'E knew what's what when 'e went for a soldier. The rest is God's will."

Which was so unusually pious for the Minotaur that Tom had no answer, and could only shake his head and bring his mind back to the night's work.

They sat and waited a good while for silence and, hopefully, sleep to take hold of the house — and spoke no more, for fear of being heard. More than once Tom found himself thinking of the Cavels, wondering whether it was for the sake of his feeble-minded brother that Adam took French money, and wishing he'd had the time to tease more about the man out of Gifford. What went on in Skeres's mind, he would have liked to know … but perhaps it wasn't much, for, when he judged that enough time had passed, and nudged the lad with a cautious elbow, the first answer was a little snore.

"Look alive, Skeres!" he hissed, as the Minotaur startled awake.

A moment later they tiptoed upstairs, a part of Tom's mind wondering how their dark shapes would appear, gliding against that alabastrine marble... But there was no one to see, and the landing upstairs was dark. No light showed under the door that led to the Baroness's quarter, nor that to the secretaries' room — and to this they applied themselves. Having been shown how earlier in the evening, Tom opened the lantern's little shutter just enough to direct a thin beam of light onto the lock's plate; Skeres knelt by it, and, taking from a pouch a ring of keys, began to explore the keyhole. There was some quiet grumbling as one strange key after the other was tried; while they all looked very much alike, they must not be, for some turned in the lock, and some did not, and at one point, Skeres cursed under his breath and pushed hard — and there was a sudden clack of metal, loud enough to awake the whole Left Bank.

The lad hissed through his teeth, and Tom froze, burning his fingers as he shut the lantern — more noise! Grabbing Skeres, he scurried back towards the stairs, waiting for steps, for calls... But no — nothing happened, Fates be thanked! Tom blew out his cheeks, and gave Skeres a little shake.

"Thought it was the wrong key — only it wasn't," the soft grumble came. "You didn't blow off the lantern, did you?"

Oh Lord... Tom pried the shutter open to see the candle stump tilted and guttering, but still burning.

"Let's go in, if you're done with the lock," he ordered, for the passage and the darker hole that gave access to the staircase felt dreadfully exposed.

Once in the secretaries' room, Skeres locked the door behind them, and, with the candle righted, went to work on the lock to the study. He was very fast and quiet this time, so that Tom knew he was done only when the lad beamed up at him, a mask of orange and shadows squinting against the lantern's glow.

"Second one's always easier," he said.

How his servant had come by such talents, or acquired his burglar's tools, Tom decided he didn't want to know. A heartbeat later, they were locked inside Stafford's study, with an empty room on either side and the curtains drawn. It would take very bad luck for anyone to see they were in there.

And now ... where to seek a secret drawer?

Tom ran the lantern's beam around the room, considering. The inlaid cabinet on the chest by the fireplace stood out as the obvious choice — and after that, the desk, but the small table laden with books between the windows also had its interest, and several sideboards. And this was assuming there weren't secret compartments concealed, say, behind the tapestries that hung from the walls.

Tom pointed to the cabinet. "Can you open this one?" he asked.

Skeres took the lantern, and went to inspect the elaborate lock-plate, sucking his teeth and muttering to himself. "I can break it open," he pronounced after a while.

Which would be a great pity, for inlaid figures and a landscape shone on the front flap as if alive in the lantern's flickering light. It was a foolish relief that no detectable mark of their passage must remain.

"You must pick it, and lock it again once we're done."

Skeres huffed and, putting the lantern on the desk, began to sift through his ring of keys.

Seen close, they didn't look like much: some bigger and some smaller, some with a hook or a straight pin instead of the bit, all of them very simple in design.

Skeres tried a small one, poking it into the hole and twisting it carefully this way and that, to no avail.

"Doors, you said," he grunted. "If you wanted to open toys, you should 'ave said toys."

"Those are too plain, Dolius. It's sure to be some devilish sort of lock."

"Ay, spoken like a locksmith!" Skeres tried another key, with no better result, and then another. "Thing is, there's the bit, and there's the wards — that's all those devilish cuts and notches of yourn, as count for naught. They let the key move inside the lock, but it's the bit as does the work of turning it open and closed. You file away the wards, like 'ere, and the bit... Ah!" A soft click, and Skeres beamed. "See?"

And indeed, the inlaid flap swung open to reveal several rows of little drawers around a square little door with its own keyhole.

"This one too." Tom pointed, and, once the lad had picked the tiny lock, began to work his way through the cabinet's contents.

Many letters — some cyphered, some not, and some in part — the notes of Gifford's papers, transcriptions, copies of reports to Sir Francis, copies of reports to Lord Burleigh, and, accordingly, two sets of cyphers, both familiar. A small pouch containing two signet rings bearing the Stafford sigil — likely variations supposed to have meaning to a particular correspondent. Letters to Stafford's mother, to his brother-in-law the Lord Admiral, to Arundel (addressed as 'My Good Cousin'), to Simier and a couple of other French courtiers, to the Protestant King of Navarre, a few petitions to the King of

France, two to Lord Paget — on very innocent matters... These last Tom tried to commit to memory, in case there was some code in use — but, on the whole, he found naught that was unknown, unexpected or very damning. Nothing, surely, that warranted Grimeston's exclusion. Tom tried to feel each hole, cranny, and carving (was he ever going to be able to afford a thing this lovely?) and, if there was a catch, he didn't find it.

"Come here, Dolius. See whether you can find some secret hole."

Skeres, who, armed with another candle stump, had been busy picking open all the locks he could find in the furniture, went to work on the cabinet, while Tom moved to the desk.

Behind the tapestry, it was as ornate as the rest of the room. Three drawers were soon searched: a few personal letters, sticks of sealing wax, a sheaf of fine new paper, a number of penknives, a small collection of anti-English pamphlets, a miniature painting of a woman who was not the Baroness... Little enough for the desk of Her Majesty's Ambassador, and nothing of consequence. As Tom pushed the last drawer closed, something stuck. He tried to reopen it, and whatever it was grazed against the top. Now let Stafford not discover this expedition because a piece of paper had jammed a drawer! Bracing both thumbs on the top, Tom slid his fingers inside to smooth down the obstacle — and a sudden memory flashed in his mind: an old and much plainer table at Scadbury that had been his grandfather's, its top too thick, its single drawer too shallow...

With an exclamation, he began to take out the drawers.

"What is it?" Skeres asked.

"Help me, Dolius. I'll wager you..." Inside the space where the centre drawer had been, he blindly felt the top, until ...

there! There was a round hole, large enough to slip in a fingertip... A panel slid half an inch aside, and a shallow tray fell into Tom's waiting hands. "Ah, here it is!" And it wasn't empty.

Four sheets of paper sewn together in a small octavo book contained yet another set of cyphers, this one using Greek letters, and a much-corrected list of code words. At the top of it, "Minerva" stood for nothing less than "Your Highness". Tom huffed in disappointment.

"What's that?" asked Skeres, coming to peer over his shoulder.

"Stafford's secret means of writing to the Queen herself. I wish him joy of it." Tom put back the booklet and manoeuvred the tray back into place. "The Queen hates cyphers with a passion. Sir Francis says she loses them on purpose."

There was a low whistle. "Slippery knave! Does 'Is 'Onour know?"

"He's always had a shrewd suspicion, and never worried about it." But this was neither here nor there. "What of the cabinet?"

"There's a false bottom inside that little door, empty as a beggar's belly. If there's others, I can't find 'em."

Tom blew out his cheeks. How many hiding places could a man keep? Many, if he had Edward Stafford's suspicious mind, and who was to say they were all in this room? Ordering Skeres to lock the cabinet and the desk, he tried the bigger sideboard by the door through which they'd entered. It was a tall thing, richly carved with an intricate confusion of winged heads, and pouting profiles, and leaves, and vines, and masks, and griffins, and enough whatnots to hide a dozen secret catches. A thorough fingering of these carvings yielded nothing, though, and it was with a dispirited mind that Tom inspected the board's contents, and his heart sank at the sight of bundle upon bundle of neatly filed papers — the topmost one bearing the legend "Lyly". Oh Lord — how was he going to read through this sea of ink and paper? What he'd been thinking to accomplish in a few hours, he didn't know. He skimmed half-heartedly through the bundles, until the Minotaur came to help by grabbing an armful of papers.

"Have a care!" Tom hissed. "They'll notice if you disorder them."

Mumbling to himself, the lad pushed the bundles back into place, craning his neck to read. "There's naught of Arundel?" he asked.

That there wasn't made for little wonder. "Burnt the day he died, I'd think," Tom said. "Or hidden better than this ... wait." Tom turned in his hands a letter from Robert Cecil, a single sheet urging caution in answer to Jove-knew-what. There was a coded passage, a string of numbers — and a little note in the margin, heavily crossed through. Still barely visible were a letter and a Roman number: lVI. A combination Tom had seen just the day before, on the verso of Grimeston's note of Gifford's letter. How had it been? *"PhilVI, Fat..."* The Sixth Philippic, the *De Fato* — and leave it to Stafford to like the works of that pompous Roman windbag, Cicero... "Book cypher!"

Had Skeres been a terrier, he'd have pricked his ears. "You found it?"

"This? No." Tom slipped the letter back where he had found it. "It just makes me wonder. It's old and easy to break, mind — but..." But Arundel had died raving — and not of his loyalty to the Queen. *Je Dirai... The Dearie...* Tom went to the table between the windows, checking the row of books. A copy of Cicero's *Philippicæ*, sure enough, several books of French poems, Hakluyt's own *Divers Voyages Touching the Discoverie of America*, *A General Rehearsal of Warres*, two volumes of *Plutarch's Lives* in English, *A Historie of Italie...* A strangely amassed little collection. "Have you come across other books?"

"Ay, in there." Skeres pointed to the smaller sideboard, a strange affair like a cupboard mounted on a chest — and indeed, there were books inside. It was more of the same strange miscellany: poetry, travels, a couple of sermon books, Latin prose, but not what Tom sought.

"*Je dirai...*" He tapped his fingers on the bottom of the lower shelf. "Help me take them out, Dolius. But mind: keep them in the same order." Once the shelf was empty, he tapped the bottom again and tried to shift it, but the board refused to budge. Jove rain on clever cabinet-makers! Was it in the carvings all around? As he began to feel vine by wooden vine the way he'd done in the sacristy, the beam of the lantern swung high over his head.

"What are you doing?" he snapped. "Down here —"

But the lad was pointing. "What about up there?"

And he wasn't wrong. It had been hard to see in the gloom, but the cupboard was topped with a carved band a span high, showing three masks of some sort, one on each side and one in the centre, and between them scenes with women and animals.

"Why, yes..." Tom reached to finger the little figures, and found them too high above. "Get me a chair."

He put back the useless books meanwhile, and, by the time he was done, Skeres was back with Stafford's high-backed chair. Tom mounted it — and when the thing tottered, made to grab for the cupboard... Only by a whisker he caught himself on the back of the chair instead, as Skeres threw all his weight on the armrests.

And then, Sir, I dragged a cupboard down on my head in the middle of the night, and the Ambassador caught me buried under his secret cyphers...

"Cuds-me, Mr. Tom!" Skeres hissed.

Tom let out a slow breath. "Light," he ordered, with as much brisk dignity as a man could who had just almost made a disaster out of sheer clumsiness. For a wonder, Skeres obeyed without comment, and Tom set to work. It was easy enough, in the end, because, once the light shone on the carvings, it showed a thin fissure between the left-side mask and the panel with Leda and the Swan. The mask, a fox's face, or a cat's perhaps, crowded by oak leaves, slid out easily enough, leaving a square black hole. Passing the mask to Skeres, Tom slipped a hand inside the hole, and eased out the panel — which was actually a drawer.

Inside was an octavo book in Latin: *The Appendix of Publius Vergilius Maro, with the Addition of many Poems of ancient Poets, never studied before.* And among those poems... Tom thumbed through the pages, until he found what he was seeking, a certain short piece called *Diræ* — after the revengeful Furies — because John Faulkes had been unwittingly more accurate than two French physicians put together, after all, and Arundel's raving last words hadn't been *Je dirai* — but *The Diræ.*

"What 'ave you found?" called Skeres from below.

"A middling poem — and..." Tom reached inside the drawer again, and fished out a little sheaf of loose papers. "Ha! Up with that lantern, Dolius."

Grousing that the good Lord had made men with knees so they could crouch down, the lad stood on tiptoe while Tom studied his findings: lines and lines of numbers, combinations of two digits, many of them carrying some kind of mark — an accent, a dot, an apostrophe. Unmistakably, a Spanish cypher!

"Master!" came another urgent hiss.

It was with nothing short of triumph that Tom grinned down at Skeres. "Lock up everything, Dolius." He waved the pages. "This is Stafford bound hand and foot!"

He kept the lantern, and began to commit what he could to memory, frowning at the rows of numbers, repeating them soundlessly.

Skeres was bustling from cabinet to cupboard. "Lord, Mr. Tom — but filch it!"

"And have Stafford know I've seen it?"

What the lad was grumbling, Tom neither knew nor cared, as he repeated number after number — until his chair tottered again, as the speeding Minotaur bumped into it, and then into the desk, making everything on it tinkle and totter.

"Skeres!" Tom hissed.

The lad reached to steady the hourglass, clumsy enough to brush it with his sleeve instead, and send it flying... Down to the floor the cursed thing fell, with the ring of a bell and a crash of shattering glass.

Jove fulminate clumsy servants!

"Quick!" In a trice Tom crammed the cyphered papers and the Virgil back inside the drawer, shoved it shut, pushed the mask into place, and leapt down from the chair, only to find Skeres gawping at the window.

"Wake up, you lack-wit! Have you locked everything?"

Was that a noise from beyond the parlour — from Stafford's bedroom? Tom caught Skeres by the arm and dragged him towards the door to the secretaries' room. It was like dragging an ox.

"Move, you fool —"

Of a sudden, Skeres shook free, and pointed to the window. "There's a creeper on the wall, ain't there?"

Oh Jove! The Minotaur gone witless — and just then someone called for Lyly. "But come away, devil pinch you!"

A furious shake of the head. "They've 'eard the rattle in 'ere." He ran to open the nearest window.

"What are you —?"

Words deserted Tom as Skeres flung a leg over the sill and eased himself outside.

"You go and 'ide," he hissed, and thrust one of his strange keys at Tom, the rest hanging from the ring. "After I'm gone, close this window, and lock the door."

In a heartbeat he was gone, and Tom leant out to see him scurrying down the climbing plant, huffing and panting... And then shouts erupted in the next room. Tom closed the window, hurried to snatch the lantern, and slid out to the secretaries' room. Now let the damn lock not clack too loudly...

A smashing of glass panes in the study cut that thought short, and a high-pitched shout of "*Tuez les Anglais*! sounded from the garden.

Lord be praised for quick-witted servants! Swallowing a laugh, Tom locked the door, ran for the stairs, and plunged down them just as a door upstairs was opened, and Lady Stafford called, "Don't be a ninny — raise Hobelot!"

Heart in his mouth, Tom flew down the last few steps. Just as he dove into the dark cranny behind the staircase, the maid Avison half-stumbled down with bare feet and loose hair, screeching like a magpie for Hobelot. Meanwhile, there was pounding and rattling upstairs — Lady Stafford seeking entry to her husband's rooms, and in the garden Skeres was shouting in his own voice for the runagates to come back. Then

Hobelot came running with a lantern, tearing at bar and bolts, and rushing out to the garden, and the maid cowered in a corner, and Stafford's voice thundered from upstairs, and there was candlelight, and shouts, and the whole household agog...

In blind haste, Tom shoved the lantern and the keys deep into the hollow under the stairs' foot, and undid his doublet.

The garden door stood wide open and unguarded, so that nobody observed Tom as he slipped out to join the confusion unnoticed: in the wildly dancing light of a few lanterns, half-dressed men and women were pouring from the gallery, running around and calling.

Tom reached the gate just as Skeres ran outside, followed by both the Cavel brothers in their nightshirts — Hobelot carrying his ancient pike. Tom glanced out. The street was dark and empty but for the three servants, the lantern staining the muddy ground yellow. They soon returned, Skeres lowering like a tyrant at the play.

"Two of them, there were!" he panted. "And another waiting outside —"

"Have you lost your wits?" Tom cut in, before the imaginary attackers became an army. "What were you thinking, going after them alone and unarmed?"

"Ay, well..." A modest shrug.

The servants were crowding around, shaking their heads, and exclaiming in admiration. The scullion Sally, it was worth noting, was armed with a spit, and there was an elderly man — the steward with a coldment, most likely — haggard-faced and muttering that the French were savages.

Then came a call: "Cavel!" and all looked up. Sir Edward Stafford, in a fur-trimmed nightgown, stood at the wrecked window of his study. "What was that?"

Adam Cavel raised his lantern. "Some men climbed inside, Master, and hurled stones. It was Mr. Abbot's man as caught them, and they climbed out again."

The flickering light from beneath aged Stafford's glowering face. "Don't shout from there, you idiot!" he chided. "Come upstairs, you and your brother!" And he was gone, leaving Grimeston to deal with the ruined window.

Because it would have been strange if Mr. Secretary's man, torn from his sleep by an assault on the Embassy, hadn't insisted on speaking to the Ambassador at once, that was what Tom did.

Making his way upstairs, he found Grimeston talking to the Cavels in the secretaries' room.

"Mr. Abbot!" The secretary abandoned the two servants at once, and hurried to block Tom's way. "Sir Edward is —"

"As aggrieved as I am, I'm sure." There was little point in playing the plain courier anymore, was there? Not if Gifford was right about Adam Cavel. "I'm sure you see that I must talk to him."

For a moment poor Grimeston stood his ground, staring at Tom, thinking perhaps of secret places in the study... Then he ducked his head. He would have gone to announce the visitor, but Tom stepped past him, and knocked on the door.

It was thrust open at once — by Stafford himself, dishevelled and thunderous.

"What do you want?" he barked.

Sparing a glance at Grimeston and the Cavel brothers — three gaping figures of Dismay, Astonishment, and Incomprehension — Tom said, as even as he knew how: "A word, please you, Mr. Ambassador."

Oh, it pleased him very little — see how his mouth worked — but truly, what could he do? Still he yielded with the worst grace: a grunt and the brusquest nod — and Tom entered the study for the second time that night.

How different it looked! The light of half a dozen candles gilded a scene of havoc: one window was broken, and a large stone lay on the floor amidst a shower of glinting glass pieces, while another sat at the foot of the writing table. Fates be thanked, it lay close enough to have hit it and caused the hourglass to fall where Lyly now crouched, picking up the pieces. Yes, Fates be thanked, and the Minotaur praised — for either his fine aim or his finer luck!

By the other door stood Lady Stafford in a blue dressing gown, her dark hair hanging down her shoulder in a braid. At the sight of Tom she moved away from the candle-branch on the mantelpiece, so that only half her face was lit.

"Mr. Walsingham," she said — neither greeting nor question.

Tom bowed, and waited for the shortest time for Stafford to beg his wife's pardon, to excuse Lyly, to suggest they spoke elsewhere... Not only did he do nothing of the sort, but Lyly rose from his crouch and went to stand at his master's elbow, staring ahead. With the Baroness on the other side, it was as plain a closing of ranks as could be.

It will always give you a fair advantage, Thomas, if you can do what your foe is not expecting. And, since these three so plainly expected browbeating hostility, let them have stunned disbelief instead.

"Is this a common occurrence, Sir?" he exclaimed, gaping at the disaster. "Ruffians assaulting your house at night?"

What effect hostility would have caused there was no telling; this other manner had Stafford in a fluster.

"You've seen what these mobs can do," he blurted. "This is how we live these days!"

And it was a quicksilver thing — but Tom caught the warning flash in Lady Stafford's eyes. A warning come too late?

"Yes, Sir — I've seen it. Twice in five days against your own house — and so much ill blood towards the English. It appears..." *It appears that matters here are rather worse than what you are pleased to write to Mr. Secretary. Are we to expect another St. Barthélemy?* But that would have cornered Stafford into owning himself either a fool or dishonest to his duty — and what would it help, besides alerting the man that he was under suspicion? Instead Tom shook his head, with the greatest show of dismay. "In truth, I don't know what to think. Surely the King's Justice..."

It worked well, for Stafford liked to see Mr. Secretary's upstart man at a loss.

"I'll write to the Royal Provost tomorrow," he assured, warming to his argument as he spoke. "And to the King himself. I'll request... I'll *demand* that more is done for the safety of Her Majesty's representative, and Her Majesty's subjects. I'll send to the Châtelet first thing in the morning."

Would he, though? The last thing Stafford wanted was for the French Court to regard him as trouble. But that was for Stafford to decide: what mattered was that he didn't seem inclined to question the night's doings. Fates send the Baroness, thin-lipped and marble-faced, was just as convinced; that she had not seen through what Tom hadn't said. As for Lyly... He stood by in silence, hooded eyes wary — much in the way of one watching a match of chess. And just as silent and aloof he remained as Tom bowed himself out.

At the last moment, Stafford called him back — as though he had remembered to be very severe.

"In one thing you're right, Walsingham," he said, one forefinger raised. "No lack of respect towards Her Majesty's Ambassador can be tolerated. And tolerate it I shall not."

And, not sure whether he was being warned or chided, Tom took his leave without another word.

Tom hurried to the kitchen and asked for a light. Skeres was there, basking in the women's admiration as he told the tale again. Tom hardly listened, all the time repeating to himself the numbers from the cyphered letters, and, as soon as he had a candle stump, he rushed up to his room. He was sitting on the bed, busy jotting down figures and marks — Jove, but the marks were hard! — when Skeres barged in, eyes alight.

"I've trampled the mud by the wall," he began in that breathy thunder he called a whisper, and stopped short when Tom waved him quiet, but only to walk close, crouch down, and begin again, a little softer. "Came and went twice to make it look like two men. Made a footprint on the wall, too —"

This time, Tom's hiss of impatience earned a spell of rumbling quiet — the quiet of deep offence — long enough to note down and double-check all that he remembered: ten lines and a half of a Spanish cypher. More lingered at the edge of his memory; he could almost see it if he closed his eyes... He added another line of figures, and another — but, curse it, it had slipped away as he'd spoken to Stafford, and the more he tried, the worse the numbers ran into each other. With a sigh, he left the last two lines unmarked. It would have to do. Hopefully, knowing where to seek the Latin key, Phelippes would have no trouble breaking it.

Only then did he grin at his pouting servant. "Nick Skeres, I'm sorry that I called you a lack-wit — tonight or ever."

Even in the candlelight, Skeres could be seen blushing. "Worse, you should call me! If I 'adn't smashed that cursed 'ourglass…"

But wonders never ceased! For all his bragging in the kitchen, behold: the Minotaur abashed.

And a sound scolding would have been in order, perhaps, but Tom was too relieved to do worse than scowl a little. "That's because you're a clumsy beast. But it might have ended in disaster — and you were quick enough of wit and foot that it did not. Stafford is complaining to the King that the Embassy isn't kept safe."

A grunt. "Not that it ain't true." And, dismissing his own faults and merits together, the lad jutted his chin at the page of scribbled numbers. "Is that what you were after?"

Was it, truly? Tom drummed his fingers on the paper. Of a sudden it seemed little enough to show for the risk they'd run. "It's not much — but it's a Spanish cypher, most surely, and now I'm sure that Arundel knew…"

"Spanish?" Skeres hit a triumphant fist to his thigh. "Lord love you, Master, then go to Stafford and tell 'im, 'Look what I've got 'ere, you lackey of Spain!'"

"I told you before: he'll say he's tricking Mendoza — and go cry to London that Mr. Secretary's men broke into his study at night like thieves."

"'E's the one doing things at night like thieves! What of those Spaniards you saw? And all the 'ugger-mugger with the book?"

"Yes, and Mr. Secretary will believe it, but there's no proving just what game Stafford is playing. Why, how do I prove that I was tricked out of the way the other night?"

"But you weren't tricked, and you saw them," Skeres cut in, with an air of much approving his master.

"Even *that*, Dolius, I cannot prove: my word against that of the Ambassador — who happens to be Burleigh's man, and step-cousin to the Queen!"

"Cuds-me!" the lad muttered, and plopped down onto his pallet. "Then all the make-a-do, what was it for?" And hear the reproach, as he pointed at the paper. "You called it 'Stafford bound 'and and foot'."

"Did I?" Tom swallowed a smile. "Perhaps I was a little eager — but it will be proof enough for Mr. Secretary. Who knows what Phelippes will find once he uncyphers it — but even if it's just the recipe for blancmange, it shows that Stafford has been conducting secret dealings with Mendoza when he was roundly told not to. Let him think he's doing it safely, and he'll pass on whatever Mr. Secretary feeds him."

"Whatever Mr. Sec'tary feeds 'im..." A slow grin spread across Skeres's face. "I've always said you weren't born no fool Mr. Tom!"

And how did one react to that, but with a laugh? "Why, thank you, Dolius. It must be a relief that you're not serving a complete dolt, after all." He folded the list and held it out. "Sew it into my cuff, will you?"

It was a mark of the Minotaur's uneasiness at his part in the night's doings that he began at once a task he despised. *'Tis women, tailors and sailors as sew*, was his constant complaint whenever he was forced to ply a needle. Tonight he snipped and stitched away with quiet alacrity, lips twisting as he worked at the doublet's cuff.

It would make a good enough hiding place until Skeres left for London — which Tom had no intention of discussing with the lad, who was bound to protest. Yet, things had come to a point where Sir Francis must be advised. And he must know that perhaps — just perhaps — there were the means to rearrange the balance with Lord Burleigh. As he prepared for bed, Tom composed in his mind the letter he would send to his great cousin: Stafford *in primis*, with his lies and his Spanish venture — and a chance of murder; then Gifford — a lost cause if ever there was one; and last Arundel, whose death might have been natural, but for the murder of Pierre Jourdain... A weighty letter enough, and one that he'd better code, if not cypher. But were his own cyphers safe, now that Gifford's had been found and broken? It was with this matter going round in his head that he went to bed, and he was still sluggishly debating it with himself when Skeres called to him in a hiss sharp enough to startle him, wanting to know what had become of his ring of keys.

It was a moment before Tom remembered and, having remembered, drew in a sharp breath. "Oh, curse it: I hid them under the stairs, and the lantern too. You'll have to recover them tomorrow, and get rid of them."

"Get rid of them!" the lad exclaimed. "Do you know what they cost?"

And trust Nick Skeres to think of that! "Put it in your expenses and throw them into the Seine. I won't be caught with a dark lantern and a bunch of false keys." Tom propped himself up on his elbow to glare with more efficacy. "And neither will you."

There was a sniff. "Ain't no wonder that you're up to your ears in debt. A spendthrift, Mr. Tom — that's what you are!"

Not bothering to answer, Tom drew the blankets up to his ears, and fell asleep to mutterings about the cost of things.

He awoke in darkness, dragging himself out of a dream in which Lyly was sewing the note with the Spanish cypher inside a cuff that was made of fur, like that of Stafford's nightgown

— and, as he did so, he stitched the sleeve closed at the wrist. A most foolish dream, he thought, and curled on his side with every intention of going back to sleep — only sleep wouldn't come, banished by that image of Lyly stitching and stitching...

William Lyly, this most devoted of secretaries by all appearances and by the Reverend Hakluyt's account, Stafford's right-hand man. *William* to the Ambassador, trusted so well as to excite Grimeston's jealousy, privy to all of Stafford's less wise hazards, sternly loyal...

Or was he?

Gifford wasn't alone in doubting the falsehood of Lyly's Catholic allegiance, and there had been the matter of Mary Stuart's pension... All of it a dangerous pretence in the service of England, according to Stafford — but how shrewd could the Ambassador's judgment be? For one thing, he hadn't known of Lyly's closeness to Arundel; for another, he'd been unaware of the Scottish pension, and if it was true that Mary Stuart was dead now, there remained her English friends — the Pagets among them.

The glass pieces in Tom's mind shifted into a new pattern, one where Lyly was the Pagets' man more than he was Stafford's. Intimate with Arundel, Jourdain had called him, and it was true that Arundel and the younger Paget had been at each other's throats more often than not — but who was to say that Lyly couldn't have become intimate with Arundel and friendly with Stafford better to spy on both?

This duplicitous Lyly could have warned Paget of Gifford's arrest, passed on whatever Stafford learnt of the confiscated papers, and discovered Arundel's panicked attempts at buying himself back into the Queen's favour at all costs. And certainly he'd had the chance to kill Arundel for the Pagets — either to poison him in the first place, or to finish him off when he took ill. And, of course, he could very well have told Paget of Mr. Secretary's man's interest in Jourdain, if not of the appointed meeting at the Cordeliers.

Tom sat up. Even after finding that the Pagets had been at the Cordeliers at the very moment of Jourdain's death, the timing had bothered him. Would they have decided to have the poor man killed on the spot, after just glimpsing him in conversation with a stranger? But if Lyly had warned them, then the matter was very different.

Again, none of it could be proved, and yet it made the Pagets — and Lyly with them — more likely murderers than Sir Edward Stafford.

CHAPTER 13

In the end Stafford did send to the Châtelet first thing in the morning. He sent Lyly with a letter for the *Prévôt Royal* — whose contents Tom would have loved to read — and Lyly wasn't happy, when he emerged from that fortress of grim towers and bleak walls, to find Tom waiting for him.

He checked by the *barrière des sergeants*, eyes darting around.

Oh Jupiter... Tom sauntered close, one brow raised. "You're never thinking to run, are you?" he asked.

Skeres was right: Lyly never looked one in the eye.

It seemed gruesomely fitting that the meat markets should sit right in the shadow of the King's great prison — with blood fouling the air, and staining the mud underfoot. Lyly's gaze stopped on something in the distance, and Tom glanced around to see a butcher's lad emptying a basketful of offal right into the street.

Still staring at the grisly heap, the secretary gave a sigh. "What do you want to hear?" he asked.

"Arundel's death, again," Tom said, earning a huff, and a slumping of French-caped shoulders.

"Walsingham's hound, sniffing murders everywhere... I've told you all I know, and maladies happen in this world. Now, I must go to the *Hôtel de Ville*."

He strode away without a by-your-leave, and Tom followed him into a narrow, stinking street.

"Maladies happen, yes. And so do poisonings." A sideways glance revealed Lyly quiet and glum. "I don't know that I believed it, when your master wrote of it — but then Maître

Jourdain was killed, murdered beyond doubt. I'm sure you see that changes the way of things."

"Why? Couldn't that poor fellow have been killed for other reasons?"

"So soon after Arundel's death?"

"Why not?" Lyly glowered at the filthy alley, the crooked houses with rot in their timbering, men and women scuttling about like rats. "You know, as a boy, back in England, when I thought of Paris, I used to imagine a city of great beauty, a place of elegance, refinement, and learning, glowing under a perpetual sun." He gave a hoarse little laugh. "Never once did I account for winter, and for the works of war and intolerance."

Having seen some of it these past days, Tom couldn't help a mirthless huff. "Most Catholics here would gladly dunk all Protestants in the Seine — starting with the English."

"True, but most Protestants are no better. You've seen for yourself how little it takes to spark off havoc, on one side or the other."

Reaching the large street that led to the Pont Notre-Dame, they picked their way across, and Lyly took from his sleeve a kerchief — a perfumed kerchief he held before his nose as they dove into another, even narrower, darker alley, where the jetties of the rickety houses all but touched overhead.

Any temptation Tom could have had to sneer at the notion vanished with the first breath he took — the stench of piss was so strong it caught in his throat and stung his eyes. A street of tanners... And, in the unspeakable mire, two urchins were tormenting a lame cat, and the little girl who tried to protect the creature. It was more than Tom could help to box the nearest bully on the ear.

"Leave her alone!" he shouted.

The children fled — the girl one way, scooping up the cat, and the boys the other, stopping at a safe distance to jeer "*Anglais! Anglais!*"

When they showed a propensity to fling mud together with the insults, Tom put his hand to his rapier's hilt, and the two little ruffians ran, yelling "*Kill the English*" at the top of their lungs. They were still cackling in the distance when, without so much as a cry of "*Gare-à-l'eau*", a window banged open, and a chamber-pot was emptied, sending Tom and Lyly scampering out of harm's way.

It was a relief to emerge into the open vastness of the *Place de Grève*, with its fine half-timbered houses all around, the stately City Hall with the builders' scaffolding, the seagulls keening in the grey sky, and the Seine on one side, blowing its cold breath inside Paris. Numberless Parisians went about their business like ants in the stone-flagged Place proper, but the long, muddy slope that descended towards the river was somewhat emptier at that hour, with rows of boats moored in the water, and the bales of goods piled along the bank. Lyly led the way there, stopping well away from a clutch of men unloading hay from a barge and onto a cart.

"For the Provost's stables," he murmured, and then jerked his head towards the tanners' street they'd just left. "Children and elderly, men and women... You see how it is. Your physician could have died just because he found himself where he was."

"That being a church where many English traitors worship. Including the Pagets."

At the name, Lyly stiffened. "Yes, many go to the Cordeliers, and just as many hear Mass elsewhere."

"But, you see, many others weren't there as Lord Paget was, not a dozen steps away when the murder was done."

This made the secretary whip around. "And you think...?" He stopped, shaking his head. "But what a mindless thing to do, to have a man killed right before him."

"He may have had little choice, if he wanted to silence Jourdain before he told me what he should not. And ever since I've been wondering who might both have warned His Lordship about me, and had the means of poisoning Arundel. I'll confess it's taken me a foolishly long time to think of you."

All colour drained from Lyly's face. "Of *me*!"

"You were a good deal closer to Arundel than you owned to me or to Sir Edward. Poor Jourdain told me, and also that servant, Faulkes... A very fine way to spy on him to the last!"

Lyly spun on his heel and stalked away a few steps with a bitter laugh, loud enough that the men with the hay cart turned around.

This was becoming far too public. Tom took the fool by the arm, and steered him away towards the river. "Are you mad?" he hissed, and stopped short when he caught a glistening of tears.

Poor Lyly was distraught, Jourdain had said. *It's in his arms that Monsieur Arundel died.* "An intimate friend —"

Lyly cut right through. "Intimate — yes!" There was a quiver to the ragged whisper. "It's one way of describing what he was to me. A great sin, you'll be thinking..."

Great, and ugly, and... Tom was surprised at how faint, how far away the voices of his upbringing sounded — worn thin through his Service years. "That's between you and God — none of my business, for sure. Unlike treason and murder."

"You think I'd kill him? Poison him and watch him suffer?"

The retort stayed in Tom's throat. Would Lyly know how to pretend that tearful fury? And, even more, would he pretend sodomy, which was a great danger in France, and an added weapon for Mr. Secretary's man?

Then again, perhaps the fellow *was* addled in his head, for the next thing he said was: "But then, I did kill him."

There. Just in case he hadn't compromised himself enough. Tom blinked, trying to gather his rather scattered thoughts into some reasoned order.

"You killed him — but not by poison?" he warily asked.

"Oh, curse poison!" Lyly choked out. "I wish I knew where you got this notion of poison, besides from Sir Edward's letter. Is this what Hennett says?"

"He isn't sure. Nobody can be, he said."

Another of those sobbing laughs. "That's where he's wrong. I can be sure, because I know where Arundel caught what killed him. Whether it was the purple ague or something else I don't know, but there was much of it in … in a place where we went. That was two days before he fell ill; he caught it, and I did not…" He faltered to a halt.

Well, there was no blaming him, was there? Not for wanting to keep some ragged semblance of secrecy. For the rest … well. "Only, you couldn't tell, because it would reveal that you were with him when and where you should not have been."

Lyly nodded and stood there, watching as the men with the hay, having finished their work, dispersed — some trudging up the slope with the cart, the others back to the barge — exchanging cheerful greetings. When he spoke again, his voice was raw. "And now, awake and asleep, I never cease cursing my fear, and tormenting myself: had I talked, perhaps he could have been saved?" He turned his back on Tom and covered his eyes, sobbing quietly.

Distraught indeed — not that it made him innocent, except of Arundel's murder, whatever guilt he heaped on his own head.

And yet, supposing it was true, and Arundel hadn't been poisoned...

"Then what of Jourdain?"

Lyly whipped around like one bitten.

"What of him?" he asked through gritted teeth. "I tell you, there was no murder he could have witnessed, and no need for anyone to silence him, or for me to warn anyone that he could talk to you."

"All of it very well — supposing you're not lying. Oh, never look so incensed, Lyly. It wouldn't be the first time, would it?"

"I told you why —"

"You told me why you wouldn't dispute the poison, yes. What of John Faulkes, though?"

"Faulkes?"

And, Jupiter rain on him, the dolt backed away, shoulders poised for flight. Did he truly think that running would help him?

Tom took a step forward, just in case. "Arundel's English servant. The man you hardly noticed. And yet he knows you quite well, and when Lady Stafford wouldn't hire him, it was your help that he sought." A piece of glass shifted. *He even managed somehow to interest Mr. Lyly in his case*, the Baroness had said — and this, more than anything else, spoke for the secretary's truthfulness. "Does he know of you and Arundel?"

There was a piece of rotting wood half-buried in the coarse sand. Mouth working, Lyly crushed it under his toe. "Damn him — damn him!" he snarled. "He said he'd ruin me for a sodomite, since I was already uncovered as a traitor. Sodomy ... they hang and burn you for it, here. I tried, and Her

Ladyship wouldn't hear of it, and still Faulkes pressed and pressed... That's when it occurred to me that he must be a spy."

"Whose?"

"The Pagets', I thought — and was fool enough to tell him so. Oh, he laughed in my face, but he wasn't happy. He said that I must never speak ill of him, that he would know if I did, for he has a friend under Sir Edward's roof..."

Ah, there went again Faulkes's friend — someone placed at the Embassy by the same people who had found Faulkes for Arundel. And therefore not the Pagets, for, even if there were a *Madame*, Arundel would never want a servant openly sent by them. But from the Guise? What if Jourdain's *Madame* turned out to be a Guise lady, even *Madame* de Montpensier herself? A she-devil, Stafford had called her. Tom wanted to laugh: poor Stafford, worrying about what Gifford might say, when he was beset by spies from all quarters in his own house!

Just as Gifford had said, come to think of it — or at least in part, for it was hard to imagine Grimeston as a man of evil life. Yet, if so much about Lyly was true...

"Tell me this, Lyly: Sir Edward is kicking out Adam Cavel, isn't he?"

The secretary had been waiting as Tom thought — waiting and watching, but this took him aback.

How do you know? He wasn't quick enough in masking surprise under a frown. "On the grounds of Gifford's lies?"

Which was answer enough, in its own way — and lo! as soon as suspicion of the coachman was seeded, *Madame* had tried to replace him at the Embassy with Faulkes... Now Stafford ought to be warned, surely? Not through Lyly, though, who still waited for an answer, and wouldn't have one.

"Go on your errand," Tom ordered instead. "And, Lyly, I'd keep quiet in your place: I know enough to make your life a misery in half a dozen ways."

A slow shake of the head. "And you such an obedient mouse, in your cousin's shadow!" Lyly held Tom's gaze for once. "You make much bolder with his authority than in his presence."

Devil pinch the fellow's gall! Tom made himself hold the bitter glare — and Fates send he didn't blush. In the end, with a muffled curse, the secretary strode away. Malicious dog!

Unus ... duo ... tres ... quattuor...

It took some counting in Latin before Tom brought his mind back to the cold reasoning he needed — for, unless Lyly was the finest play-actor in England and France, it seemed very possible that nothing more sinister than sickness had killed Charles Arundel.

It was a relief of sorts — and yet there remained the death of Pierre Jourdain, made all the more mysterious now that it was unmoored from Arundel's.

Leaning back on his heels, arms crossed, Tom took a great breath of river air, and tried to think of accident, and chance, and causeless mishap. No matter how hard he tried, though, no matter how he whittled away all that could have just happened for no reason, two facts remained: one, the physician had been stabbed while talking to Tom; and two, the Pagets had been there.

Tom had already pulled the bell at the Embassy's door before it occurred to him that there was a third fact, that might or might not bear on the Cordeliers: John Faulkes was a spy, although a considerably clumsy one, who had betrayed himself to Lyly, and failed to worm his way into Stafford's household.

And Faulkes had known Jourdain. What was more, Jourdain had known Faulkes, known him as an Englishman recently sent by *Madame*. What was to say that Cavel hadn't warned Faulkes about Tom's inquiries?

He'd just decided to pay another visit at the Hôtel d'Hercule when the door was opened — but not by Hobelot. In his place stood the elderly steward Tom had seen last night, all smiles and bows, and more than a little deaf. Hobelot was attending Her Ladyship, the fellow said.

"It takes strong young men to move chests, eh, Master?"

At least the Cavels hadn't been turned out yet, Tom thought, as he extricated himself from the old man's cordiality, and then, shoving away the thought of poor Hobelot out of roof and work, he made his way to the Rue des Augustins.

The same haughty porter admitted Tom to the flagged hall, his vexed countenance belying the pretence of not remembering him, and answered his request by announcing that Jean Faucon didn't belong to the house.

"He did, the other day."

"Yes, *Monsieur*, and then yesterday morning his kinsman came with tidings that Faucon's father had died, and he must go home at once."

And why Tom should be surprised, he didn't know. "I didn't know that he had kin in Paris."

Still less surprising was to hear that the kinsman was a huge young man, with hair the colour of ginger.

"He'd come here before. He had many English visitors, had Jean Faucon," sniffed the porter — to whom, plainly, the loss of Faulkes was no great hardship to the household.

Well, there went any hope of finding the fellow again. It was in some annoyance that Tom left, carrying with him the impression that Hercules mocked him from his perch over the lintel, and the belated confirmation of what he'd already suspected: Adam Cavel was Faulkes's friend at the Embassy and, as Gifford had said, another spy for the Queen's enemies. Jupiter, but, for a traitor, Edward Stafford must be the greatest gudgeon on this earth!

Debating with himself the need to warn the Ambassador and the usefulness of questioning Cavel, Tom turned his steps towards the Embassy again. He hadn't gone far, picking his way through the mud amidst the usual hubbub of passers-by, begowned students, barrows, running children, stray dogs, and beggars, when he found himself at the mouth of the Rue de la Serpente, with Joyce Blundell's door in sight. He squinted up at the windows: was Anne Gawdy there, frail and wild-eyed, curling and uncurling her thin hands? The more he thought back to that rather extraordinary supper, the more he felt convinced that it had not been Lady Gawdy, and much less young Clement, who had issued the invitation, but their Cousin Joyce, who had been talking to Lord Paget at the Cordeliers.

The Pagets, the Guise, the Queen Mother through Lady Stafford, who was so keen on keeping Tom away from Faulkes and from the Framlinghams — or from Joyce Blundell, after all? And then Mendoza, about whose cyphers Arundel had been ranting...

Devil take it, what a tangle! *Consider the joints and flexures of a matter*, was Sir Francis's constant advice — but here there was nothing of the sort, for every answer only added more knots, each tighter than the last. How did that Roman history go? *Several knots, all so tightly entangled that it was impossible to see how they were fastened.*

Tom had always loved the tale of the Gordian knot — not the one where Alexander cut through it with a sword, but the story where he pulled out the linchpin to find the cord's end, and undid the knot.

Well, unlike the fugitive Faulkes, Joyce Blundell was one linchpin he could try, and so he made his way towards the sign of the Three Ships: Alexander tackling the Knot, and feeling all the better for a little ancient history in his mind...

Only, he was sure, the linchpin had never jumped out to meet Alexander the way Joyce Blundell did, appearing on her threshold when Tom was still a dozen steps away. Which was a good thing, for that ancient linchpin hadn't been in league with a pack of possible murderers the way this woman was, no matter how primly she descended the steps, followed by her servant-boy carrying a basket...

And surely the Great Alexander never stopped before the linchpin like one who, going about his business, had come across an acquaintance in the street.

"Why, 'tis Mistress Blundell. Good day, Mistress."

She stopped short, flaxen brows drawing together under her coif and plain hat, as she curtsied. There was little cordiality in her even voice. "Mr. Abbot. You weren't coming to visit?"

"I wouldn't presume, Mistress. I was just passing by, and never thought... But yes." Tom squinted at the sign. "There are your ships. Places always look different by day."

She'd peered up at her own windows as he spoke; now she turned briskly. "You'll forgive me, Master. I'm on my house errands."

She made to walk away, but Tom kept abreast with her. "You'll let me escort you a while, Mistress. These are unquiet times, and I don't like to think of you alone in the streets."

That she'd be just as alone on her way back, that she had her servant with her, that she went about Paris on every unquiet day — it all flitted across her countenance. In the end she just nodded, and took off at as fast a clip as her wooden pattens would allow, lips pressed together in a manner that said: *then suit yourself, and be merry.*

They hadn't gone far, though, before she had to slow down to wind her way around a press of women at a baker's door.

"Paris has grown such that we never know, from one day to the next, what shopkeepers will procure," she said. "And at what price."

It was an all but unmannerly thing to say to one who had so recently eaten at her table. Tom ignored the brusqueness.

"The whole of France is simmering, it seems to me. Hardly the first time — and, I fear, not the last, with these Lords of Guise ever stirring discontent." He checked, as though catching himself in a blunder. "Your pardon, Mistress Blundell. You're Catholic, I think? Your notions of who stirs discontent won't be mine."

In her pattens she was as tall as Tom, so she didn't have to look up to frown at him. "No, they're not, although…" Having passed by the crowd at the baker's she resumed her fast pace, the servant trotting at her heels, and Tom at her side.

"*Although*," he echoed, "you'd like to know how I learnt of your faith? I saw you attending the Epiphany Mass at the Cordeliers, the other day."

Not being one for sideways glances, Joyce Blundell gave him a full, round-eyed stare. "*You* were there?"

"Only to meet a physician called Pierre Jourdain. Perhaps you knew him? He, too, used to worship at the Cordeliers."

Could it be that she had gone pale? Yes, and she looked away, although she covered it with a pretence of greeting a passerby.

"The one who was killed in the brawl?" she asked, and the evenness was forced. "Lord rest his soul. So you see, it's not just the Catholics playing havoc."

"Lord Paget will agree with you on this, I'm sure..." *I'm hunting the murtherer, villains come hither!* Ah well, if Joyce Blundell was a villain, this was naught she didn't know already.

And, whatever she knew, she was no fool. She stopped at the corner of the crossroads — just under the shrine that presided over it — and levelled at Tom one of those frank gazes of hers.

"Yes, Mr. Abbot, I'm known to His Lordship. He is good to me, as he is to many of us who left England behind, following the dictates of conscience."

"You will admit, Mistress, that it's a strange conscience that will dictate treason and regicide..."

The grey eyes flashed for a moment — and then the anger was gone, replaced by a curious agitation. "You're young," Joyce Blundell said at length. "You've only known a Protestant England — but think of living where your faith must be kept hidden, and each Sunday you must betray your conscience or go to ruin. Wouldn't you seek a place where you can worship openly and freely? Where all can do so — for the Huguenots enjoy this liberty in France."

"Until your Lords of Guise give orders that they be massacred in houses, palaces and streets," Tom snapped, and half-regretted it when her face creased in sadness.

"I was a child here in Paris on the night of Saint Bartholomew," she said. "In the horror of it, my mother's Huguenot brothers threw us out of the house, in fear that sheltering my English father would bring on them a greater danger. A Catholic neighbour took us in, and a Catholic midwife, a stranger, saved my mother when she miscarried a baby that night."

Sir Francis's bitter stories of Saint Bartholomew crowded Tom's mind, and Frances's memories, child that she'd been in her father's Paris house. And yet... "You call me young, Mistress, but I'm old enough to know that good and evil are never all on one side."

It was almost in anguish that she burst out: "No, they are not — nor charity, nor right, nor truth, nor virtue, nor the contrary of all those things. We're not all traitors, thirsting for blood and revenge!"

For a moment they stared at each other in the middle of the street — the servant-boy gripping the basket to his chest, eyes darting between his mistress and the stranger.

"Does Lord Paget agree with you on this, too?" Tom asked under his breath.

To this there was no answer. Joyce Blundell held his gaze a moment longer, lips pressed together, then pointed at a shop across the street.

"There is my poulterer," she said. "You need have no concern for me now."

Not *for* her, perhaps, but *about* her? Tom bowed a little, and she, with a brisk curtsey, crossed the street and entered the shop that, Tom would have wagered, wasn't her poulterer at all.

He hied himself back to the Embassy, all the way trying to untangle perplexity from perplexity. And, most vexing, he couldn't shake Joyce Blundell's question: if his own faith were all but forbidden, how would he choose between it and his loyalty to the Queen? So taken with it was he that he hardly acknowledged Hobelot, back in his place at the door. In fact, he only remarked on it when he met the old steward in the hall. The man bowed, and smiled with such a manner of acquaintance, it would have been rude to walk by without stopping.

"You don't remember me, do you, Mr. Thomas?" the old man asked with a chuckle, loud in the way of the deaf. "It's been a long while, and I grow old."

The deep-set eyes in the thin face, the domed forehead, the stoop to the tall frame... "Why, surely..." Tom cast about in his mind for a name.

"But I remember you, Master, from back in Sir Henry's days. Then we saw no more of you — but you were never one to remain just a courier."

It was the Devon in the old man's speech that jogged Tom's memory: Ambassador Henry Cobham had called him his majordomo. "Osgoode, is it?"

The old man chuckled. "Ah, you do remember, then. I knew you when you arrived, but what with all the ado... I'm glad you haven't gone before I could greet you."

Osgoode, yes. A personage of importance in the household, but kindly.

"You were always tolerant of us young fellows," Tom remembered. "Are you well recovered now? I heard that you were ill, though I didn't know it was you." He had to repeat it louder.

"It's good of you to ask, Master. Maître Hennert called it a coldment, but..." Osgoode sobered, his face changing like day and night without the smile. "I think it was those bullies at the gate that discomposed my humours. That poor young lady chased in the streets — and then last night again! Paris was a kinder place when you were here, eh?"

"A little, yes, from what I've seen," Tom said, and would have gone his way, but Osgoode caught him by the sleeve.

"And is the poor lady recovered? She trembled so, when I helped her to the bench! And the poor gentleman, too. Hit with a stone, was he?"

It occurred to Tom that he'd never inquired after Clement's injury. "They were both quite well, when I saw them last."

This eased old Osgoode's mind. "Good, good," he said. "It must have been a great comfort to have a kinsman with them."

Much as he wondered what comfort brisk Joyce Blundell would be, Tom said, "A kinswoman, in truth — but yes, I'm sure it was." And he repeated it a little louder when Osgoode's high forehead creased in puzzlement.

"A kinswoman, Master? Good for them if they have one — though it's of yourself that I was thinking."

"Myself!"

"Well, yes. Aren't Lady Gawdy and her brother Walsinghams like yourself?"

"No, they…" Tom stopped short, seeing again Clement's awkward manner and his sister's coldness on the morning after their arrival. "Framlingham is what they're called."

Poor Osgoode's face fell again. "My stupid old ears!" he moaned. "I caught it wrong, Master — but, what with you being here, I thought…"

"And they never corrected you?"

"Why, no…" A frown. "With the lady I hardly spoke. It was to her brother that I talked a little, as I led him upstairs. Oh, I fear that I called him Mr. Walsingham, then, and told him of how I'd known his cousin when he wasn't older than himself…"

Oh Lord… "And he said nothing?"

"He just stared, all befuddled — but then, poor gentleman, what with that stone he'd taken to the head…"

"So perhaps he didn't understand you well, when you called him Walsingham."

Tugging at his earlobe, Osgoode thought well before answering. "I can't say that he did, not for certain — but when I asked whether they'd travelled all the way from England with their cousin, he made me ask again…" Of a sudden, the majordomo turned grey. "Goodness above, Mr. Thomas, I'm a babbling old fool! Have I spoken out of turn? But, Master, they'd arrived with you, and I thought…"

A babbling old fool indeed! And he so discreet and precise back in Ambassador Cobham's days… Jove rain on ageing servants! But then, it was all of a piece with Stafford's twopenny household.

"It's nothing, Osgoode." Swallowing a rebuke, Tom dismissed the old man with a suggestion that there was no need for Sir Edward to know.

And, when the majordomo had scurried away, very thankful, and more relieved than he had a right to be, Tom sat at the foot of the stairs, leant back against the carved column, and contemplated several things in a new and most dismaying light.

Clement Framlingham — and most likely his sister — had known who Tom was for a week, and pretended to call him Abbot all the time. Did Cousin Joyce know as well? Of course she did, and the knowledge had prompted that unpleasant supper. Tom went back to that evening, raking his brains for what he'd said that shouldn't have gone back to the Pagets — and although he remembered nothing alarming in his own words, he found much in those of his hosts, Lady Gawdy's most of all, that should have alerted him, and had not. Why, even Joyce Blundell's conversation, not an hour ago, now took a very different meaning…

"Are you unwell, Master?"

Tom startled out of his recriminations to find Hobelot peering at him uncertainly from the garden door.

"I'm not, thank you." With as much dignity as a man can muster who has been caught slouching on the stairs and brooding, Tom rose, and almost bit his tongue as a thought occurred to him of the hollow under the step: had he been sitting on the thieving tools from last night?

And, while I escaped discovery at the moment, Sir, the next day I all but led Stafford's people to where my false keys were hidden — oh, and a thieves' lantern too… It was a good thing that guileless Hobelot had surprised him, for another might have noticed the blood rushing to Tom's cheeks. But no suspicion disturbed the doorman's placidness as he held out a folded paper tied with string.

"A lad brought this for you."

"What lad?" Thinking of Joyce Blundell's young servant, Tom snatched the paper and undid the knot. On the outside it bore the name of *Thomas Abbot, Esq.*; inside were three lines, carefully penned in French.

There are things that you ignore and instead should know, it read. *If you would learn them, come alone tonight after dark to the church of Saint Eustache, by the market of les Halles, where the chapels are being built.*

That there was no signature came as no great wonder.

"You said a lad brought it? A servant?" Tom asked, and Hobelot's round face scrunched up in thought.

"A small lad." He gestured at a height just below his hip. "A beggar urchin, or the like, all rags. He threw the letter at me, and ran like the wind."

The sort anyone could hire for a *double*, and would never be found again to answer questions.

Well, here was something: were the ends of the cord to this knot of knots showing at last?

Skeres laughed bitterly on being told the gist of the letter, as they partook of bread and cheese in the empty kitchen.

"I'm not even asking," he groused. "A good thing that I didn't throw ... well, you know what I didn't throw into the river."

Which set at rest, at least, one recent worry: the lad's telltale possessions had been recovered, if not disposed of. A servant's due obedience, of course, was another matter.

"You're a disgrace, Nick Skeres. What if they're found? What have you done with them?"

At times the Minotaur had this way of looking at Tom as though he were an innocent. "You worry none, Mr. Tom. You'll be glad we 'ave what we 'ave, come night." He peered over both shoulders in turn. "For, mind, you're never going alone."

"What if I say that I am? Will you disobey again?" Tom held up a silencing forefinger. "And spare me the sermon on my sparrow's wits — for yes, you're coming, but not coming along. You'll follow at a safe distance."

A grunt. "Ay, *safe*! I mislike this 'ugger-mugger, say what you will."

Not that he liked it very much himself, Tom thought, as he cut another wedge of Stafford's middling cheese. "What I will say, is that I'm very curious, and you won't spoil it by scaring our man away. Or our woman." He took the note out of his sleeve, and held it to the rushlight's sickly flame, peering for the dozenth time at the neat handwriting.

"Lady Gawdy's cousin?" Skeres asked, craning his neck to study the few lines.

"Well, there aren't that many people here in Paris who know me as Abbot." Tom counted on his fingers. "Joyce Blundell, Lady Gawdy, young Clement; the whole household here; Maître Hennert; Faulkes, wherever he is now ... also Commissaire Langlois and a sergeant or two."

"Ay — and those Pagets, and Adkin Cavel's *Madame*, as like as not — and Lord knows who it is they all 'ave told!" Skeres tore off a bite of bread and chewed it as though it had done him wrong. "And one of them's the murtherer."

There was that, yes — but was it likely? Tom was about to vent his doubts when a kick to the shin under the table stopped him. The change in Skeres's face alone would have been more than enough to achieve the same effect: see how the lad glowed — if in splotches — beaming most tenderly at someone beyond Tom's back.

"Salkin, chuck!" he called, gulping around his mouthful of bread.

And see how the scullion blushed, eyes on the floor, bobbing a curtsey and then another as she crossed the kitchen in haste.

"Please you, Master," she said. "I'm sent to fetch..." She disappeared into the scullery, while Skeres still coughed up breadcrumbs.

"You'll choke yourself, Dolius!" Tom slapped the lad between the shoulders.

A moment later young Sally reappeared carrying an empty pail, and curtsied herself out awkwardly — a progress Skeres followed with calf-like, if teary-eyed, tenderness. The Minotaur in romance — or was he?

As soon as Sally had gone, the lad favoured Tom with a most severe scowl. "Now don't go thinking things, Master: she can't write."

Not that Tom had ever thought the girl a spy, and much less a stabber of physicians.

"Loyal of you," he observed, for she hadn't so much as looked at poor Skeres in return for his pains.

Shrugging one shoulder, the lad took another bite of bread. "Still pining away over Adkin, she is," he muttered. "She's taken to saying she drove 'im away 'erself, what with talking to me."

"Don't you think it's just as well? We'll be off to London again, as soon as we find this murderer."

"Unless 'e finds you first tonight, when you go a-wandering 'alf-alone in this Saint Whatyoucallit."

"A very cheerful thought, Skeres, thank you. But in truth, it would be very foolish to lure me all the way to Saint Eustache to kill me. If they meant to dump me in the Seine, there are plenty of more convenient places. The river stairs, for one, or the ports, or…"

"Or else, they'll dump you in some 'ole they've dug, bury you under those chapels as they're building, and who's to know?"

"You'll know!" Tom tapped the unsigned note. "You'll have this, and the cypher, and know what to tell Mr. Secretary."

With a snort, Skeres leant low across the table, jabbing a forefinger on the greasy wood before Tom as he spoke in a hoarse whisper.

"Ay, so 'e'll send someone else to find who did away with you, and you'll be dead all the same. And 'Is 'Onour'll want me 'ide for letting you walk into their arms, and right 'e'll be, and 'Er Ladyship will break 'er 'eart!"

Well now … the Minotaur protective! "Are you finished?" Tom asked, and Skeres blinked, snapped his mouth shut, and coloured from the neck up.

"'Tis just —"

"'Tis just that you worry and I need watching — I know, or I'd never hold with your boorish ways, but truly!" Tom huffed, half-impatient and half-amused. "I won't be alone, not with you there within hearing. Besides, I'll wager you: whoever waits for me at Saint Eustache, it won't be Jourdain's murderer."

The chiding had been half-hearted enough that Skeres took heart again. "Why not?" he wanted to know. "'Tis not like you've asked your questions in secret. Why, it only lacks for the town-crier to shout it at the crossroads!"

"And, because of that, what would killing me help? Unless the murderer thinks I've told no one what I have found out."

"Ay, and who is it that you've told? Meself, you've told — for you can't trust a soul in 'ere — and there's far too many people as know that — that corner-creeping Lyly of yourn, for one!"

And this couldn't be quite discounted, for, besides what one knew, there always was the matter of what others thought one knew. "Careful, Dolius: if you're right, then you're next after me. Still, if it *is* Lyly, he's betraying himself, and if it's not, can I discount the chance to learn something I don't know?"

Humming discontentedly, Skeres picked up the letter, turning it this way and that. "But who is it?"

"Faulkes, for one, or anyone from Stafford's household who wouldn't like —" Tom broke off as the cook entered, Hobelot following with a large basket — more escort than carrier, surely, it being another sign of the times that few in Paris went to buy food alone.

Whether Skeres was right or not, he'd given Tom a thought. Once in the little room upstairs, he ordered the lad to unstitch the Spanish cypher out of the cuff, while he sat and wrote the belated letter to Sir Francis. It took some work, for there was much to say, and most of it still vague enough to require a good deal of guesswork and explanation — and, in the end, it seemed prudent to code it all.

Meanwhile, he sent a grumbling Skeres out to buy a pair of lined gloves and, by the time the lad came back, Tom had his coded letter, the Spanish cypher, and the unsigned note ready and folded small.

"Sew them inside the gloves," he instructed, and, when this was done, the gloves were as good as butchered, but they would do.

Armed with them, Tom went in search of Grimeston and, as luck would have it, found him in the room above the gallery that he shared with the chaplain, busy at one of those small writing desks where one worked standing, pushed by the window for the sake of light.

He hunched his shoulders at the sight of Tom, and, with a smile so brittle it was painful, held out the book he'd been reading: *Histoire de Portugal.*

"A most interesting book," the poor fellow stammered. "I borrowed it from Mr. Hakluyt. A French translation from the Portuguese, most interesting, truly — and I thought I'd try my hand at turning some passages into English..."

"Mr. Grimeston..."

The smile fell, and the secretary put down the book. "There was another letter this morning," he muttered. "Our friend had a visitor. Paget." This last barely a murmur.

"I know," Tom said. "I was there, but couldn't hear as well as I would have liked. A copy would..."

Catching his breath, Grimeston shook his head in a frenzy. "I don't dare! After last night —"

Oh Jove — all they lacked now was for the man to lose his head! "A most unpleasant affair, yes," Tom said. "Is Mr. Ambassador very discomposed?"

The purple cheeks quivered. "He sent Lyly to the Châtelet this morning, with a letter for the Provost."

"So he said last night, though how the Provost can find again three drunken fanatics in the whole of Paris, I don't know. Unless Mr. Ambassador thinks otherwise?"

Another shake of the head, a hand wiping down the livid face, a croak of "No."

"Well, then." *What the devil have you to fear?* Tom went to lay his ill-stitched gloves on the desk, across the *Histoire de Portugal*. Had it been a pair of snakes, Grimeston wouldn't have startled more.

"Mr. Grimeston, I'll leave these gloves with you tonight, for safekeeping. It would be best to hide them securely. Pleasing God, I'll ask for them back tomorrow morning — or my man Skeres will. If anything should befall the both of us, you'll find a way to have the gloves conveyed to Mr. Secretary in London."

Grimeston gasped. "Mr. W— Mr. Abbot, for mercy's sake! What…?" *What other burglary are you going to do?*

If he truly did expect an answer, he wasn't going to have one. "And, Mr. Grimeston, my master knows to expect the gloves from you, if I don't come back — and he will know if anyone tampers with them."

As he took his leave, the last Tom saw of Grimeston was the man staring, glassy-eyed and sweaty, at the gloves on the desk.

CHAPTER 14

Saint-Eustache stood in the windy darkness like a shipwreck —
with its unfinished, scaffolded walls and empty windows, the
transept pillars soaring like colossal bare masts.

Not knowing where the chapels were being built, Tom took
a careful turn around the apse — wary of the *barrière* not far
away — until he found a roughly boarded section in the
transept wall. One of the boards had been pushed aside,
making a gap just large enough to squeeze through.

Inside, the darkness hung blacker, and the silence thicker, the
cold air sour with stone, and sawn wood, and mortar. The
lantern's finger of light warily touched now the foot of a
cyclopean pillar, now the ropes of a pulley or a heap of ashlar-
stones — and, when pointed upwards, was swallowed by the
yawning gloom.

While the apse was roofed, there was no vault yet over the
transept, much less over the naves — still only rows of
columns pointing up towards the winter sky.

Tom hadn't moved three steps, nose in the air, before he
stepped onto a layer of rubble that crunched under his shoes.
Cursing, he stopped short, shuttering the lantern, and listened.
Nothing but the wind outside. Well, whoever was waiting in
the dark had heard him now — why, they'd likely strewn the
rubble so the noise would warn them of his coming. Well, he
was an unwary fool, and the ploy had worked: there was little
point left in secrecy.

The whole north half of the transept was filled with
scaffolding, a cage-like frame of poles and walk-boards tied
together, with an inclined ladder here and there, reaching up

into the darkness. At its foot, towards the nave, sat a stack of rough boards, together with a sawing trestle, and on this Tom placed the lantern, wide open, so he would see whoever approached. In this little island of light, back pressed against a pillar, he drew his rapier, and disposed himself to wait. As his eyes grew accustomed to the half-darkness, he could see a little more: the row of pillars stretching on one side and curving on the other like Titans on parade, sawdust on the floor, a pile of empty sacks, the skeleton-like shadow of another scaffold around what remained of the older choir...

The quiet had seemed very deep at first after the wind outside, but it was not: a rattling, the creak of wooden beams, a flurry of wings above where a pigeon was disturbed in its sleep ... and then a step.

Where had it come from? Somewhere down the dark apse, perhaps, although echoes ran and bounced in this shell of stone... Tom held his breath, listening — and there it went again: the soft scrape of a leather sole in the grit, somewhere deep in the apse. And now someone who had no ill intentions would come forward, surely? But fear was unreasoning...

Raising his guard, Tom placed himself between the light and the noise, and called softly: "Faulkes?" It echoed in the darkness, far louder than he'd intended. "Whoever you are, show yourself."

More scraping, a loose stone rolling... Tom took a step forward, eyes darting this way and that. What if there was more than one person hiding in the gloom? What if Skeres had been right? What if they had pistols? He stepped into the shadows just as more steps shuffled a little closer, away on the left.

"Come into the light," he called. "Let me see you —"

A clatter on his right made him spin around. More than one man, then... He never finished the thought, as a dark blur rushed him from the left side, and he barely had time to raise the rapier in an awkward parry before blades clanged together, and edges scraped off each other.

Damn the fellow — and damn himself, Tom thought sourly, falling for such a trick as a thrown stone! For there was just one foe, circling three wary steps away, with his hat low over his face. Well, Skeres had been right — but at least it was an ambush of one. Besides, this solitary ruffian only wielded a dagger, shorter by inches than Tom's blade.

Taking heart from all that, Tom leapt forward in a thrust that had his foe skittering out of harm's way and, at once, stepping sideways and thrusting back. Graceful he was not — but quick and reckless, pressing wildly again and again with his shorter blade. He never checked when the rapier's edge sliced through the heavy fabric of a sleeve, thrusting instead under Tom's guard.

Tom jumped back — and cursed at finding himself caught among the scaffold's beams and the dangling ropes. The advantage of the long rapier was half-lost in the cramped space, but not so much that he couldn't lunge, making his foe career backwards into the sawing trestle. The trestle toppled, bringing down the lantern with it. There was a tinkle of broken glass, and the flame guttered down.

Devil take it! Tom checked his advance, warily squinting in the sudden darkness, trying to hear over the cooing of the disturbed pigeons. And was that...? Yes: steps, farther away than they'd been, moving around the scaffold, circling... The murderous scoundrel was trying to get the back of him.

Not on your life, fellow. Tom backed against the nearest pillar — and as he did, somewhere behind him a flame whooshed to life with a great rush of sparks. In the burst of light the nameless foe was gilt copper and black for a heartbeat, as he dove inside a shallow chapel, a dozen steps from Tom's right.

"Are we playing hide-and-seek?" Tom called. "You've lost your taste for doing murder in daylight, have you?"

This earned a telltale growl, and he advanced towards it, pushing aside a knotted rope-end, the dark maws of a row of empty chapels showing clear in the flickering red light... It was the crackling, though, that made him turn and draw in a sharp breath: fire!

Across the scaffolding, the fallen lantern's dying ember had found food in the sawdust, and now green and gold crests of flame ate at the toppled trestle, licked at the stack of boards...

And then, Sir, quite by accident, I burnt down a church...

It was a moment's hesitation, then Tom ran for the fire. He snatched up a piece of sackcloth, with a wild intention to beat down the flames — but it was only fools who stopped in the middle of a fight to put out a fire... There was a rush of steps behind Tom's back, and he spun around just in time to hurl the cloth at his attacker, who caught it on his dagger's point, and wasted a moment in extricating himself.

"Do you want to burn to death?" Tom shouted. As though the murderer should care how his victim died... Little wonder that there was no answer.

Thrusting aside the sack at last, the man kicked the burning trestle towards Tom, and made to circle around, only to find his way barred by a glittering point. They were out of the scaffold now, where the long rapier was an advantage. The fire was high enough to let them see each other well, and Tom advanced. The murderer backed in a half circle, until he broke into a run and plunged under the scaffolding again.

He made for the nearest ladder, climbing up like a squirrel, Jove fulminate him! Tom gave chase, the rapier awkward in his hand as he climbed, but he wouldn't spare the time to sheath it. As he reached the first deck, the fellow was already scurrying up the next ladder, but not so high that Tom couldn't jump up a rung, then two, and snatch for a leg — but he lost his footing when a backward kick hit him in the shoulder.

Hell and Hades! Crashing down to totter on the roughly laid boards, Tom caught himself on a beam, gasping at a glimpse of the ground a good fifteen feet below, and the fire crackling greedily beyond the scaffolds amidst billows of smoke. Above, the ruffian was hauling himself towards the second deck.

Oh, what a night — and where the devil was Skeres?

Winded, Tom followed up the ladder, and was halfway when he saw something hurtling down towards him — a bucket. He leant away, just enough that the bucket missed him as it tumbled down, bouncing and clattering, and spilling sand. He held onto the ladder somehow, but he lost his grip on the rapier. It caught the firelight as it fell, and clanged onto the lower deck, the hilt caught between two crossed beams, the blade glittering in the air. Oh Lord! Tom jumped down after it, landing on hands and knees, wood shards biting into his palms. He scrambled for the rapier, and hadn't gone a foot when a great weight fell on him, squeezing the breath out of his lungs. He squirmed under it, rolling away just enough that his attacker's dagger only grazed his arm instead of pinning it to the walk-boards. The murderer shifted his weight, one arm pressing across Tom's throat, growling low as he freed the dagger's point from the wood. Blackness crowded at the edge of Tom's vision, as he grabbed wildly for he didn't know what — and yet... The frantic hands, the sour smell, the quiver in the choking arm...

The murderer smelt like fear.

Tom pushed then, with all his might, with knees and elbows, just as the dagger came free, and the man swayed backwards, unseated. The cap flew from his head, and in the wavering firelight, Tom glimpsed a young face, distorted with fright and fury — a face he knew...

Astonishment made him bolt up, and reach for a handful of doublet, just as the youth toppled backwards as the walk-boards tilted under the shifting weight.

"You!" Tom grasped, and was grasped in turn and dragged across the boards... He clung one-armed to a beam, legs dangling over the edge, holding with the other onto young Clement Framlingham, who hung in mid-air, kicking wildly, and still gripped his dagger.

"Let it go!" Tom shouted. "Keep still!"

There was a tearing sound as cloth gave way, and a scream, and Clement's weight was gone, a dislodged board hurtling after him. Tom was left hanging by one hand, gasping in the smoke-laden air. He tried to haul himself up, hissing with pain when his mistreated shoulder protested — wrenched out of its socket, surely... Yet he managed to catch the edge of the deck. Now just to swing up one leg — all the more urgent because there were calls sounding above the fire's hum and crackle.

Bellowing calls of "Mr. Tom!"

Oh, Lord be thanked: the Minotaur to the rescue — at last!

"Master!"

"Here, Skeres!" Tom choked. "On the scaffold."

Or, in truth, halfway down it... Somehow Tom dragged one leg up, and then he felt himself grasped and heaved up, and found that he was lying on his back, coughing and squinting up into Nick Skeres's wild-eyed face.

"*It ain't the murtherer*, 'e says," the lad hiccupped, squeezing Tom's shoulders tight enough to hurt. "Lord love you, Master!"

The murtherer... Oh God! Tom propped himself up on an elbow. "The boy...?"

"The one down there?" Skeres tilted his head downward. "You worry none, 'e's going nowhere. Fell on 'is own sword, 'e did ... wait!" he yelped, when Tom picked himself up, and went to climb unsteadily down the ladder.

Clement lay at the scaffold's foot, curled on his side, trembling and panting, the fallen board across his legs. He cried out when Tom pushed the board away, and rolled him onto his back. The drop had broken bones, perhaps, but Skeres was right: it was the stab wound in the side that was killing the youth. Blood flecked his lips, and his breath was shallow. Tom lifted him and laid him against his knee.

"Framlingham," he called, and patted a cold cheek. It was wet with tears. "Clement Framlingham, heed me! Why did —"

"I'm sorry!" the youth gasped, and blindly reached up a hand. Without thinking, Tom took it in his own.

"Sorry that you tried to kill me?" he asked. "Tell me why!"

Clement sobbed. "I'm sorry for that Frenchman... I'm going to Hell for it. But I'm so sorry..."

Lord above! Tom's stomach clenched hard. This stripling stabbing in cold blood... "But why Jourdain?"

"Wrong man... In the press... Lost my head... Charles, I'm going to Hell — for the wrong man!" A cough brought more blood to the white lips, and Clement writhed in pain. "Forgive me, Charles — I'm sorry! I tried... Anne wanted... She won't pray for me —"

The blood-slick fingers closed weakly around Tom's, then went limp and fell away as Clement Framlingham died, head rolling against the arm of the man he'd twice tried to kill — and who'd killed him in return.

Lord have mercy on them both.

And then Skeres trotted up, carrying Tom's rapier.

"We must make away, Master…" He stopped short, gawping at the dead man. "That ain't… Cuds-me! 'E's dead?"

"I never meant…" Tom fell silent, half-formed thoughts swimming inside his head, until a snap of tortured wood came from the scaffold's other side, and Skeres jerked into motion.

"Quick, Master," he urged, tugging at Tom's arm. "Before folks come. Or the sergeants."

The sergeants not being folks to Skeres's mind… But he wasn't wrong: all that Tom lacked was to be found with a murdered corpse for the second time in three days… And this time he'd done the murdering himself. He'd killed this boy… He looked up, blinking through the smoke at the flames that were eating their way up the dangling ropes, lapping at beams and boards.

"It will all burn down!"

Another tug. "Want to put it out by yourseln? 'Alf the neighbourhood will be 'ere in a wink."

And Tom looked down again at the body. "We can't leave him here to burn…"

"'Ave you 'it your 'ead? 'E tried to do you in, and 'e's stone-dead besides — rest 'is soul…" Seeing that Tom wasn't budging, Skeres slapped his thighs. "'Ere!" He thrust the rapier at Tom and, taking Clement's body under the armpits, began to drag it towards the apse. Tom followed — and perhaps Skeres was right, and he had hit his head, for all he could think was that all this time Clement Framlingham had meant to kill *him* — and Charles ... who was Charles, that he should forgive this failed murder? Arundel? Paget? But, Lord God — he'd killed the boy!

"Master!"

Skeres, having laid the dead Clement by an open door in the apse, was beckoning wildly. He ran back, grabbed Tom by the arm, and dragged him out into the wind again, just as the warning-bell began to toll from some church nearby.

It was like a slap in the face — the chill air, the jangle of the bells, the shouts as people poured out of houses, running for the churchyard — and it was with a clearer mind that Tom led the way up towards the deserted market, away from the ado. As he went, the glass pieces in his mind shifted from a shapeless heap into a pattern of sorts, so absorbing that it wasn't until Skeres stopped at a street corner, and dug a candle stump from his pocket, that it occurred for him to ask, "And what the devil took you so long?"

"Cursed Watch stopped me." The lad stood on tiptoe to light his candle from the shrine's lamp. "Lost the lantern, 'ave you?"

The Guet — of course, and yes, the plaguey lantern... "It fell while we fought. That's how the fire started." Over the roofs towards Saint Eustache, the sky wasn't quite black. Was that a red hue touching the clouds' dark bellies?

Lord, what a night, and it was far from finished yet.

They resumed their way, Tom trembling like a leaf, and Skeres sheltering the candle with his cupped hand, hissing whenever it flickered in the wind, or the hot wax dripped on his fingers. Fates keep the Guet out of their way, for carrying a candle like that would look almost as suspicious as carrying none. They skirted the Grand Châtelet, and the Pont au

Change nearby, that was sure to be guarded... And all the same a sergeant stopped them at the Pont Notre-Dame.

"My fool of a servant broke his lantern," Tom announced in high-handed French — the vexation far from feigned, though it wasn't directed at the lad. It worked well enough that they were suffered to pass, to scurry through the *Île de la Cité* with no other incident, and to cross the Pont Saint-Michel. Only once back on the Left Bank did Tom disclose his plans to Skeres — or tried to, for he had barely said "Now, Dolius —" when the lad stopped him, shaking his head most stormily.

"No," he growled. "I know your ways, Mr. Tom. Thinking to 'are off by yourseln again, when there's folks as would kill you — and I'll say —"

Oh, God give patience, for Tom was out of it! "You'll say naught, Nick Skeres, and do as you're told. Go to the Embassy, get help — Grimeston, if you can, and perhaps Hobelot, but not his brother. Then come after me. Rue de la Serpente — look for the sign of the *Trois Barques*."

Tom stalked away, drawing the cloak tighter around him — not that it helped — followed by a Minotaurish hiss:

"Master! What am I to tell them?"

"That we have spies and murderers there," he called over his shoulder.

There was a grumbling of "Ay, and you run right into their mouth!" and then trotting steps — the music of Reluctant Obedience.

Shaking his head, Tom made his dark way towards the Rue de la Serpente, trying not to think of the fear and despair of the dying Clement Framlingham.

He had to knock long and fiercely before he heard the rasp of bolts. The door flew open, and Lady Gawdy stood on the threshold, pale and breathless.

"Clement —!" She gave a little screech at the sight of Tom, and tried to slam the door in his face.

When he held fast and pushed through, she backed away, half-stumbling over the hem of her gown, and catching herself against the newel post.

"Where's my brother?" she demanded, shrill and quivering.

I killed him while he tried to kill me...

"Madam, would you call Mrs. Blundell?" Tom took a step into the light of the candle that burned in the sconce, and Anne's hand flew to her mouth.

"What have you done to him?"

He followed her gaze. His cloak was stained dark — again. Clement's blood on the front, and his own on the sleeve, where the youth's dagger had cut him. He touched the stains and the tear, and for the first time felt the sting of his wound.

"Your brother lured me into a trap, Madam. He meant me ill..."

"And yet here you are!" She had retreated a couple of steps up the dark staircase, one hand hitching her skirts away from her heels, the other on the baluster, curling and uncurling.

"Yes," Tom said, and advanced again, sparing a glance for the candle that glowed in its sconce. Take it, and he'd see what he was walking into — but he'd encumber himself, and might have to drop it. Leave it behind, and very soon they'd be in the dark in a house she knew and he did not.

Up another step she backed, and then another. "It was foolish of you to come back here, Mr. Walsingham," she said — a half-laugh trembling in her voice.

"Oh yes. You've known all the time, haven't you? Played me for a dolt the other night at supper."

Another step. "Some old deaf servant of the Ambassador mistook the names. Framlingham, Walsingham... God's will, wouldn't you say? Imagine Clement's astonishment when that man called him Walsingham, when he discovered who *you* were. Yes, God's own will."

"And so you told Lord Paget."

A toss of the head. "And what would that have helped? Cousin Joyce promised to tell him — but, you know, I don't believe she did. She said you'd saved us, after all..." The lovely face contorted past recognition, teeth bared, eyes burning. "*Saved us!*"

"And killing me? What would that have helped?"

She tossed her head, and bowed her slender waist as she climbed backwards to look him in the face. "I told you, Thomas Walsingham, but you don't listen: there's always some debt owed. And now, if it's my brother's blood on you, it will be all the greater."

They'd reached a narrow landing, where the stairs doubled on themselves. Upstairs was the room where they'd taken supper; here a narrow door opened into the house's other side, and through it Anne Gawdy backed, her dark kirtle melting into the gloom, only the pale oval of her face showing faintly. So it would have been better to take the candle, after all...

Feeling before him, Tom followed, stepping aside so as not to leave his back to the open door. Anne's retreat was little more than a rustle of skirts. Why wasn't she calling for her cousin?

Cousin Joyce said you'd saved us... "Lady Gawdy, where is Mistress Blundell?" Receiving no answer, Tom called, "Mistress Blundell!"

"She won't hear you." The shrill voice sounded different in the dark. Younger somehow, like that of a thwarted child. "She didn't understand — not when I wanted you here for supper, not when Clement..." A small scoffing sound. "Not that we told her of the Frenchman. And then this morning, I saw her through the window, talking to you. I *had* to give her the poppy. To think she'd bought it for me, because I couldn't sleep..."

"The servants, too?"

"None of them would understand — not even now that you've killed Clement." She choked on the name. "But then, what would they know? The debt is mine to collect."

It's a matter of what we owe you, she'd said on Twelfth Night.

"Your brother was trying to kill me, Madam. He murdered an innocent man, and would have done the same to me — in the dark, armed with a dagger like a common thief. It pains me that I had to kill him, but what choice did I have? I don't see that you must take revenge on —"

The laugh was so sudden, so high, so strident, it sent a shiver down Tom's spine — and he was glad he couldn't see Anne's face.

"You don't see!" she gasped. "It *is* God's will that sent you here, then, for it would be wrong if you died without knowing. Clement never spoke to you of Charles, did he?"

Forgive me, Charles... Who had Clement seen in his dying anguish? Never Paget, surely?

Tom had been in the dark long enough to make out the shape of Anne, huddling against the black square of a cupboard, and he moved towards her.

"He did. He wanted his forgiveness, and that of God, and your prayers — but, Madam, I was very far from Paris when Charles Arundel died —"

"Arundel?" That horrible laugh again. "Have you no conscience and no soul, that you've already forgotten Charles Tilney?"

All the breath rushed out of Tom. Oh, he had not forgotten Tilney, nor the other conspirators in Babington's ring. If he had, he wouldn't defend himself so angrily to this madwoman.

"Charles Tilney was a traitor. I stopped him while he sought to kill Mr. Secretary —"

"And you could have killed him in a fair fight then — gentleman to gentleman, one soldier of a cause to another. You could have put your sword through his heart — and you did not! Were you there when they put him to the rack? You should have been, for it was your doing. They tortured him so badly he couldn't walk to the gallows!" Through her sobs the question was only too clear: "Were you there, when they hanged him, and cut him open, and tore his body apart?"

I was, and it still visits my nightmares... "Was he...?"

The screech petered out to a wail. "He was my cousin, and had my heart, and I had his, but my father wouldn't hear of it, because Charles was Catholic. I changed my faith for him — and you...!"

All happened at once then: Anne Gawdy growled low in her throat, and there was a muffled, urgent call of "Anne! Anne!" and a flurry of blows upstairs, and steps down into the hall, and Tom — like the fool he was — let himself turn away. Instinct made him catch the blur of movement, made him bring up his elbow so that the knife bit deep into his forearm.

Wrong-footed, he fell backward, hitting his head and back, with Anne above him.

Over her scream of wordless fury someone shouted, and steps thundered up the stairs. Light spilled through the door — enough of it to gleam red off Anne's raised blade. Tom caught her wrist, left-handed, as she struck downward for his chest with all the strength of madness. She gasped when he crushed her slender bones, and dropped the knife. And still she hit and scratched with her free hand. He brought up a knee to push her away — just as he'd pushed Clement, hurtling him to his death — and couldn't, not with the youth's gaze burning in his mind...

"Anne, child — stop!" bid a woman's voice, imperious and viol-like. "Leave him!"

And then, Lord be thanked, the madwoman was being lifted away, and there was light, and more blows from upstairs, and voices — one grousing: "I told 'im it was daft to come alone! Told 'im till I was 'oarse — and did 'e listen?"

When Tom sat up, dazed, bleeding, and light-headed, and leant back against the wall, Anne Gawdy was sobbing, crumpled in Lady Stafford's arms.

Joyce Blundell tied the bandage with what Tom found to be unnecessary vigour, pressing her lips into a line as she pulled the double knot unmercifully tight.

Alexander himself would need a sword to undo this one, he thought — or at least he hoped he hadn't said it aloud, for he didn't trust his swimming head at the moment.

But perhaps he'd kept his wanderings to himself, because both Mrs. Blundell and Lady Stafford ignored him entirely.

Joyce Blundell sat back. "More than this I can't do, my lady. It's stopped bleeding, but the surgeon must see to it."

Jourdain lives nearby... Tom clamped his mouth shut. Jourdain was no surgeon. Jourdain was a physician. Jourdain was dead. It hurt when he tried to flex his fingers — thank God it was his left arm! — and at once a firm hand gripped his.

"Don't!"

Blinking up, Tom found that Lady Stafford had come to loom over him — a tower of green velvet and displeasure, bent over the chair to hold his wrist.

"You must not move it," she ordered, with the same imperious manner that had stopped Anne.

Tom sat up straighter, finding himself in an armchair after all. "Lady Gawdy?" he asked.

The two women exchanged a glance, and then Joyce Blundell said, "She sleeps."

Oh, yes… "Was there enough poppy left?"

The Baroness frowned. "What poppy?"

"She told me she'd drugged her cousin and the servants." And those blows from upstairs… "And then she locked the doors for good measure, didn't she?"

Joyce Blundell gave a grim nod. She looked older, with the puffy, reddened eyelids of drugged sleep, and her hair hanging in a colourless braid. "She put the poppy in the soup — and then neither she nor Clement touched it — but she didn't know how much would be enough."

The mention of Clement cleared Tom's mind, and he sat up fully. He would have stood, had Lady Stafford allowed him.

"Mistress Blundell, I'm sorry," he said, and his voice was not quite steady. "Your cousin Framlingham… He tried…"

She caught her breath, eyes gleaming wet. "Anne kept saying that she wanted your blood, Mr. Walsingham." The name stuck in her throat. "They worshipped Charles Tilney, both of them — and they both blamed you for his death, but Anne, who had loved him so… I think that meeting you finally addled her wits."

It was hard to imagine Anne Gawdy with a sound mind, without the haunted eyes and the curling and uncurling hands.

"She called it God's own will." Tom found himself very much wishing that, on Sainte Geneviève's day, he'd come to cross the Seine only half an hour earlier than he had.

"Oh, she said it again and again..." Joyce Blundell faced Tom, and there were tears on her cheeks. "Lord forgive me, I thought that was all it was: words and grief. I wouldn't have let her ask you here, otherwise, and I believed Clement thought so, too. I'd known them well enough as children in England — but that was years ago."

"And what were they doing in Paris?"

"Anne's father wanted no Catholic son-in-law, so he married her to another. Bassingbourne Gawdy... I don't know that he's a bad man, but Anne loathes him for not being Charles Tilney. And after Charles died..." She twisted her hands together. "Anne's aunt thought a spell of time away would soothe her. Time away from all that reminded her of Charles." And she scowled at Tom — as though it were, somehow, his fault.

It was vexation, surely, and not guilt that made his retort sharp? "None of which explains why Clement went along with his sister's madness."

Lady Stafford clicked her tongue, and Joyce Blundell flinched.

"Clement was a boy, and there was naught he wouldn't do for Anne, or for Charles Tilney. Mr. Walsingham —" she began to hold out a pleading hand and curled it in her lap instead — "I don't believe he would have harmed you of his own counsel."

As though it made it better that he'd done so at his sister's bidding. But this Tom bit down, seeing the young, tear-stained face again. "He said he was going to Hell," he murmured. "He said Anne wouldn't pray for him." And then he wished he'd bit down that, too, when Joyce Blundell's face crumpled.

"I should have seen it," she choked out. "Oh, I should have: he was more and more distraught, poor boy. These last days, he was all but mad himself…"

"He would be, after killing Pierre Jourdain instead of me."

Both women exclaimed at this — Mrs. Blundell in horror, the Baroness in something very much like outrage.

"I begin to think, young Walsingham, that there are many things you kept from Sir Edward!" she said.

And trust her to put *him* in the wrong! Tom wished he could rise, instead of glaring up at her, the retort spilling out of him. "Why, Madam, I never knew until an hour ago. I thought poor Jourdain was killed before he could tell me of your kinsman's murder — which was no murder, after all — and I never dreamt the blow had been meant for me —" He stopped short, out of breath, and cursed himself for discussing these matters with Stafford's wife and before Paget's friend.

And indeed see how Joyce Blundell stared at him.

"Then it *was* him!" she gasped. "I feared it when you told me this morning that you'd been there… Oh, I was so afraid!"

Good Lord — this woman! "And you never thought to tell me?"

"Tell you, so you'd take Clement, too? Take him from Anne, the way you took Charles Tilney? And now you've taken him all the same!" She sank onto the windowsill, burying her face in her hands, and sobbed — great, bitter sobs. And past her bent figure, Tom blinked at Grimeston and the servant-boy frozen on the threshold.

"Your Ladyship, I heard…" The secretary's eyes travelled from his mistress to Tom to the undone Joyce.

Was there anything in this world that discomposed Lady Stafford? "Please go downstairs, Mr. Grimeston," she ordered.

"See what Mr. Abbot's man has done with himself and the surgeon."

Which answered a question Tom should have asked much earlier, had his wits been less thick… And see, perhaps Her Ladyship was discomposed, for she snatched a steaming cup from the servant-boy, and shut the door in his face. When she thrust the cup at Tom, it was with enough force to make some hot wine spill on his fingers.

"If only you'd stayed away as you were told!" she exclaimed.

And wasn't this the rankest unfairness! But then a memory stirred deep down in Tom's mind: weren't the Tilneys and the Howards related?

"Ah, yes!" he muttered, with a bitterness no landless gentleman should use to address a baroness. "Because Your Ladyship knew who Lady Gawdy was — but, instead of a warning, you gave me a rap on the knuckles." *A rap fit for a seducer of wives…*

"Oh, don't be foolish! I knew these children were Charles Tilney's cousins, and I saw she wasn't right in her head. I never thought she'd have that poor boy do murder in vengeance! I only wanted you to stay away from her."

"I did, Madam, and I wish I had even more. Lady Gawdy and her brother, though, wouldn't stay away from me!"

"They wouldn't, no." Joyce Blundell had risen to her feet, red-eyed and raw-voiced. "My father used to say the Framlinghams carry grudges to their graves. Now Clement has, and Anne…" She shook her head, and frowned at Tom. "Perhaps I should have told Lord Paget who you are, after all. Begging Your Ladyship's leave, I'll see to my cousin now." She waited for no leave to curtsey herself out — her shoulders painfully straight again.

With a long sigh, Tom sat back and closed his eyes, mind sluggishly a-whirl. The knots undone: Stafford was a traitor but no murderer, and Arundel a traitor but no victim, and the one murder that had been meant was his own out of revenge — but two others had died because of it, and one of them he'd killed himself…

"What do you intend to do?"

The Baroness's question startled him enough that he made the cooling wine slosh in the cup — not that he'd ever drink a drop under Anne Gawdy's roof now. But yes: what did he intend to do?

And what an addled fool must he be, that the first thing he blurted out was a plea of his own guilt? "I killed a man…"

"A man who would have killed you otherwise," said Lady Stafford, dismissing Clement's killing just as she had dismissed the fretful secretary. "No, you were never there. I think it was that silly boy who was lured … where was it?"

"Saint Eustache, but —"

"Yes, he was lured to Saint Eustache, and God knows who it was, and why. We all know what Paris is like these days: besides, poor Clement Framlingham was hot-headed and a little thoughtless. It's little wonder that he found a fight somehow, and was killed. Mistress Blundell will see it's for the best."

This had Tom exclaiming in disbelief. "Whose best, Madam?"

Head tilted, the Baroness studied him. "I'd say yours, too — but in truth, I'm thinking of poor Anne Gawdy."

Poor Anne Gawdy… Tom scrambled to his unsteady feet. "Poor Anne Gawdy caused two deaths — three deaths, had she had her way with that knife — and all over a murderous traitor —"

"Don't you dare, Thomas Walsingham!" The Baroness drew tall — the most severe Juno. "You did what you must to Tilney, and to that poor youth tonight — but what have you done to Anne? Men never think of that. If you ever loved someone with all your heart, think: what would you do if someone took her away from you? What would *she* do, if you were taken, and she blamed someone for it?"

Frances.

He was my cousin, and had my heart, and I had his, but my father wouldn't hear of it... Anne's words — but they could be Frances's. Not quite, for Frances was too much her father's daughter to utter such thoughts to anyone, and yet ... how many times had she thought so to herself? And if he were taken, sent to a traitor's death she deemed unfair...

"She'd never do murder," he said, wishing he could summon something stronger than this hoarse whisper. "She'd never go mad."

Which in itself, his blood-let wits dully objected, was too much of an admission to make before this woman.

Lady Stafford watched him so intently that, for a moment, he feared to hear that then, perhaps, *she* didn't love him enough. But this was Douglas Howard, who'd loved Lord Leicester, and lost him, and kept her wits sound and sharp, so she only nodded, as though whatever she saw in his face satisfied her.

"Sit down, before you faint," she said — and Tom found he'd been swaying. He sank rather gracelessly back into the chair, hissing as he jostled his wounded arm.

"If I was never lured to Saint Eustache, how do I explain this?" he asked, and it sounded peevish to his own ears.

"I told you: we all know what Paris is like, these days. But..." A frown. "Lured, you say. You had a letter?"

Back at the Embassy, ready as proof, had I not come back... "I burnt it," he said — and, to his own surprise, he meant to make the lie true as soon as he could. Jove rain on Lady Stafford — did she have to make him see Frances in Anne Gawdy? Then again, he carried her husband's ruin stitched into a pair of gloves...

As though summoned by this thought, steps floated up from the stairs — and voices. Grimeston's and Skeres's, and another...

"The surgeon." The Baroness gathered her skirts around her and went to the door. "Take heart, young Walsingham: an hour, and all will be right."

All will be right. Tom closed his eyes again — and didn't like it when he did, for he saw Anne Gawdy's vengeance-mad grimace, and Jourdain's blood on his cloak, and Tilney limping to the scaffold, and Joyce Blundell asking what he'd do if his faith were forbidden, and, most of all, poor dying Clement's pleading, tear-stained face...

It would all fade away, no doubt. For the moment, though — the weary, sad moment — he couldn't think that all would be right ever again.

HISTORICAL NOTES

*[S]urely, Sir, I must confess that I can never serve with a goodwill in a
place that I have seen such a mistrust of me in, nor where I shall be so
disgraced [... when] it shall be seen to my disgrace what a mistrust is
made of me at home. [...] I promise you Sir, I am so much grieved withal,
and so ashamed of my hard fortune, as with all my heart I rather wish to
be dead than alive.*

Edward Stafford to Francis Walsingham, 2 January 1589

Sir Edward Stafford, whose father had once been married to
the Queen's aunt, and whose mother had Elizabeth's ear and
great influence at Court, served as English ambassador in Paris
between 1583 and 1590. He was recommended for the post by
Lord Treasurer Burleigh, likely as part of an attempt to
undermine Sir Francis Walsingham's control of intelligence and
diplomacy.

Personal allegiance to the Cecils apart, I'm not sure quite
what qualities Burleigh saw in Stafford. The surviving letters
show an excitable, sullen, rather petty man, who apparently
thought that everybody had it in for him — Secretary
Walsingham most of all. It's true that Sir Francis was, in turn,
less than thrilled with Stafford, and never trusted him, trying
more than once to have him removed from his post.

One thing is certain: during his Parisian tenure, the
ambassador did little to earn Walsingham's trust. He constantly
reported to Lord Burleigh, of course, but also tried to deal
directly with the Queen behind Mr. Secretary's back — an
attempt Elizabeth seems to have discouraged. What's worse,
Stafford strayed well beyond underhand Court politics: he sold

secret information to the fiercely anti-English and anti-Protestant Duke of Guise, and very likely did the same for Bernardino de Mendoza, the formidable Spanish ambassador. Diplomatically kicked out of London after his involvement in the Babington Plot in 1586, Mendoza had been sent to France, where both he and his king, Philip II, thought he could keep up his work. They were right, it turned out. Even half-blind and in poor health, in Paris Mendoza worked feverishly to acquire damaging intelligence against England.

Did Mendoza truly manage to snag Stafford as an informer at some point in 1586? It would have been a remarkable move in his bitter, titanic duel with Walsingham. While there is no indisputable evidence for it, the correspondence between Mendoza and King Philip strongly suggests that's how things stood, and Stafford's precedents with the Guise make it more than plausible. Besides, Stafford was a spendthrift and a reckless gambler: by 1586 his debts were enormous and, according to one of Walsingham spies, had put him very much under the thumb of at least one prominent French diplomat and courtier tied to King Henri III. At this point, it wouldn't have been overly hard for exiled Catholic leader Charles Arundel to draw his harried kinsman into Mendoza's well-paying orbit.

Of course, Stafford could have claimed he was tricking Mendoza with false information. In fact, he did claim something like it — although for the recently dead Charles Arundel rather than himself — when Gilbert Gifford was arrested by the French and began to sing like a bird. One of Walsingham's more questionable informers, Gifford oscillated between versions, describing Stafford now as the worst of traitors, now as a complete fool in the hands of the traitorous Arundel. The ambassador, torn between gloating at what he saw as Walsingham's blunder and bemoaning his own undeserved disgrace, made a point of complaining bitterly: Gifford painted Arundel as Spain's agent, when actually the poor man had been trying to extract intelligence from Mendoza in the service of England. Of course, this was supposed to exonerate Stafford himself in the first place... In truth, the evidence is inconclusive. Information about the Spanish Armada and England's countermoves leaked both ways: in both directions it was incomplete, and sometimes downright false. Was Stafford innocent? Was he mistrusted both in Spain and England? Was he playing false on both sides? And, if he was, what on earth was his game?

Whatever the truth, Stafford wasn't recalled from Paris until 1590 — and afterwards never held any post of trust or responsibility again.

All through the twentieth century, historians have never quite ceased to debate Edward Stafford, alternately painting him as guilty or innocent. I've espoused the "guilty Stafford" theory, because I find it more convincing, and because it makes for a better story — together with the notion that Sir Francis, once certain of the ambassador's guilt, would leave him in his post, blissfully unaware, to leak carefully fabricated information to Mendoza and Philip.

And, of course, whom would Mr. Secretary send to deal with the matter but his trusted young cousin Tom?

There is no evidence of any involvement of Tom with the Gifford disaster or the whole Stafford affair. Actually, we know nothing of Tom's whereabouts at the time, so he might well have been in Paris on a very confidential mission. Almost everyone on this side of *A Matter of Blood* is historical: Stafford and the Baroness his wife, of course, but also his secretaries Lyly and Grimeston (both really, if reluctantly, in Walsingham's pay), and the chaplain Richard Hakluyt. Stafford really sent his own "very honest, learned" physician to attend the very ill Charles Arundel; I gave the man a name and made him a Protestant Fleming — just as I gave a name to the Embassy coachman who, according to Gilbert Gifford, was a Catholic spy. The Pagets and Charles Arundel are, of course, historical, as are Phelippes's blunder, the suspicions of poisoning, Lord Paget's visit to Gifford at the For-l'Évêque, the mess with Stafford's notes and money, and the woman of ill repute and Lord Essex's supposed man Cotton, who were arrested together with Gifford: it all comes from Gifford and Stafford's letters. I made up everyone else — or rather Anne and Clement Framlingham did exist. Anne was married to Sir Bassingbourne Gawdy, and Clement died aged eighteen or thereabout — and they were related to the Tilneys and, therefore, quite distantly, to Lady Douglas Stafford. That Anne was ever in love with Babington's crony Charles Tilney, that she and her brother were ever in Paris, that Clement died there, that they had a cousin named Joyce Blundell, is all the work of my imagination.

A NOTE TO THE READER

Dear Reader,

Thank you for reading *A Matter of Blood*. I hope you enjoyed it. In these notes to you, I like to share little stories of how research goes into Tom's adventures. This time, instead, I'd like to tell you of a bit of research that didn't make it to the novel's pages — and for good reason.

Of the three physicians who vainly tried to save Charles Arundel's life, one was sent by ambassador Stafford himself. The other two I made up: Arundel's habitual physician (the sort of inexpensive young fellow a penniless exile could afford), and another sent by the Duke of Guise, Arundel's powerful French patron. I found myself wondering about this Guise man: could I find out the name of someone tied to the family in some way?

You know about falling down rabbit-holes? In no time at all I was researching French medical history, and the Guise family — and finding nothing especially useful... Then, in a footnote to Stuart Carroll's *Martyrs and Murderers: The Guise Family and the Making of Europe*, I discovered the existence of Hubert Samier, a Guise agent who, under the name of La Rue, posed as a physician to travel undetected, and even visited Mary Stuart in England. There! I thought: the Duke of Guise didn't actually send a physician, but an agent with enough medical knowledge to find out what was wrong with this useful but troublesome English exile. It seemed perfect — provided that Samier was in France in January 1588, because the man seemed to have been quite the traveller. Imagine me falling down another rabbit-hole...

It was very late one night, and I was making myself a cup of tea between bouts of reading, when the voice of reason at last spoke up. Arundel, it pointed out, was to be already dead at the book's beginning — and, whoever else Tom was going to question about it, it would never be the physician sent by the very hostile Duke of Guise. We'd never meet this man, and there would be neither the chance nor the need for him to be discovered as a disguised enemy agent. Fascinating as the idea was, did I really need him to be Samier/La Rue? Did I want to deal with all the backstory for the sake of a not terribly relevant detail? *No!* clamoured the voice of reason — and it was right. So I climbed out of this particular rabbit-hole and gave up: the Duke's physician is only mentioned, Tom steers well clear of him in his investigation, and really, that's all there is to it.

My point? Research is such a siren! It's very easy to get lost in it, endlessly chasing after details and people — but in the end what matters is the story: while historical accuracy is all-important, research should never overwhelm or hijack the story. Next time I'm tempted, I'll tell myself to remember La Rue!

I'd love to hear from you — about this or Tom's adventures generally — through my **website** or **via Twitter**, where I tweet under the handle **@laClarina**. Meanwhile, if you enjoyed *A Matter of Blood*, I would truly appreciate it if you'd drop by **Amazon** and **Goodreads** to post a review, and let other readers know that you enjoyed this novel.

Thank you, and we'll meet again in the next Tom Walsingham book!

C. P. Giuliani

Sapere Books is an exciting new publisher of brilliant fiction and popular history.

To find out more about our latest releases and our monthly bargain books visit our website:
saperebooks.com

www.ingramcontent.com/pod-product-compliance
Lightning Source LLC
Chambersburg PA
CBHW070726280626
47159CB00023B/2750